# A Vase of Lilies

BRIANNA WEBB

Order this book online at www.trafford.com
or email orders@trafford.com

Most Trafford titles are also available at major online book retailers.



Printed in the United States of America.

ISBN: 978-1-4669-5898-2 (sc)
ISBN: 978-1-4669-5900-2 (hc)
ISBN: 978-1-4669-5899-9 (e)

Library of Congress Control Number: 2012917083

*Trafford rev. 09/14/2012*

Trafford PUBLISHING www.trafford.com

**North America & international**
toll-free: 1 888 232 4444 (USA & Canada)
phone: 250 383 6864 • fax: 812 355 4082

For Mom:

We have a bond that is hard for most to understand. You have always seen my potential and put a special stride in my step. You're the best.

Love you forever and for always.

# Acknowledgments

To Dad, the tough love you have given me over the years has pushed me to be the best I can possibly be. Your strength and work ethic has been the most inspiring. The biggest thing I am grateful for is your patience and support with all my dreams—there has been and still are plenty. "Bring on the doubters!" I love you very much.

Jordan, Konner, Chase—I have the best siblings in the world. I will always be here to push you to your potential (even if you don't always like that).

FB, ON, MC, TF, thank you guys for your input. Your opinion means the world.

Finally, I would like to acknowledge my grandpa, Ron Webb, for this ambitious blood you have provided. We miss you every day. Endless love. Our lives are forever changed. Thank you.

*In every girl's life there is one boy she will never forget and a summer where it all began . . .*

—Anonymous

# Chapter One

Here I am, standing in front of the most horrific apartment building I have seen with my own eyes. Fiona definitely didn't put any kind of effort into this apartment search, and suddenly I completely regret giving her this task.

"I thought you said you did some research on this neighborhood?" I scold.

This is a drastic change from our gated community homes back in Palmdale.

"I did! Don't you love it? It's perfect for an adventure apartment, Vero! Sure, it's a little rough around the edges, but we will put some warmth in here, and soon we'll be calling it our humble home!" she suggests as we make our way up the stairs and into the apartment.

Keeping in mind our budget, I guess this will be it for now. I begin to burn with regret in the lowest part of my gut. Have I just made a huge mistake?

"I mean . . . you can have whichever room you want! I know it's not perfect, but we will make this work, V!" Fiona defends.

"Yeah . . . I understand . . ." I frown.

I take a peek around. It's not big; definitely, it will be cramped especially because Fiona is not the tidiest person in the world. The fridge needs a good scrub. Actually, this entire apartment needs a major overhaul.

"I guess I'll take the room on the right. It'll give me good morning sun, which helps me drag my ass out of bed," I say with an optimistic approach.

"Perfect! I'll take the one on the left! The bathroom is right in the middle, so that suits us both." Fiona smiles.

I cringe knowing I need to peer into the bathroom because I already know in advance what I'm in for.

"Why don't we get our stuff, find the proper place to park your car, and take a walk around the neighborhood? Maybe we will be able to find out where we can get some groceries and cleaning supplies close by," I suggest.

"There is no way we are diving into household chores today, Vero! We have the beach at our fingertips, the wind in our hair, and the sand at our feet! Live a little!" Fiona sequels.

This lifestyle change is about embracing the act of letting things go, living in the moment, and trying to put away the controlling side of me which always ends up taking over. So I agree to throw everything down, grab my bikini and flip-flops, throw on my Ray-Bans, and head for the beach. I don't know if people can change, but I'm willing to give this my best shot.

Fiona is my very best friend in the entire world. She has her flaws, and I surely have my own set too, but she is without a doubt the most easygoing, carefree female that walks this earth.

"Isn't this beautiful, Vero? Can you believe how close this is to home? I don't think I'll ever get sick of this!" Fiona says as she throws her hands in the air and runs toward the Pacific Ocean.

The view is actually quite amazing. A beautiful sunny day and not a single cloud in the sky, the perfect welcoming to a new life we are now devoted to. Despite the stick-of-dynamite apartment and questionable neighborhood, my regrets are beginning to fade as I lay my towel down on the sand and take a seat.

"I wonder how long it will take us to establish ourselves here. You know . . . friends, jobs, all that," Fiona wonders out loud.

"Yeah, I know. Tomorrow I am going to start looking for a job. You know how strict my dad is . . . He will be completely harassing me about my every move as far as a job goes. I was thinking maybe an authentic coffee shop or cool little surf place," I answer.

"Hmm . . . I'm not in such a rush to find a job. If something comes up, then great, but right now, I'm all about working on this Cali tan!" Fiona says as she strips down to her itty-bitty bikini and begins rubbing herself down with Banana Boat SPF 8.

After a few hours of listening to the slow crashing waves, I decide it's time for me to pack my stuff and make some progress on my room. Even if Fiona doesn't want to start the apartment organizing, there is no chance I will be able to fall asleep with that chaos.

"Well, beach babe, I'm off to sort out my room. As much fun as this is, I really can't help myself. I need to do something productive," I say apologetically to Fiona as I begin my trek through the sand.

The walk back to the apartment is not very long. Along the way, I see a little Mexican boy playing with his tricycle on the street, and his mother watching over him while watering her garden, which actually looked a little more like a mini desert. I give her a small, sweet smile and put my head down as I continue on.

I unload my two suitcases; I didn't bring much with me, just my favorite things. We traveled from Palmdale where we grew up, about two hours from Huntington Beach where we have decided to now call home. As I sit on my "new" single bed, it makes an awful creaking sound and I roll my eyes. That is going to be fixed. I grab my cell phone and dial my mom.

"Hi, sweetie! I have been waiting all day for this! Do you know how hard it has been to resist calling you?"

"I can easily imagine, Mom."

"What's wrong? You sound off. I was expecting you to be so excited! Are you okay? Is everything okay?"

"Everything is fine. I just feel disappointed. I was so excited to get out on my own and start a new life for myself. I don't think I honestly realized the amount of responsibility I am going to face. You know how much I love Fio, but I am getting the sense that we are on different pages . . ."

"Oh, honey, this is what life is about. Going out into the real world, making some mistakes, getting to know what works for you and what doesn't. You have a good head on your shoulders, Veronica; don't be hard on yourself now. How is the apartment?"

"Completely and utterly awful! I hate it! I'll have so much work to do to make this place even remotely decent. I think that's going to be an impossible task. I just want to cry."

"Vero, hold your head high and carry on with this. You can do it. Take this apartment situation as a fun project. Dad and I love you, and we miss you, but we have every piece of faith you are going to be just fine. Now, I have to run, sweetie, I have some weeds out in the yard that need some attention! I love you! Call me if you need me, honey!"

Why don't I feel any better? My mom is probably right; I do need to pull myself together.

I unzip the first suitcase and begin to hang my clothes in a tiny hole-in-the-wall closet. This apartment came furnished with some really rundown furniture. We chose the furnished route so we didn't have to worry about furniture shopping; although it will have to be done eventually. I walk into the kitchen and open a few cupboards. There are some plates, a couple pots and pans, forks, spoons, knives . . . all the things we will need. Before I touch any of it, they will need some major disinfecting.

I finally venture into the bathroom to find a pastel-colored green tub and a tiny silver showerhead sticking out of the wall. There is a toilet, miniscule freestanding white sink, and a medicine cabinet mirror. It's not as bad as I was expecting.

Off the kitchen, there is a teeny sitting area with a couch from the seventies and beachy coffee table. The floors are all vinyl with the exception of our bedrooms, which have some interesting beige carpet.

Our apartment is on the second floor of a motel-type building, suite number 202—just a short walk up the stairs from the street. The building itself needs demolishing. It's a dirty white stucco color and has a tacky blue trim with metal railings along the three entry levels.

It is a fenced-off area that has a security gate at the front entrance. It's nothing fancy, just a place for tenants to stick their key.

Fiona comes back a few hours after me.

"You won't guess! I met this really cool girl while I was tanning on the beach! She works as a waitress at a restaurant a few blocks down. Her name is Ivory and not only is she totally cool, she also plays tennis! I have a tennis partner already!" she bursts out.

"That's great, Fio. Did you ask her if we could get jobs at that restaurant as well?" I ask.

"She said they are hiring, but they only need one girl," she answers nervously.

"Oh, of course you will get it. Don't worry I will find something else," I smile.

"I can't wait! I've got to go meet up with her, she's going to bring me there to meet her boss and she thinks I'll for sure be able to get the job!" she shrieks.

"That's great, Fio. Well, good luck. I'm going to the grocery store. I googled it, it's just down the street a bit," I inform.

I pull a sweater over my head and grab my wallet. We need so many things I didn't even bother to make a list. I assume since I'm the only one who worked all summer, I will be the only one buying this round of cleaning supplies. I also need some food. I haven't eaten all day and I am starving.

At home, my parents are very structured. I had to be home every Sunday night to make dinner for them. I always made spaghetti. The house is permanently clean. I had to pick up after myself and do my own laundry. My parents really wanted me to be independent and have life skills. My dad is disappointed I won't follow in his footsteps by going to university. He understands I am creative, and he accepts and pushes me to my full potential. I am very similar to my dad; we share a lot of the same traits. I am proud of that because my dad is an extraordinary person.

Upon my arrival, I grab a big cart on wheels and throw my wallet into the child's seat. I grab a jumbo bottle of disinfectant, window wash, dish soap, a mop, a broom, a dustpan, bug spray, a bucket, and plenty of scrubbers. Looks like I'm set in the cleaning department. I'm sure the girl at the till will think I am running a cleaning service and I guess I pretty much am. Next, I pick out milk, eggs, bread, orange juice, apples, and a few bananas.

When I get home, the sun is setting and the apartment is completely quiet. I wonder how many people actually live in this building and wouldn't be surprised if it were only the two of us. Beginning with the kitchen, a full bucket gets filled up with hot water and disinfectant in it. I scrub the entire fridge out until it smells decent and appears clean. Next is sterilizing the entire kitchen from top to bottom. I'm pretty satisfied with myself.

For dinner, I have made eggs on the beaten-up stove. It switches on and seems to heat up, so that's all I can ask for at this point. I poured myself a big glass of orange juice and feast away.

Tackling the bathroom is my next step so at least the shower is useable tonight. It doesn't take too long as it's not overly big and bathroom cleaning is very straightforward. I place my shampoos and conditioners, razor, and body wash in the shower. In the medicine cabinet, I find a new home for my toothbrush, tampons, Advil, and mouthwash.

Lastly, exhaustion pours over my mind as I finish off my bedroom cleaning. I place new, clean sheets over my bed and place down a new pillow. On the rickety, old desk lives my laptop, pictures of my parents, and a vase of lilies. Fake lilies because I know I won't be faithful with buying new ones each week. At least now, it feels a little more like home.

After a long, hot shower, my pajamas feel amazing. I glance at my cell phone, no text from Fio; just some boring junk e-mails, and as usual, my friends have nothing interesting to say on Facebook. Then, I seem to creep in all the wrong places. I notice a girl back home just posted that she is now in a relationship with my ex. Is she *that* stupid? Does she *really* think he will be *any* different than how he was with me? I begin to feel my heart race, and I sense a feeling I am familiar with—a sharp knife poisoning me with heartbreak. My stomach turns into a knot, and I have to pull myself together. *Get off this page*, I demand to myself.

I exhale a triumphant sigh and decide to look online for some job postings. At least the Wi-Fi works.

"Vero! Vero! Wake up!" Fiona yells in my ear.

"What is it?" I ask with my eyes still closed.

"I got the job! I start waitressing tomorrow! Ivory is so cool! I am so excited!" she shrieks.

"Wow, good for you, Fio. I'm happy for you," I mumble.

Fiona runs out of my room and is still yelping things from the kitchen. I begin to wonder if she will even notice I spent my entire evening slaving over the apartment. Likely not. I call Fiona back into the room.

"I saw something tonight that I just have to share. Did you know that Raquel is dating Tyson now?" I ask.

"I heard a rumor about it. Please, she is a total idiot. Don't get upset and don't waste any time thinking about. He will be cheating on her soon enough. You know he will never change. You are way hotter, way smarter, and *way too good for him.* I've said it before, and I'll say it again! The very best thing you can do is move on, Vero. This is your closure. You know it's really over now," she comforts.

She points it out to me clear as day. It *really* is over. I knew this day was coming, I just didn't know how I was going to feel. Now that I'm going through it, I was right to worry before. *This sucks*.

In the morning, I get up nice and early to set up my printer and print off some resumes. First on my list is this low-key coffee shop a couple blocks down. I read that a lot of locals grab their morning coffees and bagels in there.

As I arrive, I see a giant surfboard mounted above the door reading "Beanz"—just a small blue-painted brick storefront with a couple of tables outside.

"Hi, my name is Veronica White. I would like to drop off my resume," I say to the woman at the till.

"Wonderful, I am the owner here. What kind of position are you looking for, Veronica?" she asks me sweetly.

"Whatever is available? I just moved in down the street. I love this place because it's close to home, it's a local hangout, and it's got a great vibe," I tell her as I look around.

"Excellent, Veronica, I think today is your lucky day. Why don't you come by tomorrow around nine in the morning and we can go over some basic training?" she said.

"Really? That's amazing, thank you. I didn't catch your name?" I state.

"I'm Melody Goldberg," she answers with a smile, "and I will be here in the morning for you."

"That's great, thank you again," I say and walk toward the door.

The coffee shop has a laid-back, beachy feeling with mini surfboard tabletops on all the tables. There are about ten of them, some with two seats, some with four. The walls are painted an ocean blue and the floor has light beat-up wood. She has a small stand set up with cream, sugar, and lids.

The cookies, muffins, bagels, slices of cake, and biscuits are all displayed in a glass contraption beside the till. The countertop is just a thick piece of wood. On the one wall, there is a mural of a guy surfing a big wave; and on the other walls, there are various pictures framed and all kinds of newspaper articles. Behind the till counter, there is a small cutout where you can see the tiny kitchen.

Wow, that's awesome! That wasn't as hard as I was expecting. At least now we both have jobs, and rent shouldn't be a problem for either of us. Luckily, our rent isn't so high anyway.

Fio loves her restaurant job at Joe's. She has made good friends with that Ivory girl, whom I am not sure of yet.

I need to do laundry. This is the first time I had even thought of it.

"Fio, where do we do laundry here?" I ask.

"Oh, good point!" She said obliviously.

"Really, Fio? You didn't ask?" I snap.

"Actually . . . I remember the guy saying there's a Laundromat down the street! When you go, can you do mine please? I have to go to work in ten minutes! My first lunch shift! Love you!" She smiles.

I load a big bag full of both mine and Fiona's laundry. After a quick look on Google Maps, I locate Soap Laundromat. It only takes roughly five minutes to walk there.

When I arrive at Soap. The old lady working there looks as if she could be Russian or something. She is heavy and has a large mole on her chin.

"Hello, this is the first time I am coming to a place like this, and I don't know what I have to do," I explain to her.

"That's nice," she replies in a very rude Russian accent.

"Would you mind giving me some simple directions?" I ask her again.

"You buy some detergent, put in some coins, you wait, switch the load over to the drier, put in more coins, and you wait again. The rest is pretty self-explanatory if it weren't already in the first place," she snarls at me again.

"Okay . . . ," I reply with wide eyes.

What a grouchy woman. She needs some happy pills, pronto.

After buying some Tide from her, I realize I won't have enough coins to dry my load.

"Could I please exchange this five-dollar bill for some coins?" I inquire.

"Not today. I am low on coins," she replies rudely, as usual.

I leave the load to wash and try to figure out where I can find some coins. I see across the street Floyd's Automotive, so I glide toward it in an attempt to find some help. It's a grey building with a sign revealing the name. It's a simple storefront, so I decide to go in.

"Hello?" I chime loudly, but no one calls back. To the right, there is a bell on the reception desk. I press down the bell twice. I am in a hurry because I don't want to leave my clothes sitting at Soap.

"Hello?" I call again, but no one comes.

I look through the cut square that reveals the shop. It's quite messy with a lot of scrap metal and what I would assume to be grease and paint lying around. It's a very disorganized shop painted a grey color throughout. The floors are scuffed-up black.

"How can I possibly help a girl like you?" a young guy says in a flirty manner as he wipes his hands off with a rag. He's probably a few years older than me and is wearing a navy blue mechanic suit.

"Uh, I need some change . . . I need eight quarters for the Laundromat. Can you exchange it for me?" I ask him.

"Well, sure I can. Will that be all for you?" he asks again in the same flirty tone.

"Please," I answer as I hand him the bill.

"You're new to town, I am presuming. I haven't seen your pretty face around here before that's for sure, or I would have remembered it," he states.

"Yeah, new to town and in a hurry for the quarters, so if you don't mind . . ." I realize now I am being rude, but I am in no mood for this. I am in no mood for flirting, not now, not for a while.

As I sit and wait for my laundry to finish its final cycle, I catch myself feeling regret again—that unsure feeling in the deepest part of an aching heart. I decide to call my mom again; she's the only person lately who can lift me out of this funk.

"Hi, honey! What a wonderful surprise! I am just gathering the last few things I will be sending your way! A little present! I couldn't resist!"

"Hi, Mom, thank you, that's very thoughtful."

"Oh no, I know that tone . . . What's the matter, sweetie? Still feeling the blues?"

"I don't know what I am feeling. I was expecting to be so much happier once I got here, like all my troubles and negative energy were all going to drift away with the wind. It hasn't seemed to have happened . . ."

"Not yet, my girl. You went through a lot back here at home, difficult times like that don't just disappear into thin air. You made the right choice, Vero. Even if you come home in four months from now because you have found that this is not your path, that's okay, sweetie. Dad and I love you unconditionally and are very proud of your independence. These feelings are normal, and if you weren't feeling them so strongly right now, you would be kidding yourself. Now go do something fun today, honey. When does your new job start?"

"Tomorrow."

"Good. Well, you prepare all your things and you call me tomorrow after you finish your first shift. I will be waiting. Looking forward to it. I love you!"

"I love you too. Talk to you tomorrow."

"Oh, honey. Before I forget to tell you, I had such a marvelous coffee date today with Miss Brielle. She says the studio just simply isn't the same without you! Don't you want to find a ballet studio down there? It might be what you are missing, sweetie."

"I'll think about it and let you know . . . Bye."

I danced ballet three days a week for three-hour sessions. I loved it. I felt such a relief while I was lacing up my pointe shoes, but I just don't want to do it anymore.

Fiona comes home later than I was expecting.

"How was your day at your new job, Fio?" I ask.

"It was great! You *have* to come by soon. Everyone is so welcoming and laid back!" she says enthusiastically.

"I'm happy for you. I did all the laundry, put all your stuff on your bed," I inform.

"Thanks. I can't wait to go to in again tomorrow. Ivory and I are going to hit the beach tonight, apparently there's a big party down there. Do you want to come and hang with us? You totally should!" she invites.

"Actually, I think I will tag along tonight. I could definitely use a change of scenery!" I accept.

"It won't be long until we have a new group of friends down here, V!" Fiona comforts.

I decide on a pair of weathered jean short shorts with a bright pink wife-beater. Summer's ending, but this weather would never give that away. I throw my just-past-the-shoulders sun-kissed blonde locks into a pony, apply a quick swipe of mascara to my long lashes, some clear gloss over my full lips, and meet Fiona in the kitchen.

"Ready? You look cute!" Fiona says to me as she slips on her flip-flops.

Fiona is ridiculously beautiful. She almost never wears any make up; she has flawless skin and to-die-for dirty blonde hair that grazes the top of her lower back. She has striking blue eyes, the color of turquoise almost, and from lying around in a bikini all summer, she has a golden tan to match. She has got to be every guy's dream.

"You always look gorgeous, Fio. Thanks for inviting me, I am pretty excited surprisingly," I admit.

"When would you ever *not* be invited? You're my favorite girl in the whole world! Now let's go have some fun!" she shrieks.

Ivory meets us outside our ramshackle apartment building and the three of us walk to the party together. She explains that there are often beach parties and that everyone is really easygoing and is always welcoming to new faces around. This is the kind of town where everyone knows everyone and no one can keep a secret to save their life. Sounds like a crime scene I just fled from . . .

"In high school, we had a lot of problems with backstabbing bitches. You can only imagine the amount of peace we are trying to keep here, so we won't be causing any drama with anyone this time around," Fiona explained to Ivory.

"I totally get you. I grew up here, so I will always have some of my past lingering around me, but I don't live with any regrets," Ivory answered.

Just as we walk toward the huge blazing fire, I spot a face I recognize. That guy from the auto body shop, that totally cheesy, obviously trouble kind of guy.

"Didn't think you were going to see me around here again, did you?" he says as he approaches the three of us. Fiona gives me a questioning face.

"Honestly, it didn't really cross my mind," I reply.

"Ouch! You know, a girl with a stinger doesn't intimidate me. I'll leave you with your girls tonight, but this definitely won't be the last time you see me," he says with a sly grin and walks away. I'll admit, he looks pretty hot.

"Oh my god, V! Why didn't you tell me you met a guy! He is *cute*!" Fiona gushes.

"I barely met him! I asked him to change my money so I could get some quarters for the laundry. He is so cheesy. Don't even try to tell me different!" I argue.

"So what, V? No one said he was your ultimate Mr. Right! Maybe he's just Mr. Right Now! Just be nice! Poor guy, you totally gave him the playing-hard-to-get card!" she scolds.

"Really, Fio! What makes you think I am ready for games already? After the summer I have just been through . . . I forgot my phone, I'll grab it at home and come back." I lie.

I can't help but get completely annoyed with Fiona about things like this. She is almost too easygoing sometimes. Fiona has always stuck with me, since our first day of grade two together. She has always taken my side and always defended me in situations. I am the reason her high school life was so intolerable.

I recently broke up with my ex-boyfriend at the beginning of the summer after a few years of complete and utter dramatics. Between girl fights and fights with him, I was always in a battlefield. There were always rumors going around about him, our relationship, or me because my ex was desirable and had his way with words. I was purposely naïve because I was crazy in love with him and never believed he was seeing other girls behind my back, but he was. I put my family and my closest friend through hell defending me. They knew my ability to see the truth for what it was, but I was hiding in the dark. I was a mean girl; in fact, I still am mean, and because I lived with a broken heart for so long, I have lost my carefree side—a side I want back.

Imagine having girls know secrets about your boyfriend that you will never know. I may be young, but that kind of betrayal has got to feel the same whether you're twelve or ninety-two.

Our break-up was extremely quick and shocking. One day, he sent me a text message and told me he liked someone else and there was nothing I could do anymore to make it work with us. Instead of freaking out and harassing him, I took the news and dealt with it on my own. I cried enough tears to water a small lake, but I never went back. I haven't spoken to him since, and I don't plan to ever again.

Now, when I meet other guys, I don't want to know their story. I need time for myself, not another player who uses my trust to form schemes. That's highly understandable and intelligent, but Fiona would love nothing more than for me to move on from it all with a snap of my fingers. It's not that easy. She's never had a serious relationship; she is the heartbreaker, the girl who pulls away when she's in too deep. She goes on dates and has her fun, but she never gives her heart away; yet she is the most amazing friend I could ever have.

I sent Fio a text when I got home.

-Vero: Hey, I just got home and feel tired. I think I'm just going to crash. Have tons of fun! Love you.

-Fio: I knew it! I'm sorry for the comment, V. Love you like crazy! Mwah!

I brush my teeth, put on my pajamas, and drift off into a deep sleep almost right away.

Eight seemed to have rolled around fast. I turn around for a few more minutes before I finally pull my ass out of bed. Another beautiful sunny day in California, but I'm glad to be starting my new job today. I plan to stick this one out until I find another one that's more stable. I still haven't decided what I want to do with the rest of my life as far as school or a career goes. I know for sure, it's not serving coffee.

I arrive ten minutes early, and Melody is waiting for me. I wore a pair of conservative jeans and a white t-shirt. The dress code for the job seems to be very casual and comfortable.

"Excellent! I am excited to have you here today. Have a seat, let me grab you something to drink. What would you like?" Melody offers kindly.

"This is kind of strange I'm sure, but I don't drink coffee. Maybe just an orange juice?" I replied.

"I'm not worried about the fact that you don't drink coffee, more for the customers! I will gladly grab you an orange juice. Have a seat, make yourself comfortable," she welcomes.

She returns with my orange juice and what looks like plain black coffee in her mug. We went over the whole job description—what she expects from me, what I should expect from her, my hourly wage, and my expected hours. After all the paperwork, I started my first day on the job.

Four-hour shifts are not so bad. Especially because everyone seems to love coffee, so the store always has people on their laptops or having catch-up coffee dates. Melody makes fresh muffins and cookies in the back kitchen and I stay up front monitoring the place and silently learning all the different drinks I'm expected to make.

When I got home, Fiona was there talking on her phone. I came in, took off my shoes, hung up my bag, and went into my room. There was an embarrassingly large display of real white lilies beside my fake ones. They are in a beautiful glass vase. Wow . . . I am puzzled and totally lost not having a single clue where they came from. I wait for Fio to finish on the phone, and as soon as she's done, I ask her.

"Oh, well, last night when you left, Kirk, the guy you were so rude to, came up to me and started asking a lot of questions. He asked what you like, what you do for fun, just wanted to know what your story is. You know, I asked Ivory about him. She said he's actually really nice and that she hasn't seen him with a girlfriend for a while. Apparently his ex-girlfriend used to live here, but she moved," Fiona explains.

"So you told him I like lilies, gave him our address, and let him into my room? That seems totally understandable and appropriate, thank you for your discretion!" I snapped back at her. So inappropriate! What was she thinking!

"No, he said he works down the street and he wanted to give you a gesture so you know he's sincere. I told him you like lilies. He said he would come by and drop some off before he started work this morning. For the record, I did not let him in your room," she snarls with focused eyes.

"Well, what am I supposed to do now? I am not interested in him," I say nervously as I flick my hair from one side to the other.

"Veronica, you need to let some of the tension go. No one is perfect. Kirk is making a real effort with you, and I made sure he is not some creep. He seems legitimate," Fiona insists.

"How annoying," I grumble under my breath.

"I heard that! Here, I wrote his number down for you. I didn't give him yours, I told him I wouldn't do that to you, but you have his, so in the event the polite Vero would like to thank him, you can."

I look at the lilies again. Gosh, they are pretty gorgeous. I debate my opinions in my head. I could easily not call him, totally avoid any further interaction, or I could call him. If I call, for sure I will be stuck on the phone with him and his effort. I finally decided that I am going to wait a few more hours until I make my ultimate decision. Wow, my life is pretty boring if this is my biggest worry.

I check my Facebook, text back a friend from home, eat an apple, take a nap, and when I wake up, I decide I won't call him. If I call, I will look interested, and since I am not, I won't pull a Fiona and lead him on.

* * *

Another week passes us by, Fiona and I both working at our new jobs, and more apartment rearranging. Nothing interesting has happened this week. She decided to drag me to the tennis courts with her. I'm dreadful at tennis, so as collateral, she treated me to dinner at Joe's on her night off. The whole time, she continued to nag me about Kirk. She can't believe I didn't call.

In the morning, I wake up early to get ready for work. Fiona is up too, all decked out in her tennis gear. She was meeting Ivory to sign herself up at the tennis club. She takes tennis pretty seriously; she really enjoys the game.

"I was thinking tonight we could take my car and just drive around, I'm in the mood for that," Fiona suggests.

"Sure, I would like that too," I answer.

"So since I have today off, obviously I want to hit the beach later. When you're off, do you want to meet me?" she asks.

"Yeah, I don't see why not. It's just a short shift today. Melody said it's been slow lately, so she doesn't need me that much," I said.

"Okay, ciao, bella, enjoy work!" She smiles.

"Ciao!" I call back.

# Chapter Two

After work, I meet Fio at the beach. She has an ice-cold water bottle in hand and sporting her tiny bikini and her overly large sunglasses. She has mastered the beach look.

"It's so funny, you totally suit the beach. It just looks like you belong here!"

"That's because I *do*!"

"Do you think I should join a gym or something? I've never really worried about it since dance has always given me more than enough exercise," I ask.

"Start dancing again, Veronica! You're a gorgeous ballerina! Why don't you want to dance?"

"I'm not tall enough, I don't float like the other girls."

"Oh, whatever, Miss Perfectionist! Get some tennis shoes and I'll show you the ropes on the court once and for all!"

I lay down my towel beside her, strip to my bikini, and pat on my sunscreen. My skin isn't the tone of Fiona's. I can burn easily, but I'm not ghostly pale. My mom was always a freak about sunscreen, so I've always applied it.

"So I saw Kirk today, V," Fiona starts.

"So? He lives in the same town as us, you're bound to see him," I defend.

"He asked why you never called," she informs.

"Okay? Did you tell him it's because I'm not interested?" I ask.

"No, I told him you are stubborn as hell and I thought it was so rude that you didn't call. I'm not going to stand behind you on this one. Usually, when you are being treated unfairly or need defending, I have no problem. But this, this is just mean," she scolds.

I don't respond, simply because I really don't know what to say. Obviously Kirk has no interest in being just friends with me, and I have no interest in being more, so what kind of situation is that?

"Vero, I love you. I want to see you happy! Maybe Kirk is the answer to all of this. Why don't you just give him a chance? He seems like a really nice guy!" she starts again.

"Fiona, I appreciate you, and I know you are just trying to help, but I *am* happy. Maybe if Kirk is so hungry for some attention, you could give it to him. Maybe you can change your own ways and have a serious relationship for once. Maybe Kirk would be perfect for you. I *am* happy!" I suggest.

"If you think I would go for a guy who is clearly much more into you, you are dead wrong!" she cheekily states.

"Fine, so let's just leave Kirk be, and we can both be single and happy together!" I suggest again.

"Kirk is not going away. He lives here and so do you! You need to find a resolution for this. Either tell him you are definitely not interested and to please stop, or give him a chance," she snaps.

"If I see Kirk again, I will say something, okay? Does that make you happy, Fio?" I ask.

"Race you to the water! Loser has to jump in!" she yells as she gets up and runs for the ocean. Great, I clearly lost.

After such a fun afternoon tanning and swimming with Fio, we finally get home to have a much-needed shower. As we walk up to the door, there is a note.

Veronica,

Can I please take you on a date this week? You're driving me crazy.

Kirk

Oh my! I look at Fiona, and she glares back at me.

"Can you not see?" she hisses as she walks inside.

I grab the note, and a small part of me becomes flattered. Okay, maybe larger than a small part. I put the note on my desk and shower off my salty body.

Fio and I get ready for our driving adventure, as we climb into her '96 blue Volkswagen Rabbit. Her car won't start. That's not surprising considering she takes care of absolutely nothing she owns.

"What the hell! This would happen to me right after it leaves my dad! What's wrong with it?" she asks me franticly.

"You're asking the wrong person. I only ever borrowed my mom's car. I know absolutely nothing about cars . . . but I know someone who does," I say reluctantly.

"Kirk," Fiona says. "Call him or I will."

This is so embarrassing. I really don't want to call him, but difficult times call for difficult measures.

"Hi Kirk, it's Veronica."

"This must be a prank call."

"No, well, actually, I am calling on completely different terms than what you are expecting."

"Oh . . . then why are you calling?"

"Fiona's car just broke down in front of our apartment . . . I was hoping you could maybe come and have a look at it. Of course we would pay you for your troubles, I'm not looking for any favors."

"Funny, I definitely am. I'll close down my shop and I'll see you in ten minutes."

He hangs up. *Thanks a lot, Fio*, I mumble in my head. She better hope this isn't some kind of trick.

When Kirk arrives in his old, battered white pick-up truck, the atmosphere gets awkward. He looks under the car, pops the hood, checks some parts out, and eventually has a verdict.

"So it's just a few old parts that need replacing, you're lucky this thing got you guys through your two-hour trek without any problems. I don't mind doing this for you, Fiona, won't take me much. However, it'll cost that green-eyed cutie," Kirk says as he points at me.

"It'll cost me how much?" I tease.

"I'm not talkin' dollar value, sweetie. I'm talkin' time," he replies.

I roll my eyes at him.

"Your effort is admirable, trust me, but I don't have what it seems you need right now," I say boldly.

"I just need to spend some time with a quality girl. I find you intriguing. I like what you're about. Now stop with the mind games and just agree to a simple hangout," he says.

"I'm not playing mind games with you, Kirk! If you want to simply hang out, fine, but don't be expecting a good-night kiss," I reply.

Seeing as though Fiona's car is out of commission tonight, I agree finally to spend some time with Kirk, one on one, as he specified.

"So where are we going to spend our quality time, Kirk?" I ask him.

"I don't know, Veronica. Somewhere warm and dark where we can spend the evening making out and you can admit you are secretly in love with me," he replies.

"What the hell!" I react to him. "Maybe in your wildest dreams!"

"You're right, those are in my dreams lately," he smiles.

"What's your story, Kirk? Are you always so upfront with girls like this?"

"I haven't been for a while. I grew up with a womanizing father who couldn't commit to a cell-phone plan let alone a monogamous relationship. I royally fucked up with my last girlfriend who treated me like gold, and I tested her limits every day and made her life hell. I took all her dreams, all her trust, everything she had going for herself and squished it like a bug under my shoe. Eventually, she packed up her shit and moved away on me. Haven't talked to her since," he tells me.

"See, I knew you were that kind. Ew, you make me want to be sick right now," I snarl.

"Veronica, this was two years ago. Since then, I have put everything I have into opening my auto shop. That shop is my life. I have different priorities now. If I were still that way, trust me, I wouldn't be talking about it," he says. "Listen, and there's something about you that I dig. You're not like most girls. Yeah, I can see, your last boyfriend totally fucked you up too. Made you feel like a loser with nothing going for yourself. Maybe it's my guilty conscience, but I'm not interested in that again," he continues.

"I feel bad for your ex," I reply.

"My ex-girlfriend was sweet, but she wasn't totally innocent either. I don't want to dwell on my past. I'm over it. Now, you need to get over yours," he said.

For a minute, I think maybe Fio has something to do with how honest he is being. She probably told him about what happened to me this summer. She probably told him why I'm so emotionally turned off and defensive. He probably already knows everything and he's trying to break the ice so that I don't have to hide it from him.

"I didn't move here to dwell on the events of my last relationship. I want to move on," I said to him quietly.

"Great. I have ghosts in my past, but I want a fresh start," he said.

For some reason, I believe him.

The whole night, Kirk and I sat on the beach with the waves in the background as we admit our most intimate insecurities and buried memories. He comes forth with the fact that he spent time in the strip clubs and had sex with a couple of the strippers in town. How he encouraged his ex-girlfriend to have an abortion when she became pregnant at seventeen. He admits he did her wrong by pursuing her best friend and winning. He admits all the things he did to drive her away, and how he is finally okay with her choice to leave him after four tough years together. He talked about his dreams of his auto shop and how he hasn't spoken to his father in almost a year because he is nothing but a bad influence with too much money. I share with Kirk the hurt I have felt in the past, the betrayal, and the effects of all my fears.

"I'm sure he regrets it, believe me," Kirk reassures.

"He already has a new girlfriend," I shrug desperately, trying to hide my disappointment.

"Who cares? For what it's worth, I think a lot of guys do that just to hide their pain. It doesn't mean he doesn't ever think about you or has regrets. Don't take that kind of shit personally. Guys are just dumb, and I am a guy, so you have no choice but to believe me," he comforts.

"I think I'm more mad that a girl who saw what he put me through all those years would have the audacity to try and step in and fill my shoes," I argue.

"You're overthinking all of this. The guy's just a dud, I don't want to talk about him," he says as he attempts to flash a genuine grin.

"Can guys really change?" I ask doubtfully.

"Only if we want to. When we find a real game changer sometimes we don't have a choice. A lot of chicks just fill in gaps and let us walk all over them so they're not a reason. I mean, some girls are real dumb and allow us guys to repeat things from our past relationships that we were into. Even if they know it's been done before, they don't seem to even care. Those chicks aren't game changers. One-nighters aren't classy, they don't leave us wanting more, but they are fun. I shouldn't be telling you stuff like this, it's guy code," Kirk teases and changes the subject.

We pull in at six in the morning, exhausted, knowing I have to work at nine. I give Kirk a hug, and I tell him I was sorry for being such a bitch before. I tell him I hope we can hang out again and that I had a nice time. I crawl into bed and fall fast asleep.

I wake up to a text from Kirk sent around six in the morning.

-Kirk: I'm not going anywhere.

I am far too exhausted to reply as I am sure he is fast asleep and I am now just over two and a half hours rested. Not a good look. I head to work and arrive just on time.

I contemplate a coffee—that's how tired I am. Melody initiates small talk about the weather, her daughter, and the shop—nothing excessively exciting. I tell her a little about my small family, my two dogs, and how I miss them so much already.

I get home from work and immediately am aching for my bed. I dive in, and it feels as if I've hit a miraculous cloud. It doesn't take long before I'm into a wonderful nap. I don't think I even moved once while I was sleeping. My mind was so excited to shut off. I had not even begun to process the amount of material my brain was going to have to digest about Kirk. It was still astonishing to me how honest he was; so vulnerable and yet still so confident.

When I wake up, I stagger around my room, changing into something more comfortable, and then decide to spend some time on the computer. I received an e-mail from my mom.

**From: Jacqueline White**
**Subject: You didn't call**
**Date: September 3, 2011**
**To: Veronica White**

It's Saturday morning and I didn't receive a call from you! I am worried! I have some exciting news that I guess I will have to write instead. Dad just surprised me with a three-week cruise around Europe next month! Maybe there are some benefits of you moving away from your momma after all;)

Love you forever and for always,

Mom

Wow. My dad *never* takes any time off of work. He is a defense lawyer and is always so busy and stressed out; vacation is never an option. Good for my mom. This e-mail puts a smile on my face. My parents are pretty cool.

I find Fio who is absolutely dying to talk about my night.

"Tell me! Tell me *everything*!" she asks excitedly.

"You will be disappointed if you think I have anything interesting to say. He is nice, nicer than I initially thought. He's cute, which I will now admit, and I'll probably see him again, but only on a friendship basis. There was no kissing, no intimacy besides a hug, and that's that!" I inform.

"Oh, but he obviously so badly wanted to plant one on you, don't deny!" She laughs.

"Yeah you're probably right, but he didn't! Now leave me alone!" I joke.

I decide to finally reply to Kirk's text after twelve hours of letting it sit.

-Vero: I enjoy your friendship, Kirk Floyd. You entertain me with your confidence.

Within about thirty seconds, he replies.

-Kirk: So . . . She does reply . . . Good to know . . . Can I see you soon?

I read the text and strongly sigh. I am not against seeing Kirk again, I just don't know how long his interest is going to last before things have to move in one direction or the other.

-Vero: I guess so. Can I sleep before 6 a.m. this time? Please.

-Kirk: We'll see, pretty lady, we'll see. I'll pick you up at 8.

I have about two hours before I can expect Kirk; something tells me he'll be on time. I tell Fiona I am going out with Kirk tonight and inquire about her plans.

"*Again?*" she freaks out.

"Stop that nonsense! It's Saturday night; I have nothing else to do, unless you have something better to propose? In that case, I will gladly ditch Kirk!" I offer.

"No . . . Actually I've been so tired lately I am going to read this new book I've been meaning to start and I'm hitting the hay at a decent hour!" she tells me.

"Okay, I definitely won't wake you when I get home. I won't be late like I was last night or I will definitely be in trouble by Melody tomorrow!" I inform.

"You need at least one weekend day off! You work at that place all the time!" she whines.

"Sleep tight!" I say as I hug Fio and leave her room.

Kirk is on time, and he looks so cute in his grey polo, fitted jeans, and flip-flops. *Stop it, Vero*, I tell myself.

"Like what you see, little lady?" he winks.

"What does that even mean?" I tease.

"It means . . . Do you like what you see?" he repeats.

"You don't completely kill my eyesight. Where are we going?" I admit.

"That's a surprise!" he winks.

We drive about fifteen minutes. The car ride includes a lot of over-the-top singing coming from Kirk's vocal cords, some reckless driving, but all in all . . . a lot of laughs.

"Kirk, is your CD available for purchase?" I taunt.

He just looks at me and laughs. I don't think I could offend him even if I tried. He's so laid-back.

We arrive at a little restaurant—not many tables outside, not many inside.

"Kirk!" the owner shrieks. "What brings you in this fine evening?"

"Dex, are you blind? Do you not see this beautiful young woman I have been lucky enough to take out?" he said cockily.

"Indeed, I see her. What's your name?" the owner asks me.

"Veronica, you can call me Vero," I reply.

"Pleasure to meet you. Now please, allow me to give you the best seat in the house," he said as he ushers us to a small table by the window.

He seems to be fairly young, I would say midfifties, and has a warm presence.

"My best friend's dad," Kirk rationalizes.

"Seems like a lovely man," I nod.

"You seem lovely," Kirk flashes a silly grin and grabs my hand.

"You must not know me then," I smirk and pull my hand away.

We continue to tease each other, and Kirk continues to make me blush by having inappropriate outbursts, which are beginning to grow on me oddly enough. He orders fish n' chips and insists I have them as well. He claims that they are the best thing on the menu. He convinces me, and together we sit, eating fish n' chips and drinking ice-cold root beers, getting to know each other. For the first time in a while, I feel stress free.

"Now, I was thinking we could probably polish off a mean banana split for dessert, but not here," Kirk plans.

"Sure . . . Give me a few hours to digest that food first! I haven't ate that much in a while," I reply.

"A few more hours? I have that long?" he asks me jokingly.

"No, smartass, you don't. I was implying a rain check! I am stuffed! Just take me home and I would be forever grateful," I smile at him.

Kirk pays the bill and off we go. At dinner, I learned about his best friends, how one has a gardening business and is very successful, and the other goes to school for architecture. I told him I'd love to meet them, and he told me he has to wait until he's sure he has me all to himself before I can meet the competition. He seems to really love his friends and holds a lot of respect for them . . . I like that.

We arrive at my apartment, and Kirk gives me a sad face. I laugh at him.

"I would invite you in, but I'm just not that kind of girl," I tease.

"Come here," he said to me.

Kirk takes my face in his hand and puts a loose grip on my jaw line. He moves toward my face and turns it, pressing a light kiss against my cheek.

"I enjoyed mowing down on fish n' chips with you, Vero. I hope we do it again," he says to me.

My heart shifts in my chest.

"I don't know, Kirk . . . It will depend on whether or not I spend the evening with my head in the toilet from food poisoning," I tease.

"Yeah, yeah. Run along now, Princess Vero, and leave my heart in the truck this time!" He smiles.

I jump out of the truck and walk to my apartment with my warm heart—a feeling I thought I'd forever lost.

As suspected, my phone buzzes with a text.
-Kirk: Dammit! I told you to leave my heart in the truck!

What a goof. I roll my eyes at him and reply.
-Vero: *Rolling eyes*

I wash my face to make sure it's free of makeup, brush my teeth, put a brush through my hair, and put on my pajamas. I feel peaceful. I will sleep like a baby tonight.

# Chapter Three

As I jump into bed, Fiona swings open my door and appears to be drunk. I thought she was in bed.

"Fiona, are you drunk?" I ask her.

"I just got home from a crazy party with Ivory! I totally would have invited you but you were with Kirk!" she mumbles.

"You didn't answer my question, Fio. Are you drunk?" I ask again.

"I may have had a couple of drinks," she admits.

Fiona was never a big partier back home. In high school, she always was the one who preached that drinking was bad and not necessary to have fun. Her grandfather suffered from alcoholism, and she was always against it.

"Hmm . . . sorry to hear that," I say.

"I had so much fun! You are coming with me next time! Wahoo!" she yells as she leaves my room.

I follow her out because I have a suspicion she has had more than a couple of drinks.

"What exactly did you drink?" I ask her sternly.

"Just a few coolers, a few beers, nothing hard," she answers carelessly.

"Okay, well if you begin to feel sick or anything, just yell at me, k?" I say to her as I go back into my room.

I decide to phone Kirk and get the story on Ivory. I didn't feel the need to until now.

"Hi, sorry to call, I just want to know what you know about Fiona's new friend Ivory?"

"She's a pretty heavy partier, likes to pop a few pills now and then. She's a bit of a slut from what I've heard. I'm sure she's a great gal to have fun with but not best friend material. Why?"

"Fio just came home drunk, and she told me she was taking a night off to sleep. I'm just worried about this new friend. Fiona never drinks, she's always been against it."

"She's growing up, and she has independence now. She's going to experiment, and so are you."

"Thanks for the info. I hope you have a good sleep."

Now I am worried about Fio. Oh, how the tables turn.

When I wake up, I head into Fiona's room to make sure she is okay. She is fast asleep with her mouth open and her arm draped over the side of her bed. I prepare some water for her and place it on her side table. She will be in need of that.

I remember one night in high school I completely overdid it with vodka and juice at a house party. I got totally drunk, my mom had to come and pick me up. I felt so ill in the morning my parents said that was my punishment. The deathly hangover that lingered around my head and my stomach all day long was enough to keep me away. I figure Fiona will have one just like it today, but I don't think it'll keep her from her new circle of friends.

I get ready for work and arrive on time, as usual. Melody is there, and she tells me today her daughter is visiting her for the week. She is one year older than I, and Melody suggests we all do something fun after work. She says her daughter is a lot of fun. I agree because I have nothing better to do, and another friend can't hurt.

After work, we decide to all go bowling at the lanes in town. Melody's daughter's name is Mandi, and she is very pleasant company. She tells me all about her life, her friends, her dad, and her job. I feel like I know her better than her mom does. Mandi enjoys talking, which is great, because at this point, I only want to listen. My life is so complex and confusing; I really don't feel like getting into it.

Throughout our bowling games, Kirk had been texting me nonstop, wanting updates on my night. I figure he was bored, but I also figure he really was interested, seeming as though he is pretty into me. I agreed to let him pick me up since I definitely didn't want to take the bus and I did *not* want to ask Melody to drive in the opposite direction. When Kirk arrives, I am grateful for his generosity and am actually pretty excited to see him. I leave Melody and Mandi inside the lanes and run to meet Kirk.

"Looking gorgeous as usual, Miss Vero," he says with a mischievous grin.

"Smooth talker," I tease.

"I've missed you," he starts again.

"Yeah, yeah . . . Just drive!" I laugh.

"Can we go for that banana split now? You left me hanging, remember?" he insists.

"Yeah, I could go for some of that," I agree and shake my head with defeat.

When we get to the ice cream place, Kirk runs around the truck and opens my door. Acting like such a gentleman, I don't buy it for one second. We enter the ice cream place and the girl at the counter immediately recognizes Kirk.

"Hey, Kirk! Long time no see! Let me guess, banana split with extra milk chocolate?" the girl says.

"Great memory, Alexa! That's wicked. Yes, banana split with two spoons this time," Kirk replies.

I feel like everywhere we go together, everyone knows him.

"Why does everyone know you everywhere we go?" I ask.

"Probably because I've been around a lot longer than you have, and that's just what good business people do to keep their customers," he replies nonchalantly.

The split was amazing. I usually don't go for one when it's my choice, but it was definitely a pleasant first. The ice-cream melted in my mouth, and the banana was fresh and flavorful.

"Yummy! Thank you for that," I say to Kirk.

"My pleasure, I'm glad you enjoyed it. I had a feeling you might dig it. Pretty much everyone does. It's the best thing they offer here. Basically famous for them around town," he replies.

"You know the best dish every place around here," I assume.

"Vero, I've only taken you to two place so far, and in both, I seem to have a pretty decent reputation at. Maybe this has been a plan of mine to make sure you're becoming a bit smitten with me," Kirk winks.

"Again with the blatant honesty, Floyd. That's growing on me."

After we leave the ice-cream place, we head back to my apartment so Kirk can drop me off.

"Thank you again for picking me up and taking me for a delicious dessert, my tummy is grateful too." I smile at him.

"Wouldn't have it any other way. I wouldn't have wanted you to take interest in some random guy at the lanes and have him drive you home. He might take priority over me, I can't be having any of that," Kirk flirts.

"Is that your jealous side coming out and expressing itself?" I tease.

"Yeah, get used to it. Now run along, Vero, I don't want to keep you."

"Thanks, Kirk, see you soon," I say as I jump out of the truck.

In the morning, I feel like going for a run around the neighborhood. Let off some steam and get some exercise. I pull on my runners after I've dressed myself head-to-toe in running gear. I start out around the block, and after about twenty minutes, I find myself at Kirk's auto shop.

"Good morning, Kirk," I say in a pant.

"Vero! Look at you! Getting some fresh air I can see," he replies.

"Yeah, decided to stretch my legs, haven't been out for a while." I smile.

"The good news here is, I also love to run and would love to race you sometime and see how you match up in comparison," he initiates.

"I don't do races. I run strictly for fun and exercise. I'm not so competitive, but I'm almost positive I'd beat you! If you ever want to run for fun, I'm your girl," I comeback.

"You sure are." He smiles.

I look around; it seems that he is working on some type of BMW. The shop is very disorganized, with parts lying about. It needs a feminine touch.

"You know, Kirk, I could come by one day and really give your shop some organization. Looking around, it kills me to see how disorganized this place is. It would make your job so much easier. You probably have no time to do any work like that, you're your only employee," I offer.

"I would love if you wanted to come in here and give me a hand. Yeah, I've been messy, because every day when I finish, I just want to leave and do something else. I don't want to hang around to clean and organize. One day, I will run a bigger shop with employees who do all my dirty work. For now, I will take your free labor as a gesture of kindness," he accepts.

"Great, it's settled then. I will come by soon and organize all your tools and parts. You will be much happier with that. Anyways, I've got to get back. I have today off though, so maybe if you want to come by when you're off, we can go do something?" I ask fearlessly.

"Unreal . . . I can't wait. Anything for some time with you, beautiful. For the record, I don't mind you a little sweaty. I have yet to see you in a state I would not prefer you," he teases.

"Whoa, is that not a little forward, Floyd?" I reply.

"My tongue says outrageous things when it's around you, Vero, I swear!" he teases again.

"See you later," I chuckle.

When I arrived home after my long run, I see there are some people beside us moving in. It seems they are a young couple that didn't bring much along either. It's not usually my nature to approach strangers and be outgoing, but I am in a respectably blissful state this fine morning, so I offer a hello.

"Hi there, I'm Vero. I see you guys are moving in next door to my best friend Fiona and I. Please let me know if you need anything," I offer.

"Pleasure to meet you, Vero. My name is Konner, this is my fiancée, Bridgette," Konner responses.

"Yes, hi, this place seems to be a little rough around the edges, but what can you expect for the price?" Bridgette adds with both her hands wrapped around a large box.

"When we first arrived a few weeks ago, I was downright mortified with the state of the building and the apartment. I just wanted to cry. I was so upset with my friend, but surprisingly enough, after a couple weeks now, it feels safe and sound and you'll both be adapting quickly too. Good luck with your move in!" I beam.

"Thanks, see you soon," Konner says and continues on.

I found Fiona in the kitchen making toast and peanut butter when I came in. She looked sickly and tired.

"How are feeling today, Fio?" I ask her.

"Like death, to be honest. I don't know what got into me last night. I was totally exhausted, but I didn't want to hang out here alone all night. When Ivory invited me out, I didn't see why not. Everyone was drinking, and I just felt like it," she answers.

"It's fine, you are human, you mess up, you get drunk, and now today you will be nursing a nice hangover to remind you!" I say with a wink.

"Thanks for the water, I noticed it right when I woke up. It was like an answer to my prayer! Love you!" Fiona said.

"I thought that might be just what the doctor ordered. I'm in the shower," I chime.

As I stand under the water deciding whether to go with my KMS shampoo or Morrocanoil, I begin to think about how happy I am. All summer I was feeling gloomy and disorientated, barely finding food attractive, not feeling the urge to go for any runs, and I lost all my hobbies and interests. I woke up this morning with a runner's itch, with a tune in my head, with a smile on my face. Could this be because I have finally decided to give it a go with Kirk? Are all my walls coming down because my heart has allowed me another chance? I really didn't come here expecting this at all. In fact, I tried really hard to avoid it. I hate clichés like "things happen when you least expect it," or whatever that saying is. Then I begin to think, these sayings wouldn't exist if they had never happened to someone else. I need to learn to just embrace this.

I continue on with my unusually long shower, switching over to the conditioner debate. I am so indecisive lately; it's just bizarre. Today I want to go all out and blow-dry my hair, lotion up my body, refresh my face, give myself some TLC. The TLC I have been depriving of for the last three months.

Once I am out of the shower, I take one towel for my hair and wrap it. I snatch another for my body and dry myself off. I wrap the towel around my body and tuck it in, the ever famous "towel dress" all girls use religiously.

My mom gave me an amazing Chi blow dryer for Christmas last year, but since my hair is wavy, it's always a battle with the hairbrush, so I never bother with it. I always just let it air dry and fall how it may. Releasing my towel wrap, my wet hair hangs and I dose my hands with a generous amount of leave-in conditioner and run it through the ends. Reluctantly, I take my hairbrush and begin to fight through the knots. Once my hair is smooth, I take a roller brush in one hand, my dryer in the other. After what feels like hours, my hair is dry and bouncy. It looks clean and shiny—just the look I was going for.

Next, I drop my body towel and squirt body lotion into my hands. Beginning at my chest, I work my way down, even applying lotion to the soles of my feet. There is no feeling better than being fresh out of the shower clean, smelling heavenly, and feeling divine. I clutch my housecoat and put it on.

The bathroom is still steamy when I open the door. Fiona comes out of her room to meet me.

"Wow, I heard the blow dryer and I thought someone else was using our bathroom! That's a first in a while, wouldn't you agree?"

"Yeah. I don't know what came over me. I'm just in the mood to be good to myself today."

"V, you look happy. You have a wicked glow to you. You're inspiring me. I, however have a headache the size of Texas! I have to lie down. What are you doing today?"

"I'm pretty sure I am meeting up with Kirk. We didn't decide what we're going to do yet, but probably just something low-key."

"Yeah, now I understand the blow dryer and the self-love. I'm so happy for you, Vero, I think this is going to be blamelessly good for you."

I give her a lighthearted shrug and head into my room. She always has my best interests at heart even if we tend to battle at times. She is the one who pushed Kirk on me, and I wouldn't have pursued him, as I made clear before.

I find a place in front of my full-length mirror positioned on a bare wall. I apply my face moisturizer, lip balm, and then my tinted sunscreen my mom has forced down my throat instead of foundation. As I begin my simple eye makeup, my phone buzzes.

-Kirk: I'm done for the day. Got better things to attend to;)

-Kirk: Can I pick you up in 10?

I quickly feel rushed and finish up. I run to my closet, choose a flower-printed sundress, quickly throw it over my shoulders, and smooth it down my body.

-Vero: Sure, Kirk, see you in 10.

# Chapter Four

I put my things back in their place and close my bedroom door. In the kitchen, I toss some almonds into my mouth and slide on my flip-flops. I take my purse and opt for a piece of mint gum. Nervously, I head down the stairs to meet him.

"You look angelic today," he winks at me.

"Cleaner look than earlier in the day, I would say." I smile.

I notice Kirk has also had time to take a shower and change. He has on his regular black Lacoste flip-flops, khaki shorts, and a white tee. He has thrown some gel in his hair to make it look a little neater and Oakley sunglasses cover his bright blue eyes.

"Where are we going today?" I ask.

"The sun is out, I think we should spend some time at the beach. I hope you're hungry, I put together a picnic for us, and I know a good spot we can go to eat it. I also arranged a volleyball court for us to throw a ball around," he suggests.

"Sounds good," I smile.

When we arrive at the beach, he parks his truck and gets out to grab whatever it is he has packed. In his arms, I can see a blanket and a literal picnic basket. I get a sensation that feels like butterflies as I watch Kirk. He gives me a big toothy grin and I reciprocate.

"Shall we?" he smiles.
"We shall!" I answer.

We walk down some big rocks, a little bit past some weathered logs, and finally after our trek through the sand, he presents a quiet, secluded place for us to sit. He lays out the blanket and places the basket down.

"Come sit," he says as he pats the place beside him.
"This is a beautiful spot," I state.
"Yeah, I like to come here alone and think," Kirk admits.
"I don't blame you," I offer.

For lunch Kirk packed us two turkey sandwiches and two lemonades. Inside, I also find a giant chocolate chip cookie in a brown bag.

"I hope you're satisfied with this picnic selection, I threw it together last minute." Kirk grins.
"It's wonderful! I'm pretty easy to please, but turkey is definitely my favorite," I reply.

After we ate, Kirk split the cookie in two, and we each ate our halves. The beach is so peaceful with the waves and the sounds of the birds calling each other. I feel peaceful with Kirk even if I don't know him well. He has a comforting presence. As our afternoon progresses, we tease each other and we laugh. Kirk threatens to throw me into the ocean and I beg for him not to. He asks me about work, Fio, and my parents. I ask him more about the shop and how it's operated. He is running everything on his own, but his grandparents help him out a lot. He talks more about his absent dad and how he sometimes wishes they had a better relationship. I can't relate. My dad and I are on great terms. We don't talk that often because he's always really busy, but he's always kind and supportive, and that's all I need from him.

"You have nice teeth and startling eyes, Kirk," I compliment with a smile.

Kirk moves closer toward me and looks me in the eyes. Within a second, he places his lips on mine and we begin to kiss each other. My stomach has what feels like a thousand butterflies fluttering around hastily. My eyes are closed, and before I even know what is happening, I drop my defenses and give in to Kirk. The electricity between us is hard to deny.

Our kiss didn't last a lifetime. Although, I can't say I would mind. We come back to reality, and I giggle nervously. He smiles at me and lies down on the blanket. He signals me to lie beside him, so I do. We lie together visibly cuddling, but we say nothing to each other. I snuggle my head right onto Kirk's chest, and he strokes the side of my face and runs his fingers through my hair. I am immediately grateful I went the extra mile with it this morning. I am so relaxed, and time passes us by in no hurry.

"You have soft lips," he compliments as he clasps my chin and runs his thumb along my bottom lip.

"Thanks." I smile.

"All right, time for some volleyball. Have you played before?" he asks.

"Yes, once or twice," I smirk.

Of course I have played volleyball before. At school, they made our all-girls phys-ed class play all sports imaginable, including lawn bowling and archery. Kirk takes off his shirt to reveal a large tattoo inked across his upper back. It's all different designs; it almost looks tribal. I wasn't expecting that, but I definitely think it looks hot.

"I'll serve!" he calls from the opposite side of the net.

"Are you really good at this, Kirk? Am I about to get my ass kicked?" I inquire.

"I'm all right." He smiles.

"I didn't know you had tattoos," I state.

"Yeah, a back piece, and I'm working on both sleeves eventually," he answers, "I got them when I was eighteen, I haven't decided if I'll add to them or not, who knows."

He sends a spike right toward me, and I react by defensively throwing my forearms over my face. This causes the ball to ricochet off of me and fly far to the right toward the water. Kirk runs after it and re-serves a lot gentler.

"Sorry!" he yelled before he served.

This time the ball floats toward me, making it easier for me to return. I volley it off my wrists and it makes it over to Kirk. Expecting to see the ball float again, I approach the return in proper form but the ball comes zooming toward me and hits me right in the face; actually, right on the bridge of my nose to be exact. It didn't tickle. I fall backward onto the sand immediately covering my face with my hands.

"Oh my god! Vero! Are you okay? I'm so sorry!" Kirk yells as he runs over to me.

"Ow . . . ," I mutter.

We decide to leave the beach as the game is clearly over. Kirk picks everything up off the sand, and we walk to the truck. I feel drowsy and calm as I sit. My face doesn't hurt anymore. He pulls out of the parking lot, and within a few minutes we are back at my apartment. I'm disappointed because I've had such a wonderful afternoon with Kirk despite the tiny accident. He tells me he has to meet up with some buddies later at his place and he needs to grab some food and clean up. I get out of the truck and before I completely leap out, Kirk grabs hold of my arm and pulls me toward him. He plants a kiss on my lips and says he can't wait to hang out again. I smile at him with sad eyes because I wish we could spend more time together right now. He asks me again if I'm sure I'm okay. I tell him it's all good. I jump out of the truck and walk toward my place. The debate to look back or not comes over me, but I hear him reverse and drive away.

When I get home, I decide to give my mom a call.

"Hi, Mom."

"Hi, darling! How are you?"

"I'm good, just at home. I went to the beach pretty much all day."

"What a hard day you must have had!"

"What's going on at home?"

"Just an average Monday evening. Dad is still at the office. Listen, honey, I ran into some ladies today when I was at Zumba. They said they haven't seen Fiona's mom in quite some time, and there had been some talk around town that she is going through a divorce. You know how those ladies are. They know everything about everyone. Has Fiona said anything about her parents lately?"

"Before we left, things were not good between them. A lot of fighting, and Fiona's thought is that Henry might be having an affair with his secretary at work. That's upsetting that people are gossiping about her family. That's not very fair."

"Talk to Fiona, she might need a modest ear and a genuine hug right now. Call me tomorrow, sweetie."

Part of me is not surprised to hear this news. I am sad for Fiona. She has never had a functional family life. Her sister Jordan and Fiona have always been each other's only family who actually enjoy each other. They get along great, but her sister is older and always away. She has a new boyfriend every week, and they always seem to be exceedingly wealthy and head-over-heels in love with her. In comparison to Fiona, Jordan is even more breathtaking.

Henry, Fiona's dad, is a hard man to take. He is judgmental and sharp; and Fiona's mom, Gwen, is sweet but demanding. I agree to ask Fiona what's going on with her parents and ask her how she is.

"Good evening, Fio. Still in bed I see," I said.

"By choice tonight. I feel much better. It's amazing what Advil can do. How was your day?" she asks.

"It was awesome. I had a phenomenal time. Listen, we haven't really talked lately about you and what's new in your life besides Ivory and your job at Joe's. How are your parents? How is Jordan?" I inquire.

"My parents are getting a divorce. My sister is in Europe with her newest boyfriend. That's really it. Anyways, I think I'm going to make some dinner, what do you feel like? Should we order pizza?" she changes the subject.

"Fiona, I realize this probably isn't something you want to talk about, but I am like your family, and I want to always be here to support you, and you need to know I love you and want you to be happy," I say.

"You are doing more for me than anyone else by ignoring this drama and letting me carry on with my own life. I don't want to talk about my family. I have been ignoring my mom's calls for days. They have their own issues. Their marriage has been over for a long time," she answers.

"Pizza it is. Get pepperoni and cheese!" I suggest.

My phone buzzes in perfect timing.

-Kirk: Missing you.

-Vero: That's so sweet. Hope you are having a good boys night.

-Kirk: We are having fun, always have fun when we have a generous amount of beer.

-Vero: Cool. Call me tomorrow. I have the day off at the coffee shop again.

-Kirk: Want to spend the day with me at the shop?

-Vero: Sure. I will organize tomorrow while you work.

-Kirk: Big kiss.

Looks like it's girls' night for Fiona and me; sincerely needed girl time with my best friend.

"Which movie should we watch?"
"Your choice this time, Fio."
"Okay, I say, 'He's Just Not That into You.'"
"Sure, sounds good to me."

We get cozy on our beat-up couch with an awfully old television and the DVD player my dad gave me when we left. The color is awful on the TV, and it's definitely not a big screen, but it does the trick. We also scarf down our medium pizza from Domino's in record time. I painted Fiona's toenails a red shade, and she painted mine hot pink. As the movie ran in the background, she and I joke around and laugh—something we are really good at. After she felt she could, Fiona cries, finally letting it all out.

"I'm just so sad. I knew it was coming, but I didn't know how I would feel when they made the call!"

"Everyone's parents have problems, Fio. No one is perfect, and maybe now they can both be happier and make you a bigger part of their lives. Jordan is amazing to you, she really loves you, and you're lucky to have a sister like that."

"I feel like I will always have relationship issues after perfect Mr. Malcolm being such a selfish asshole all these years and putting all the girls in our house last."

"You can be angry with your dad, you have all the right in the world to be extremely mad at him, but not all guys will be like this. You're a total package for any guy, but you always feel the need to hold back because you don't want to get hurt."

"I see you get hurt too. Everyone in my life is constantly being screwed over by bad guys in their life. You are a relationship girl, so what saves you is the relationship. What tends to save me is my independence and my ability to call all my own shots. I don't know if I will ever be happy with a guy."

"You will be, Fiona Malcolm. I promise," I reassure as I give her a tight hug.

She seems to be feeling a bit better. Nothing I say will take away any of her pain, and I know that. We both head off to bed with another hug. Looking at the living room, at the couch, and at the TV just makes us both start to laugh. What a month it has been.

I call Melody in the morning to confirm my day off; she tells me I am off for the day and that tomorrow I can start at nine again. She also asks me if I would like to come to a barbeque at her house tonight; it's her daughter's last night before she goes back with her dad and she wants to make it a special evening for her. She tells me I can bring whomever I like. I agree and tell her I will see her later. I wonder if I want Melody to meet Kirk just yet. I also wonder if Fiona would even be interested in coming to the barbeque. She's living in her own head lately, which I get, and seems to be doing whatever she wants to make her happy. I figure I won't invite her to the barbeque.

After exchanging texts back and forth with Kirk, I get ready and head over to the shop. When I arrive, I see Kirk in his mechanic coveralls, hair a mess, and a streak of grease across his left cheek. He smiles at me, and at that moment, he looks absolutely adorable; the ultimate American boy.

"Hi there." I smile.

"Finally." He smiles back as he drops the tool in his hand. He comes to embrace and greet me with a big kiss.

I guess we're at that point now.

"Are you sure you want to organize this pigpen?" he asks.

"If you want me to visit you at work, I see no other choice," I tease.

"All right, well, I'm workin' on some guy's old Chevy right now. He's looking to restore it, so all the parts I need today are here on this tarp. Over there are all the toolboxes. I don't know how you want to organize those, but be my guest as long as I can find them when I need them," he instructs.

"The whole point of organization is being able to find things when you need them," I say sarcastically.

We walk around the shop, he explains to me what he does and the schooling he took. He went to Golden West College and took their Automotive Mechanics course. His grandparents support him and his decisions, although they really wanted to see him apply himself to a career that's more academic. They live in Palm Desert and he visits them every so often. For a twenty-two-year-old, he has things figured out.

After a full day of sorting wrenches and other miscellaneous tools, I am finally done. It looks so much better; the shop needed a little femininity. An auto shop is probably one of the most masculine places in the world. Kirk seems to have every tool under the sun. He has hung various pictures of different cars throughout his working pad. He has a car lift, three giant red toolboxes, cabinets, and the doors to the bathroom and reception painted the same grey as the walls. The bathroom is surprisingly clean.

"You have a real handle on that organizing stuff," he says, impressed.

"I labeled pretty much every drawer so you can easily find what you're looking for," I smile.

"I'm lucky I work here alone or else I'd get my balls busted for letting you do this," he laughs.

"Oh, whatever! Everyone needs a little organization in their life!" I fire back.

"Cute. You want to come over to my place finally? I figure by now I can trust you're not some crazy serial killer." He winks.

"I would love to come over." I laugh.

He changes into some jeans and a fitted V-neck white shirt. He cleaned his face so it's free of grease and his sun-kissed, clean-shaven face is back in prime condition. We climb into the truck and drive about ten minutes. We pull into some wickedly beautiful luxury apartments; so much for hoping off the gravy train when he left his dad. I immediately become so embarrassed of my apartment and make a silent vow to never invite him over.

We park the truck in his designated spot and head up to the apartment. It is so nicely laid out with a ton of space. He shrugs it off as if it's nothing, and I give him a questioning look.

"My grandparents bought this place as an investment. I live here and take care of it for them, and when they want to come down to the big city, they crash here. Want a tour?" he offers.

"Yes!" I cry.

We walk into a large living room right off the bat, which then opens to a dining room with a tucked-away kitchen. To the right is a spacious deck with deck furniture. Off to the left are his spare bed and bath, separate bathroom, washer and dryer closet, his big master bedroom, and master bathroom.

"You are never coming to my dreadful apartment!" I declare.

"This is just an apartment, Vero. Does my shop seem top-of-the-line to you? Do I have an expensive truck sitting in the parking lot?" he asks rhetorically.

"So what? This place is amazing. No wonder all your buddies want to hang out here for their boys' nights!" I cry.

"Relax. It's not so shabby, but I'm not some trust-fund money sucker. I figure if I can live here, then why not?" he shrugs.

He opens a beer for himself and offers me whatever I want. Opting for lemonade, I make my way to the deck. I open the sliding glass door and step out. I sit on the dark-brown chaise lounge he has sitting out and make myself comfortable. This is exactly what I wish for myself one day.

He joins me on the deck and lies behind me on the chaise so I am rested on him.

"I love this place." I sigh.

"You are welcome here anytime you want," he offers and kisses my forehead.

We lie on the chaise for a few more minutes, and I ask if we can go see the pool area. He agrees to show me, and we walk there hand-in-hand.

The outdoor pool area is so beautiful and clean. There are plants surrounding and sprinkler systems to keep them fresh and alive. The pool is empty; it hardly seems like anyone is around. It's so serene and quiet. I notice a stunning hot tub too. The pool area is situated on the first floor of the condos right in the middle. You can peer up and see all the condos surrounding it.

"We're going in next time I'm here!" I cry.

"Deal," he grins.

I continue to look around in astonishment, and Kirk watches over me with crossed arms and a smitten grin. I remove my shoes, bend down, and take a seat at the edge of the pool. I dip my feet and calves in and turn my head around to find Kirk.

"Well? Aren't you going to join me?" I smile.

"I guess I could," he grins.

Kirk sits beside me and drops his legs in too. I let my head fall on his left shoulder, and he doesn't move a muscle. I see what looks like a fitness gym through the glass windows.

"Do you work out there?" I ask.

Kirk is in good shape, I can tell he works out and takes good care of himself.

"From time to time, I'm not as committed as I should be," he answers.

"You look like you spend a lot of time there," I wink.

"I like to play soccer. I played in high school competitively, but now it's just more for fun," he explains.

He whirls his feet so they meet mine in the water. I get butterflies again. I can't imagine how Kirk could have treated his ex-girlfriend with so much disrespect. He treats me like gold.

# Chapter Five

We are smiling at each other until Kirk breaks the electricity.

"Should we head back?" he questions.

"Sure," I answer as I lift myself off the ground to find my shoes.

We go back to Kirk's apartment. My feet feel clean from the pool, I rub them against the carpet in the living room as we walk to the couches. He has two monster-size black leather couches and an oversize black leather chair to match. I imagine it reclines like every guy's dream. I can picture Kirk with a bag of chips, chair fully reclined, beer in hand, while watching the big game. I smile and hope to see it one day.

"What are you thinking about?" he asks me.

"Oh, nothing," I reply.

I hadn't realized I was so obviously in my own world. I hope my eyes didn't do that horrific zombie look.

"Liar!" he yells and smiles.

"Oh, whatever!" I laugh.

"Turn on the TV, anything you want to watch. Just please don't make me sit through any of that girly bullshit, please," he begs.

"You said whatever I want!" I laugh and stick my tongue out at him.

"Whatever you want within reason," he corrects himself.

I flick through the channels. I don't find anything exciting. I don't watch a lot of TV. I can imagine that Kirk probably does. He has an incredible big-screen TV with clear-as-day resolution. Okay, Kirk is *definitely* never allowed to watch my TV. I stall for a second and realize I hate my apartment more and more as I sit here.

I decide on the movie *Fifty First Dates* with Adam Sandler, guaranteed to bring in some laughs.

"What do you want to do for dinner? I'm not much of a chef, my diet mainly consists of fast-food and all the other shitty stuff you can put in your body," he says.

"I don't mind. I had pizza last night, so preferably none of that," I respond.

"Okay, little angel over here doesn't exactly eat from the fruit trees either, huh?" He grins. "Let's order a foreign cuisine. What do you feel like? What's your favorite?" he asks.

"Sushi!" I cry.

"Really? One of those types . . . Fine, sushi," Kirk agrees.

Kirk gets up off the couch and grabs his cell phone. He calls up the sushi place and asks them to deliver a variety for us.

"Should be here within the hour, but who knows with that? They're always late," he states.

"It's fine, I'm not starving." I smile.

"Come here and give me some love." He winks as he opens his arms.

I move over closer to Kirk and face him. He pulls me toward his face, and we begin to passionately kiss. Things start to get heated pretty quickly, so I push him away and gasp for air. I smile at him sheepishly and move away slightly. He looks at me with a puzzled expression on his face.

"Did I do something?" he asks.

"No, of course not. I just don't want things moving at the speed of light, that's all," I answer.

"Okay, fair enough. I might get carried away sometimes, so be clear with me when you're not feelin' it. I find you to be irresistible and I absolutely can't help myself," Kirk says in an honest tone.

"I will let you know." I smile. "I'm just not one to jump the gun on anything. I don't want to get carried away."

"Veronica, I'm not going to jump on you and strip you of your clothes. I get it, you're not the whore type. I dig that, don't be feeling badly," he says as he strokes my cheek.

I begin to feel a rush of warmth within my cheeks. I hate talks about sex. It makes me squirm and I totally clam up. Of course I had sex with my ex-boyfriend, but we didn't talk about it on the regular. I haven't been with anyone else since, and I get nervous when I think about it. Kirk will be the second guy I've been really attracted to, but I'm only eighteen. I think that's normal.

"Listen, look at me. Give me those sweet green eyes. I am not pressuring you, don't get the wrong idea here, all right?" he asks.

"I don't feel pressure, why are you saying that?" I begin to get hostile.

"I can tell. Your cheeks are turning red, your eyes are concentrated on your thoughts. I get you're not going to tell me. Forget this, okay?" he says as he looks me deep in my eyes. "I love spending time with you, that's it," he adds.

Oh, what does that mean? That he doesn't want to . . . with me?

"Oh?" I say with a puzzled face.

"I mean, I'd love to . . . ," he pauses, "ah, forget it! This conversation is over!" he laughs and kisses me softly.

After an hour passes, the sushi finally arrives. Kirk jumps up from the couch, grabs his wallet, and takes out some cash. He arranges the sushi for us and brings it over.

"Forget good manners, these babies are leather for a reason. Real easy to keep clean and black so you'd never know this is where I eat all my meals," Kirk says.

"At least get some napkins so we can feel remotely civilized!" I laugh.

My parents strictly forbid eating anywhere besides the dining-room table with a fork and a knife. I'm an only child; of course, I had a strict upbringing, they only had to do it once.

"Do you have any siblings?" I ask Kirk.

"I have an older brother. He lives in Canada. He met an awesome Canadian girl while he was traveling in Mexico. He fell in love with her, and she changed his life. He had to marry her; he just wouldn't have it any other way. He tried the long distance thing, and it wasn't working out. He moved to Vancouver two years ago now. He loves it," Kirk tells me.

"Good for him. Do you see him often?" I ask.

"Not so often. He doesn't visit a lot. They have a newborn. She's four months old now. My brother's wife, Grace, got pregnant right after their wedding last fall," he informs.

"What's your brother's name?" I ask curiously.

"Chase," Kirk answers.

I wonder to myself if Chase looks anything like Kirk. I grew up wishing I could have someone in my life that looked like me. I always wanted a little sister, but never got one. I don't think having more than one kid was ever an option for my parents.

"Do you guys get along?" I quiz.

"Of course, he's my big brother. He's actually the reason I decided to stop talking to my dad in the first place. My brother is nothing like my old man. He's happy, he's successful, and he did the opposite of what my dad did. Chase showed me I don't have to be a total douche bag to get what I want. He encouraged me to open the shop when I was first thinking of doing it. He gave me some money, told me he was proud," Kirk expresses.

"Do you mind if I ask you what happened to your mom?" I shyly ask Kirk.

"My mom never married my dad. My dad has commitment issues. He drove her away. Her parents encouraged her for years to leave, and my dad told her she could if she wanted to. He's a mean son-of-a-bitch. He has no conscience. She left, and she never called, never wrote, never made another attempt with us," he tells me.

"That's terrible, Kirk. I'm so sorry," I offer.

"That's that. I'm not mad at her, but I wish she were around. We'd treat her right, you know? Chase wishes she were here to see him now. She'd be proud of him," he says.

"She would be proud of you both," I confirm.

After sushi, I ask Kirk to give me a ride home. I tell him I'm tired and I need to do some stuff at home. After an entire day and night together, I figure I need to give some attention to my gross apartment, and to my best friend. I send Fiona a text.

-Vero: Hey, are you home?

I didn't get a reply. I figure she might be at work, so I leave it. Listening to Kirk talk about his mom made me realize I will never meet her. Maybe he will be able to reconnect with her. It makes me think of my relationship with my ex's mom; she is so wonderful, and I know I'll never have that again. Then, I think of how awful Fiona must be feeling about her parents. I have never struggled with this before, but I'm aware a lot of people do every day. I decide to tell Kirk about Fiona's parents.

"Fiona's parents are getting a divorce. I just found out last night," I blurt out.

"Is that right? That's too bad," he says sympathetically.

"Her dad is an arrogant man. He cheats on her mom all the time with multiple different women," I disclose.

"He is like my dad—egomaniacs. The funny part is, they're actually the most insecure people inside. Her mom deserves better," Kirk states.

He didn't give me any more than that. I was hoping for some better advice, but he didn't seem to want to give me any. I didn't push it. First of all, he barely has met Fiona; and second, he probably doesn't know what else to say either.

When we arrive at my apartment, I move closely to Kirk. I give him a kiss on his lips and tell him thank you for the lovely day. He kisses me again, and we sit in his truck for another five minutes kissing and caressing each other before I finally escaped his grasp.

Fiona is not home when I get in. I expected that since she never texted me back. I have a frightening realization right there and then. I completely forgot about Melody's barbeque. I panic! I reach for my cell phone and I call her. No answer. I leave an apologetic voicemail.

"Hi, Melody, it's Veronica. I'm so sorry! I feel terrible, but I got caught up in some plans today and I just got home now. I sincerely hope you are not too mad at me, and if you are, I completely understand. Please give Mandi a giant hug for me. See you in the morning."

I arrive at work at eight forty-five, really hoping that Melody is not mad.

"Good morning, Melody," I chime as I walk in.

"Good morning," she answers.

She has a cold tone in her voice. I decide to avoid any further communication and I begin to work. She doesn't make another effort with me all day. Finally, when I get off at one o'clock, she comes out from the kitchen.

"I'm really disappointed you weren't able to make the barbeque last night, Veronica. I thought I would have given you enough notice. Mandi was devastated," she tells me.

"I'm really sorry, Melody. I have a lot going on in my personal life right now. I really wanted to come, and I had good intentions, but I wasn't able," I explain.

"Yeah, well have a good day. Tomorrow should be pretty slow, so you can take the day off. Oh, and your paycheck is in the top drawer," she says and turns back toward the kitchen.

Shit! She's really mad. I begin to regret mixing my work life with my personal life. I gather all my things, take my check from the drawer, and I leave the coffee shop. As I walk out, I throw my sunglasses over my eyes. To my surprise, Kirk is waiting outside the coffee shop for me.

"How was work, babe?" he asks curiously.

"I'm surprised to see you here. I don't remember telling you what time I was off?" I state.

"You mentioned to me before the typical hours of your shifts. I have great memory. I closed the shop early today. It was slow and I just wanted to see you." He smiles.

"I'm glad you did, I'm having such a terrible day. I forgot last night I committed myself to a barbeque at my boss's place. Obviously, I didn't go. She is not happy with me today." I sulk.

"Forget it. It's not mandatory to become friends with your boss. It's probably better if you don't anyways," he advises.

We get into the truck and Kirk drives us to get lunch. We go to a little café and steal a table outside as two people were leaving. Kirk comes back with two turkey sandwiches and two lemonades. Tradition, I guess.

"So I have an idea. I have to visit my grandparents this weekend in Palm Desert. It's about a two-hour drive. What do you say you come with me? They like me to throw a few beers back with them and stay in the guest room, but if you're not comfortable with sleeping there, I get it," Kirk proposes.

"I would love to visit your grandparents with you," I answer.

"Yeah? It's usually pretty fun. I don't bring people with me regularly. It's always just been my buds who join me, but I think my grandma will be pleased to see me bring a girl by," Kirk says.

"Sure, just tell me when. I work Saturdays until one, but I'm off every Sunday and Monday," I tell him.

"Let's go Saturday afternoon. I'll call my pops today and tell him to expect us for around four," he answers.

"That sounds cool. I'm excited to go with you." I smile.

"They have a wicked pool, and I always take the golf cart for a spin. They have a pretty nice pad over there; I have a feeling you'll be into it. Plus, my grandparents are super laid-back," he adds on.

"I'm convinced, don't worry. I'll be going with you." I smile again.

We carry on with lunch and talk more about the shop and how it hasn't been so busy lately. He said a lot of his customers are repeats and he's been lucky to have a lot of referrals. We also talked a lot about my job at the coffee shop and how I'm already beginning to get bored. He suggests I start looking for a new job that's more stimulating for me.

"Do you like working with cars?"

"I love cars. I have always loved cars, but more so now. I know it'd be way easier to just give in to my grandpa and take up a job at corporate. I'd get in easy, but I want to control my life. I don't want some asshole boss who walks around with his head held high. I can't stand guys like that. I want to be in control. He can get me corporate, but he can't get me CEO."

"Yeah, but maybe if you start from whenever you can, the CEO position is something you could work towards."

"Nah."

Kirk likes things that come easily, it seems. This conversation surprises me, as he was so persistent with me. He wouldn't take no for an answer, but I guess in his career he will.

After lunch, Kirk said he needs to get his haircut and asks if I'll accompany him. I agree to watch him and tell him it'll be the first time I've done something like that. He grins and says he likes company while he runs his errands, makes them seem less boring. Kirk stops by the bank and gets cash out for his hairdresser. Apparently he's had the same one for the last eight years, and she cuts out of her house.

We arrive at his hairdresser's house. It's a small place with a sign on the lawn that reads, "Cuts by Cynthia." I am assuming her name is Cynthia. Kirk knocks on the side door, and she runs to answer it. An older woman answers. She greets Kirk and gives him a hug. Kirk introduces us, and she pulls me over a chair to sit on while Kirk gets his hair cut. The whole session they talk catch-up while I sat and played with my phone, obviously bored. He tried to include me into the conversations, but since I've only known him for so long, I find it hard to follow along. He is sweet to his hairdresser, and she seems to enjoy having him in her chair. She gives him a long shampoo, and when we are done, he gives her some money; another big hug and off we go.

Kirk is very polite. He always treats the people who serve him with such a high respect. He remembers everyone's name and makes him or her feel as if they are doing an amazing job.

The clock reads five. I still haven't heard anything from Fiona. She never texted me back last night. I lose my train of thought as Kirk grabs my hand and we walk to the truck. He opens my door for me and I climb in. He pauses and moves toward me, putting his grip on my face and kisses me eagerly right there in his hairdresser's driveway. He thanks me for coming with him and asks me what I feel like doing.

"I don't care!" I answer.

Basically, he makes me feel shy, and I just want to spend time with him. Even just sitting in the truck, I am happy to be in his company. Every day I am becoming more smitten with him, and he is beginning to overtake my every thought. I think about him all the time; if I'm not talking to him, I am wishing I were. I am under his spell without a single doubt in my mind. I am becoming obsessed with him mind, body, and soul.

"Should we go get dinner and head to my place?" he asks.

"Honestly, anything you want!" I reply.

We go to the grocery store, and Kirk picks out some salad fixings, chicken breasts, and wild rice. He tells me he knows how to cook a dish like this, but not to expect any Gordon Ramsay results.

We arrive back at Kirk's place. He goes into the kitchen and switches on the oven, fills a pot with water, and places it on the stove. As the water begins to boil, he places the salad fixings in the fridge. I walk to the couch, fall gracefully, and spread out all my limbs. Kirk meets me with two ice-cold lemonades and places them on the coffee table.

"After dinner, I think we should head to our spot at the beach," Kirk suggests.

"Yeah we might be able to catch the tail end of the sunset," I add.

He cuddles up to me. He smells heavenly; whatever cologne he sports, I like it. I take a deep breath and close my eyes. I am relaxed once again. The thought of moving seems like a grand effort. Kirk begins to play with my hair and I open my eyes to find him staring at me.

"You're pretty," he smiles.

I blush hard.

"Just say thank you," he says.

"Thank you," I repeat.

"What is it with girls and getting embarrassed with compliments? Just embrace them. I hate insecure girls, not that I'm suggesting you're insecure at all," he says.

"I don't think it's necessarily insecurity. I find it to be more awkward than anything," I reply.

I try so hard every time I meet Kirk to look, smell, and seem my best. Each time I see him, it becomes more and more important to me that he finds me irresistible, yet I still cringe at the thought of things moving any faster sexually than they already are.

The oven timer beeps a loud reminder that it's ready, and Kirk heads to the oven to prepare the chicken breasts. I turn on the TV because I know we will be eating on the couch. Again, I have little luck finding something I assume we will both like. I settle on *Storage Wars* and wait for Kirk to come back.

"Another surprise," he smiles.

"What? You didn't think I like *Storage Wars*?" I ask.

"Just didn't think it'd be a program you'd migrate to," he answers.

"It was this or *Miss Congeniality*," I tease.

"You made the right choice, or you would be eating dinner in front of the TV alone." He smirks.

"I want to see your room, you didn't show me on the tour," I point out.

"Yeah, because it's a real mess, and I know girls are weird about that. Especially an organizing freak like you," he teases.

I jump up from the couch and walk toward his room. The door is slightly open, so I gently push it and enter. His queen-size bed is not made; the covers are half on the bed, half on the floor. I find some clothes scattered on the carpet by his dresser and some loose change and receipts on his bedside table along with a steel lamp and clock. His room is modern; there is no headboard. He has dark bedding and white pillows. His dresser and bedside table are both black, and he has another giant TV hanging on his wall across from his bed. Kirk has a very plain and unpretentious room.

I make my way to the bathroom. He has two mirror closet doors, so I slide them open to see. They reveal a large walk-in closet. He has a shoe rack, more clothes both folded and hanging—a typical closet. In the bathroom, he has his toothbrush resting on the counter of one sink. The other sink looks untouched. There is a large mirror on the wall above the bathroom vanity and Kirk's cologne sits on the countertop; he wears Chanel. There is a separate room with the toilet and shower.

I feel a sense of intrigue as I walk through the most intimate room in Kirk's life. This is all new to me. A guy's very own apartment, his own shop, and his own truck. I want to spend more time here. I feel so comfortable and at ease.

"Vero, are you done snooping or what?" he yells to me.

I come out of his room and head back for the couch.

"I like your room." I smile. "Who decorated it?"
"Of course I did! Look how boring it is." He laughs.
"It suits you, I think. You smell nice," I change the subject.
"I'm glad my scent appeals to you, now come here," he says and grabs my hips.

Kirk pulls me so I am lying on top of him with my stomach on his. He reaches his hands under my shirt grazing my lower back and begins to tickle lightly. I drop my head on his chest and close my eyes.

"You have soft skin," Kirk says.

I say nothing and relish in sensation.

A few minutes later, the oven chimes again. I secretly curse it because I was enjoying the attention. Kirk moves up and climbs off the couch to attend to the stove. He makes some racket in the kitchen, lets off some swear words, and seems to settle things down finally. I hear him open the fridge and I predict he is starting to make the salad. This is a first for me—having a cute guy cook me dinner in his amazing apartment, just the two of us. I am so used to my lame juvenile relationship that consisted of plenty movie nights with popcorn. I never got the best of Tyson. He always wanted to be somewhere else when he was with me. It seems with Kirk, he doesn't want to be anywhere else, and I love that impression.

Kirk comes back with two steaming hot plates.

"Be careful, hun, these plates are really hot," he warns.

I take a plate from his hand and put it on the coffee table. The food looks good, but it smells even better. Kirk hands me a knife and a fork and sits down beside me.

"Thank you for making me dinner," I smile.

"I hope you don't get any kind of poisoning from this," he teases.

I realize I am famished as I dive into the plate. It's just a simple lemon pepper chicken with mixed greens and wild rice. I don't take long to finish, and neither does Kirk.

"Yum!" I express.

Kirk smiles at me and grabs the plates from the table. He puts them in the kitchen and comes back.

"You want to head out?" he asks.

"Whatever you want," I shrug.

He finds his keys and slips on his flip-flops. I join him by picking up my purse and slipping my shoes on too. Just like that, we are out the door and on our way to the beach—on our way to "our spot."

I regret not bringing a sweater because the breeze is uncomfortable, but I don't dare to tell Kirk that. I am always cold! He takes the blanket from the truck and tucks it under his arm. He frees one hand and reaches for mine. Suddenly the draft is secondary.

Kirk lays the blanket onto the sand. There is no one in sight. He flicks off his shoes and walks toward the water. I quickly hope he is not going in. He stops before the waves and begins searching around. I watch him with interest and wonder what he's up to.

He doesn't seem to find a stick, so he crouches down and begins tracing his finger along the damp sand. I can't tell from where I am what he is writing, but I continue to watch him, intrigued.

"What are you writing?" I inquire.
"You'll see," he answers.

I wait patiently for him to call me over.

"Come," he says.

I flick off my shoes and I run toward Kirk. I look curiously and see, "I'm crazy about you" with a giant heart around his chosen words.

I gush. I look at Kirk, and I force a kiss on him. He accepts quite willingly. He picks me up so I am face-to-face with him. Kirk releases me, and I take his hand to pull him toward the blanket. We sat side-by-side, and Kirk lifted up one corner of the blanket and draped it over my shoulder.

"You're cold," he states.
"I'm fine." I smile.

Kirk leans in toward me, and we begin to kiss each other. As usual, I have flutters in my stomach both attraction and extreme nervousness. I feel so inexperienced. I'm always having my guard up to try and avoid being humiliated. Kirk makes a move by pushing me down into a lying position. He then climbs over on top of me in a straddle, and we continue to kiss.

"Should I be getting you home now?"
"I want to say no, but the better answer is probably yes."
"You know, if you really hate that coffee-shop deal, you can always quit and look for something better."

I don't say anything. I don't mind the coffee shop, and it *is* my fault that I missed the barbeque.

We get in the truck, and off we go to meet the end of another amazing day together. I'm relieved to know that tomorrow is another day, and I'm sure I'll be spending it with Kirk again.

When I get to my apartment, I walk past the pathetic attempt at a garden on either side of the entrance gate. I notice that each of the terracotta pots that hold dead debris are chipped and broken. It looks likes someone used it as an ashtray more than once. I slide my key through the keyhole and make my way up the stairs. I run into Bridgette in the stairwell.

"Good evening." She smiles.
"Hi, nice to see you again. How is everything going?" I ask.
"The place is dirty, but like you said before, we'll make it our home," she answers.

"You will. We should all get together and do something sometime soon. Fiona and I would love to get to know our neighbors," I suggest.

"I would love that, and I'm sure Konner would as well. Knock on our door next time you girls have some free time," Bridgette says as we part ways.

"See you soon." I smile and continue up the stairs.

The second night in a row Fiona is nowhere to be found. No trace of her even to silence my worry. I decide it's time to call her.

"Hey, V."

"Hi, where are you? You never texted me back."

"Sorry, I've been busy with work and stuff. I'll be home really soon if you want to eat some ice-cream and catch up?"

"Okay, I'll wait up for you, Fio."

I sit on the couch in silence. I can't help but wish I were back at Kirk's warm and cozy place instead of this pathetic one. I love his place. It's sad that he wouldn't feel the same way about mine.

I go into the bathroom, lock the door, grab a towel, and run the hot water in the shower. I strip off my clothes and stand under the heat while it soaks my hair and the rest of my body. I lather my hair in a big squirt of shampoo until it's nice and foamy, and I grant myself a scalp massage, scrubbing away all the thoughts in my head. Once I rinse the shampoo, I apply the conditioner and leave it to sit while I shave my legs.

After the shower, I wrap myself in my fresh, crisp towel and take a big breath in. I love nothing more than being clean. I put on my pajamas and dive into my bed. Time to dial my mom's number.

"Hi, honey."

"Ola!"

"How are you? I was just thinking about you."

"I'm good, Mom. How are you doing?"

"Sweetie, I realized I told you I was sending you a care package. I have got completely sidetracked and have put it off, I'm sorry!"

"Don't worry. Honestly, I had forgotten all about it."

"Is something bothering you, honey?"

"No, I'm just tired. I just wanted to call and say good night. I miss you and Dad a lot."

"We miss you every minute, Vero! Why don't you do some drawing? Can I call you back tomorrow, honey? Dad and I are just watching *X Factor*, you know how we like that show."

"Call me tomorrow afternoon, tell Dad I love him and I miss him, okay?"

"I will, we love you, sweet dreams."

The apartment is so quiet and gloomy; it's never bothered me this much before. It has a cold energy, colder than usual. I continue to wait for Fiona to come home. She doesn't have the decency to call or text that she's going to be late. I call Kirk.

"Hey, babe."

"Hi, what are you up to?"

"I'm watching ESPN and having a beer, what are you doing?"

"Just lying in bed, waiting for Fiona to come home. I talked to her an hour ago; she said she would be home so we could have ice-cream and chat. This apartment is just so glum, so I called for some company."

"I hope she doesn't keep you awake all night. Maybe something came up? Do you want me to come pick you up and you can sleep over here?"

"Do you want me to sleep over?"

"I would love for you to sleep over, but you know it's your call."

"Okay. See you soon."

"Bring your bathing suit. We can go in the pool like you promised."

I hang up and realize I am already in my pajamas. I wonder if Kirk will mind, they're not the flannel kind with pink frogs or anything. *Oh no*, I say to myself. Maybe I should wear something sexier. Oh man, what have I got myself into?

I change into jeans and a tank top and pack a bag with my bikini, toothbrush, perfume, and deodorant. I choose my pink silk nightie, and fresh underwear in the pajama department, and I also pack a striped blue and white strapless sundress for tomorrow's outfit.

I send a text to Fiona as I wait down at the street for Kirk to come.

-Vero: I waited for you and never heard a thing. I'm sleeping at Kirk's.

Kirk arrives, and he speeds us off to his apartment.

"I'm so happy this has happened tonight." He smiles.

"Totally not what I had in mind when I called," I say, although I'm not sure if that's true.

"You smell marvelous, I can't wait to cuddle you." He smiles again.

We get into Kirk's place, and I feel a rush of ease.

"Put your stuff in my room," Kirk directs.

I walk to his room and drop my bag on the floor by his bed. I briefly wonder how horrified my dad would be at this situation, and I quickly drown out that thought.

I see he is walking toward the bedroom. I freeze with anxiety.

"Let's get on our bathing suits on so we can go for an evening tub and swim."

"Sure."

"Give me a smooch first," Kirk says as he pulls me in for a kiss.

I change in the bathroom and Kirk changes in his bedroom. I feel extremely self-conscious knowing I will have to my reveal my body to him. I'm not a self-conscious girl, but that setting is not an easy one. I play around with my lime-colored triangle-top bikini to try and show off my girly assets to my best ability. I tighten the strings at my neck to give my C-cup boobs an extra lift. I swear my boobs used to be bigger. I move my matching bikini bottom around so they flatter my butt. This is it . . . I open the door to find him patiently waiting, just as I thought.

"Wow!" he shrieks with hungry eyes.

My face gets hot as I swiftly grab a towel off the counter and wrap it around my body.

"Let's go, shall we?" I tease.

Kirk follows me like a lost puppy.

"I dare you to run and jump in!" I laugh.

"I'll accept as long as I get to throw a dare at you," he answers.

I understand agreeing to that puts me in a risky position, but I do anyway.

"You're on." I smile.

Kirk runs and jumps into the pool, making a big splash. I watch him with intrigue and put our towels on the glass outdoor table. I make my walk to the pool's steps and ease my way in. The water is not warm, which gives me instant goose bumps. I am immediately grateful for the generous amount of padding in my bikini top. Kirk comes my way and takes no time to wrap his wet body around me, causing a loud shriek to escape from my vocal cords. He starts laughing and dives under the water again. I'm not too interested in getting my hair wet, especially because I just showered an hour before.

"Don't get my hair wet!" I command.

"What makes you think you'll be able to keep up with me in this pool if your hair stays dry?" he asks jokingly.

"I mean it! I just showered an hour ago, my hair is still damp!" I answer.

"Yeah, yeah. Girls will be girls," he states.

"Let's go in the hot tub, the pool is chilly," I suggest as I walk out of the water.

The hot tub temperature is perfect. It burns my skin a bit, but I take a seat on the stairs and wait for Kirk.

"This hot tub is so nice, I bet you come in here often," I assume.

"Not so much. I'd feel weird coming out here alone. I wouldn't want my neighbors to feel obligated to join me," he answers.

"I'll join you whenever you want." I smile.

"Good." Kirk smirks.

He swims over and takes a seat deeper in the tub on the tiled bench. He signals me to join him, so I do.

"Come sit on me," Kirk guides.

I swim over to him and plant myself on his knee. Kirk brushes his hand along my back again. I look at him and he looks back at me. I give him a shy smile, and Kirk kisses me. I move, so I am straddling Kirk now and things get hot between us. He takes a firm hold of my butt, and I can feel his body tensing up as I assume he is extremely turned on. For some reason, I am not intimidated. I continue my bold movements, and I run my fingers through Kirk's hair and place my arms around his neck. Kirk reaches to the front of my bikini, and begins to rub me in between my legs over my bathing suit. He is still committed to our make-out session, but I can tell he is ready for more.

# Chapter Six

I do it again. I bitch out. I pull away from Kirk about a minute after he switched his position. I can see him clench his teeth a bit, but he doesn't lose his temper. Surprisingly, he smiles at me with a genuine grin as I study him. I move to the opposite side of the tub and kick my feet toward him.

"You can massage those if you want instead." I wink.

"I'll take whatever I can get." He laughs and takes hold of my right foot.

After an amazing night in the water with Kirk, we return to his apartment.

"I'm going to shower, babe," he informs.

"Okay," I reply.

"I'll leave the door wide open so you can feel free to join." He winks.

"Thanks but no thanks," I tease.

When he finishes in the shower, I decide to rinse my body off as well on my own. When I finish, Kirk is lying in bed already.

"Come," he calls.

I changed into my silky nightie in the bathroom already, so I get my toothbrush from my bag and brush my teeth.

"I've been waiting for this all night," he says.
"For what?" I ask with a raised eyebrow.
"Cuddling. I'm a softy," he says as he flashes a cute grin.

I nestle right up into Kirk. He smells heavenly. I close my eyes and relish in this feeling. I love having him close to me like this, I feel safe and wanted.

Kirk and I have a bit of flirty pillow talk as he tries every excuse in the book to touch me and get things heated in the bed. As much as I want to, I'm just not ready. I can tell Kirk reads my signals, and within minutes of our mutual silence, we drift into sleep with me in Kirk's arms; I haven't been that pleased ever.

In the morning, I am disorientated as I open my eyes to find myself in Kirk's bed. I snap back to reality and feel Kirk's grip still tightly around me. He is still asleep and making quiet breathing noises. I glance outside the window and see the sun is out shining brightly. I close my eyes again and back to sleep I go.

"Good morning, beautiful," Kirk whispers in my ear as he lightly shakes me awake.
"Good morning," I smile as I manage to open my heavy eyes.
"Did you sleep well?" he asks.
"I had an incredible sleep. How did you sleep?" I reply.
"Haven't slept that good in a while." He smiles.
I stretch out and yawn as Kirk puts his head on my tummy and lies across the bed horizontally. He looks just as cute in the morning as he does always. I look down and smile at him.

I point to my lips and move my upper body toward him to give a kiss.

After lying in bed for a few more minutes, we both get up and go into the kitchen. Kirk makes himself a pot of coffee, and I help myself to a glass of orange juice.

"What time will you open the shop today?" I ask.

"Whenever I want." He winks.

"I'm off today. Melody told me to take today off," I explain.

"What will you do with your day off?" he asks.

"Haven't thought about it. I draw sometimes, I might draw today." I shrug.

"Unfortunately, I can't take the day off to spend with a gorgeous girl. I have a lot of work to finish up today with that truck, but I would love to see you again tonight? And I didn't know you draw, I want to see something," he tests.

"I would love to show you," I beam.

After our beverages, we both got ready and carry on with our days. In the back of my mind, I keep remembering how strange Fiona is acting, and I continue to worry about her.

When I returned home, Fiona was finally there.

"Is your phone broken or something, Fio?" I test.

"No. I didn't text you back because you said you were at Kirk's," she replies.

"Well, I still appreciate a reply," I inform her.

"I know for next time," Fiona says with attitude.

I go into my room and shut the door behind me. I can't help but be annoyed by that conversation. I gravitate to my drawing portfolio and pick out my pencils. We'll see what my hands create today.

*  *  *

Reflecting on my week, Friday arrived quickly with work and a whole lot of Kirk time behind me. I am feeling better and better about my move here.

Yesterday morning, I met with Bridgette, and we walked to the grocery store together. She is very kind and soft-spoken. After groceries, I made us both a light lunch consisting of toasted whole-grain bread, lettuce, tomatoes, mayonnaise, cheddar cheese, and mustard. Bridgette is a vegetarian. We learned a lot about each other. Bridgette met Konner in high school in their junior year when she moved from Florida. He finished his marketing degree from UCLA, and Bridgette is a yoga teacher who is involved with a lot of volunteering around the community. They moved to Huntington because Konner got an irresistible job offer at a firm nearby and they decided it was time to take a plunge and move in together. They are the same age as Kirk and got engaged last summer while they were in Paris. He proposed to her under the Eiffel Tower. She said it was magical, and every time she looks at her ring she remembers their amazing European vacation—the trip that confirmed they wanted to spend their lives together.

She said Konner is a workaholic, and he often stays past his duty hours to do more work and kiss the bosses' asses. He wants to move up as fast as he can. She said she's much more calm and enjoys a much less stressful life.

I really enjoyed my afternoon with Bridgette. I confided in her about Kirk. She's the only person I have really done that with. She gave me some advice about my nerves and how she dealt with things like that with Konner.

I can picture the four of us getting along quite well. We agreed we could all go on a double date and she could meet

Kirk and tell me what she thinks of him. I know she'll like him. What's not to like?

At work, Melody apologized to me for being rude. She explained that it's been hard for her with her daughter's decision to move away a couple of years ago. She and her ex-husband lost the loving feeling, and her daughter was going through a terrible break-up with an awful boyfriend. Mandi and her dad decided to leave together. Melody gets emotional every time Mandi leaves.

I completely forgive her because that is fully understandable. I told her I won't miss the next barbeque for the world, and I thanked her for caring enough to want me there. I mentioned to Melody that I am going to Palm Desert on Saturday and wondered if she needed me the whole day. She told me I could take the whole day off and she would cover it for me. I feel badly for Melody. She is at that coffee shop religiously day and night and never takes a day off for herself.

I told my mom and dad I would be going to Palm Desert with Fiona for a day trip Saturday. I had to lie to them because my parents are not the easygoing types when it comes to guys. After watching me miserable all summer long, they would be very concerned about my choice to have another relationship, especially with Kirk's past. I could *never* tell them about that. They also wouldn't appreciate the age difference and would lecture me about older guys and their intentions. I have to wait before I am sure it's the right time to tell them about Kirk. For now, what they don't know won't hurt them.

The whole Fiona situation has made little to no progress this week either. We are never like this with each other. It feels awkward and wrong. I am never home, and neither is Fiona. She claims she is always working and that she has a group of friends she enjoys spending time with. She tells me she's happy I have Kirk and that he seems like a great guy for me. She always puts bandages over every problem.

Kirk and I make plans to have a romantic picnic dinner at our spot tonight. He told me he would bring everything we need and said he would pick up a bottle of wine and asked me if there is one I prefer.

"I don't know . . . I never drink wine."
"I'll pick something out, don't worry."
"I really don't need to bring anything?"
"Just bring a warm sweater so you're not shivering this time. See you at seven."

I don't even like wine. I agree to myself that I will keep an openmind and be as positive as I can. A million worries run through my mind. This is the first time Kirk has included the word "romantic" in anything we have done. I call Bridgette.

"Hi, sweetie!"
"Hey! Can you come over quickly? I need some help with a Kirk problem."
"Of course, I'll be right there!"

She is over within minutes, and I am so relieved I have some help with this considering my best friend is MIA all the time. She spots the drawing I am showing Kirk tonight.
"Wow, Veronica. That is such a beautiful picture. You make those lilies look so real and lush. Congratulations on such an amazing talent!" she gushes.
"Thank you." I smile and change the subject. "So we are going to have a romantic beach dinner," I explain.
"Wow, romantic is right," Bridgette laughs.
"Why am I so nervous?" I ask her.

"Probably because the big elephant in the room here is that you two haven't taken this thing to any next level yet. You're just coasting in neutral," she says.

"You're totally right," I agree.

"Tonight might be the turning point. Are you ready for that?" she asks.

"It depends which turn." I cringe.

"Sex is a huge change in a relationship, Vero. Guys love having sex, especially with their girlfriend. There is absolutely no way around it. You might need to make a choice about this. You don't want him to lose interest because you're being overly square about the topic," she explains.

"You're right again!" I laugh.

"Here, just tell me what you're so worried about. Maybe I can help with a past experience of my own," she offers.

"I'm nervous that it won't go well or he will see through my inexperience and it will ruin everything. I'm scared because he'll be the second guy I have slept with and I know he has been with plenty more. In general, the whole situation is not sitting well with me," I explain.

"If Kirk is the amazing guy you make him out to sound, you have absolutely nothing to worry about. Every girl who has morals and self-respect feels the same way you do before they sleep with the guy they're into. Don't be ashamed of that. They actually like it if you're inexperienced." She smiles.

She is so right. I am so happy I called Bridgette over. Her reassurance makes me pretty positive I have made a choice I'm confident with.

"Have so much fun tonight, girl," she says.

"Thank you so much for coming over, you just saved me." I laugh.

"Let me know tomorrow how things went, I'll be thinking of you." She winks.

I let Bridgette out and peer at the clock. It's five-thirty. It's time to get into the shower and give myself some serious prepping.

I take a clean towel and place it on the bathroom counter as I shut and lock the door behind me. I look at myself in the mirror. Thankfully, my face is pimple-free, and I've been sleeping great, so it has a good shade to it. My green eyes are full of life again. I'm excited.

After my shower, I decide to give the blow dryer another dance, in same routine as before. That task finishes, and I hydrate my entire body with lotion. I feel confident and ready for whatever tonight will bring.

I pick out a flattering strapless sundress that cinches around my waist and is a bright blue color. It's high on my thigh and shows some freshly shaven legs. I plant myself across from my mirror and finish my mini makeup application. I spray my perfume, Givenchy, once on each wrist and once behind each ear. I swipe each underarm with deodorant, and I look at my phone to catch the time. It's six-forty. Twenty minutes until I get to see Kirk. That thought put a huge smile across my face.

I take another look at my drawing. Do I really want to show him? What if he thinks it's awful? I love drawing, but I don't usually show anyone. Just my family and close friends. He's a close friend now, right?

Seven o'clock rolls around, and I can be found on the road waiting for Kirk. He arrives promptly. I am so excited to see him! I wrap my arms around his neck and give him a tight hug. I breathe in, and a familiar smell fills my nose with ease. I release him and he kisses me.

"So nice to see you." He grins.

When we arrive at our spot, we do our usual slide down the rocks and trek through the sand. Kirk's arms are full, but he doesn't let me carry anything. He drops everything on the sand and lays the blanket down. He keeps the basket closed and removes his shoes as he sits on the red and blue striped blanket. I kick off my shoes and sit right beside him.

"How was your day?" I ask.

"It was good. I arranged everything with my grandma, she can't wait to meet you." He smiles.

I blush. I had forgotten I will meet his grandparents tomorrow. I hope they like me.

Kirk ruffles around in the basket and pulls out a bottle of white wine with two wine glasses. He removes the cork and swiftly pours us each a glass. He hands one to me and toasts, "Cheers to us!" He raises his glass to cling mine. We each take a sip. It's not so bad actually; every wine I've had before I've entirely hated.

We sip and chat our way through the first glass while Kirk prepares our dinner. It looks like he brought some kind of pasta.

"Did you cook?" I ask.

"Yeah right!" he laughs.

I knew he didn't cook it, but the effort is still adorable. He sets out the foiled take-out cartons and hands one to me with a fork.

"Bon appetite!" I grin.

The pasta is delicious. It's a cream sauce with sliced chicken breast. It tastes like it could be sundried tomato sauce, but I'm not sure. It's heavy, so I'm not able to finish it all.

Kirk happily eats my leftovers, and we both lie on our backs on the blanket with our full tummies. The sunset is stunning, letting off a powerful orange, and the ocean is completely calm, reflecting the colors of the sunset. I look around to see if we have any company. I am shocked on this beautiful Friday night that we are all alone.

Kirk looks over to me; I smile at him and he rolls my way, beginning to kiss my lips. Soon, Kirk is straddling me as we take each other in. I begin to run my fingers through his hair. I can feel Kirk's erection through his khaki shorts. He places more of his weight on me as his right hand moves up my thigh. I can assume where it's ultimately going. Sure enough, Kirk penetrates his fingers into my underwear, causing me to make a quiet purr. As one thing leads to another, I let it all happen, releasing all my insecurities.

I pull Kirk's shirt up over his head. He allows me to remove it as he continues exploring me. Next, Kirk removes my sundress, leaving me lying in my matching black strapless bra and panties. The chemistry between us makes it impossible to resist. Kirk pulls off his shorts, revealing his Calvin Klein white fitted boxers. He is so sexy.

Kirk peels off my panties and makes his way between my legs. This is not something I'm used to. I lie there, on the beach, in complete public eye, curious about these sensations while they eventually win me over.

"Are you ready for this, baby?" Kirk whispers.
"Yes," I pant.

Before I know it, Kirk has removed his underwear and has peeled a condom on. He pulls me upward so he can remove my bra. We're both naked, and Kirk places me back down and works into me. The sensation is strong as it sends a thunderbolt up my body, and my legs start to tingle. We carry on having sex until Kirk reaches his orgasm.

We both lie there, panting like crazy. That happened fast, but it was so worth the stress I've been putting on myself.

We both gather up our clothes and begin to redress ourselves. I definitely have sex hair after that. I pat my hair trying to smooth it all down. I nervously look around half-expecting to find a police officer waiting there to arrest us.

The sun still has a little life left, but the breeze is coming on strong, so I reach for my sweater and put it on.

"Are you glad you brought that now?" he grins.
"Definitely glad I did," I grin back.

Kirk pours us another glass of wine, and we sit together side-by-side. It's not awkward like I was expecting.

"So do you feel differently about me now?" he asks.
"Differently?" I ask back.
"The first night we met, you told me I disgusted you—the whole nine yards," he answers.
"Kirk, I know you a lot better now. Of course I feel differently about you, you do not disgust me in any shape or form," I reassure.
"Good." He smiles.

We continue to sip our glasses as we look out at the water.

"You're the first girl I've brought here and I've been coming for at least a year and a half. Shortly before I met you, I asked myself for forgiveness. I had to move on. You came into my shop and immediately I had a feeling I needed to chase you. I'm so relieved I did," Kirk says.

I smile at Kirk and hug him tight.

"Vero, do you want to do this girlfriend thing with me?" Kirk asks with wide, genuine eyes.

"I think I'm ready to try. I've been having an incredible time with you, I trust you, and I would love to be your girlfriend," I beam.

Just like that, I have Kirk all to myself. He is my boyfriend. Thank you, Cupid, or whoever is responsible! We have a place here where no one bothers us. It's secluded, it's safe, and it has magic. Here, in our haven, we are two honest people falling in love with each other.

We arrive at my apartment. I tell Kirk he can finally follow me in. I tell him to please not expect much in comparison to his place. I tell him to please not expect much in comparison to a prison cell.

"Oh, please," he answers.

"I'm serious." I laugh.

We arrive home, and Fiona is not there—surprise, surprise. I was hoping she would be so she could be the first one to greet Kirk as my boyfriend. They don't know each other at all. I suggest to Kirk that we sleep at his place tonight considering I have a shitty twin bed that barely holds me up. He laughs and agrees that the twin bed situation probably won't work for his six feet-one inch frame and his bed is a better bet. We are leaving to Palm Desert early in the morning since I have the day off tomorrow.

I pack a bag as Kirk sits on my bed and watches me. I silently beg that the bed doesn't collapse underneath him. I show him the drawing I drew today.

"Hey, is it the vase of lilies I gave you?"
"Maybe!"
"Looks awesome, babe. Good job."

I brought my cutest black strapless bikini, my two most conservative sundresses—one strapless white, the other floral print—a light white sweater, and all my other necessities. I want to give off a good first impression to Kirk's grandparents.

I grab my phone and dial Fiona.
"Hi."
"Hi, I'm just letting you know I am going to Palm Desert tomorrow for the night. I won't be back until Sunday. I'm going to meet Kirk's grandparents."
"You definitely won't be in the apartment tomorrow night?"
"Well, no . . ."
"Cool. Have fun."
"Thanks."

What the hell?

Kirk gives me a questioning look. I don't even want to get into it. I refuse to let Fiona's moods ruin my perfect night with my new boyfriend.

"PMS." I smile.
"I see," he replies in a disgusted tone.

On our way out, we catch Konner and Bridgette on their way in.

"Hey!" I say to them.
"Hi!" they both reply.
"This is Kirk," I introduce.

"Nice to finally meet you, Kirk," Bridgette looks at me with suspicion.

"He's my boyfriend." I wink.

"Nice to meet you. I'm Konner West, and this is Bridgette Moore," Konner says as he shakes Kirk's hand.

"So a double date is in order soon?" Bridgette asks, ignoring how formal Konner is being.

"Absolutely! Do you guys want to have dinner on Sunday?" I invite.

"Sunday it is," Bridgette smiles.

"Great, I know just the place. Have a good night." We all smile and part ways.

If Fiona is avoiding me, she won't be able to for long.

Saturday morning comes quickly after an evening of movies and cuddling. Kirk and I get all of our things together and make our way to the Desert.

"I'm nervous to meet your grandparents."

"My grandparents are crazy cool, you shouldn't be."

Kirk fills his truck with gas at the first pump we find. On our way, we listen to the radio, and Kirk expresses his awful singing voice over and over while using the steering wheel as a set of drums. He looks really fine with his sunglasses on and the wind from his open window flying through his hair. It's hard for me to believe that two weeks ago I wanted nothing to do with him. The sun beaming in on him and the hilarious expressions that come across his face makes me feel like the luckiest girl in the world.

We arrive at our destination. The Desert is beautiful with immaculate streets, groomed palm trees, warm sunshine, and gorgeous views of the desert. I recognize the bougainvillea.

We finally reach his grandparents' place. I read a sign, "The Reserve." When we arrive, the guard knows Kirk.

"Steve, how are ya?" Kirk inquires.
"Hangin' in there, kid." He nods and lets us through.

We drive by mansion after mansion until he pulls into a driveway. My mouth drops at the sight of this house. It's a Mexican-style villa, with terracotta roof tiles. The house is cream stucco with two gigantic dark wood front doors at least nine feet high. Each side of the house has large windows that are separated in smaller squares by dark wood. Two enormous terracotta pots stand on either side of the front door with a fair-sized tree planted in each. I think about how pathetic the ugly pots at my place are.

Their garden is beautiful as well, with cactus and other beautiful desert flowers; I can't imagine how much their house is worth.

Kirk picks a key off this key ring and opens one of the doors. We walk in, and my awe just digs deeper. I look to the right to find a long open hallway. They have beautiful stone floors, and I can already spot a few prestigious carpets lying out. I glance up to find a large, rustic chandelier hanging over our heads. I kick off my flip-flops, and Kirk continues in through the house.

"Grandma! Pops! We're here!" he yells.

Straight across from the front door is an inviting living area with plush grey-colored couches, a wooden coffee table, a divine rock fireplace, and an oversized white terracotta lamp in the corner. This is by far one of the most beautiful houses I have ever been inside.

"Kurtis!" his grandma shrieks and hurries toward him.

Kurtis?

He lifts his small grandmother off the floor and gives her a genuine hug. His grandma is roughly five feet, with short dark hair, tanned skin, and a very slim frame. She gives him a big kiss on his cheek. She seems very gentile and sweet.

"Grandma, this is my girlfriend, Veronica," he introduces.

"How do you do, dear?" she asks as she gives me a light hug.

"I'm great, thank you. You have a breathtaking house," I compliment.

"Make yourself at home." She smiles.

Kirk and his grandma discuss what the plan is for the day. She tells him she is meeting friends for a few games of tennis and that his grandfather is playing golf for a few more hours. She tells Kirk we will have the house and to help ourselves to any food or drinks we please.

She waves good-bye and disappears into her gigantic house.

I look at Kirk with wide eyes. He knows I want an explanation.

"My grandfather is a successful man." He shrugs.

"No? Really?" I tease.

"He made some good choices when he was younger. He was high up in corporate with GMC and retired a few years ago. He's always been involved with investing. My grandma's never worked, but she's also never needed a maid. She does everything on her own—all the cooking and cleaning," he explains.

So his family has millions and millions of dollars he has never felt the need to mention. What else do I not know?

"Listen, I'm not a flashy guy. This kind of stuff doesn't get me going," Kirk says.

"I'm just surprised, that's all," I reply.

Kirk ushers me to the room we will be staying in.

"They have lots of space here in the event you want your own room," he teases.

We put our bathing suits on and head to the pool. We walk through the kitchen to get out to the deck. The kitchen is beautiful with dark granite countertops, stainless steel appliances, and dark wood cabinetry. There is an island with four wicker barstools and a giant vase with plenty of flowers displayed. At the sink, there is a large window that looks directly out to the pool area.

The pool is an infinity version with a dark blue color. They have large rocks and plants situated around, making it very private. You can look right out over the pool to a view of a luscious golf green, one of the holes on the prestigious course of Indian Wells. There is a clear view of the Santa Rosa Mountains, a simply breathtaking scenic display. They have an attached hot tub to match the pool.

There is tasteful deck furniture, including an outdoor couch facing another large stone fireplace with a flat-screen TV mounted to the stone, and an outdoor propane heater with two chairs on either side to match the couch. They have an outdoor kitchen with a very expensive barbeque. Closer to the pool, there are two lounge chairs with a round, glass table that face the pool for sprawling. By the fireplace setup, I notice attached to the house are sheer brown curtains you can pull for ultimate intimacy.

I don't mind if we never leave.

Kirk walks toward one of the lounge chairs and lays a towel out on each one. There is a pool shed off to the side that matches the house, and he opens it up and brings out two floaties for us.

"I'm having a cold beer, what can I get you?" he asks me.
"Ice water." I smile.

I apply my sunscreen all over my body especially on my shoulders because I always burn there. I make myself comfortable on the lounger, and I can feel the heat within seconds. It's going to be a hot day. I glance at the thermometer on the pool shed. It reads ninety-five degrees and it's only noon.

Kirk comes back and hands me a large glass with water and ice.

"Thanks." I grin.

Kirk takes a large, refreshing chug of beer and puts it down on the table before he heads for the pool.

"Coming?" he asks.

I follow him. The temperature is perfect.

"You're getting your hair wet today," he commands.

He moves toward me and attacks me by lifting me up and throwing me overhead into the water. I come up from the water. I pretend to be mad, but really, I'm not.

"You're going to get it!" I yell jokingly.

Before I could do anything, he voluntarily dives under the water. We play around in the pool for quite some time and then opt to relax in the sun. I lower my lounger down so I can lie on my tummy. I close my eyes and enjoy the heat.

Kirk joins me at the loungers and begins beating on my ass like a drum with both of his hands. I laugh and turn around to face him. I put my sunglasses on and stick my tongue out at him.

"You have a bangin' bod, babe," he says to me.

I've noticed since I moved from home, I've lost a bit of weight. I'm thankful for that today.

"Pops!" Kirk yells as he jumps up to greet his grandfather.

He shakes his hand and wraps his free arm around his grandpa and pats him strongly on the back. His grandfather is a big man, seems to be in good shape for his age. He has slicked-back grey hair, dark features, and tanned skin.

"This must be Veronica," his grandfather says as he approaches me.

"So nice to finally meet you, Mr. Floyd," I say as I offer my hand.

"Call me Tory," he replies and places his cigar back in his mouth.

He has a strong presence. He is wearing a blue golf polo shirt, black slacks, and black dress shoes.

Kirk follows him into the house, and I choose to stay put and leave him some alone time with his grandfather. Kirk looks up to him immensely.

He returns a few minutes later with some cut watermelon on a plate.

"I don't know about you, but I'm starving," he states.

I take a piece too. We skipped breakfast this morning. We spent that time doing something else.

I hadn't taken time to reflect on that part of last night yet. I'm glad that ice is broken, and it couldn't have been any smoother or more romantic.

"I was thinking we could spend the day out here and later go for a cruise on the golf cart. My grandparent's each have one, so we don't have to wait for my grandma to come back before we can go," he suggests.

"Cool." I grin.

# Chapter Seven

"Slow down!" I yell.

Kirk is speeding us down the hill in his grandfather's golf cart. I have an awful vision of something jumping out at us. He slows the cart down and begins to explain to me about the neighborhood. He tells me all about the infamous street called El Paseo.

"Next time we come down, I will take you around the town. This is just a short trip." He smiles.

"Can't wait." I grin.

"Do you want to drive?" he asks.

"I'll give it a try," I answer.

We switch sides, and I take the wheel. It's surprisingly easy to maneuver; it's actually quite fun!

After a half-hour cruise, we arrive back at the house. His grandma's golf cart is parked in the garage when we get there, which means she's home from tennis.

"What's your grandma's name?" I ask Kirk.

"Mary," he tells me.

When we enter into the kitchen, his grandparents are inside.

"I'm going to pour your grandmother a glass of white," he tells Kirk.

"I'm going to have a beer, but give one to Vero too," Kirk replies.

His grandfather hands me a wine glass and gives me a shy smile. I smile back at him. I notice his grandfather doesn't have a drink.

"Cheers," Tory says as he lights another Monte Cristo inside the kitchen. I recognize the cigar because my dad stores the same in a humidifier for special occasions.

I sip my wine. It's delicious just as I was expecting. Mary smiles at me and sips hers too.

"Take that outside," she scolds at Tory.

"For dinner, I am making a homemade lasagna. I hope you like lasagna, Veronica?" she asks.

"I like pretty much everything except mushrooms, I'm not picky," I answer.

"It should be ready in about an hour, but if you are hungry now, I have prepared some bruschetta as an appetizer. My boys are always hungry." She smiles.

Kirk's grandmother is so sweet; I can tell why he loves her so much.

"Thank you." I grin and politely pick up a bruschetta with a napkin.

I look around for Kirk. He is outside on the patio with his grandfather sprawled out on the couch.

"I was surprised when you called Kirk 'Kurtis,'" I expressed, leaning over the island countertop.

"Kurtis is Kirk's full name. His grandfather started calling him Kirk from a very young age. He prefers it, so that's what he has decided to call himself. Kirk can be difficult, but he's such a special young man," she explained with a small smile.

"I think by the sounds of things he has had it a little rough," I add.

"Yes, dear, he sure has," she says as she walks back to the sink and cleans off some more dishes.

Kirk yells for us to come outside. They have started a fire and the sun is beginning to lower in under the mountains. Mary and I join them on the deck. I have never seen an outdoor flat-screen TV before.

"It's interesting to see a TV outside," I state.

"It only rains about four days a year," Tory explains.

"We're in the desert, so it's hot basically every day," Kirk adds.

"The real reason there is a TV out here is because Tory is forbidden to smoke those damn cigars in the house and he's an avid sports fan. He came up with a way to enjoy both," Mary clarifies.

"Clever." I smile.

Tory nods at me.

We all nestle in by the fire, as the patio gets dark now that the sun has officially set.

"What are you doing for work, Veronica?" Mary asks.

"Right now, I work at a coffee shop in Huntington Beach. It's a small place called Beanz, it's good for now until I find something else," I answer.

I see Kirk's grandma look over at him. I instantly feel self-conscious and assume that my answer is subpar.

"She's still deciding what she wants to do, but she showed me a pretty wicked drawing she drew yesterday. She's got a gift there," Kirk says.

"There's nothing wrong with taking time off to figure it out," Tory adds.

"I have always had a passion for drawing so I might do something involving that. I'm just not sure yet. I used to dance ballet, but I gave that up not long ago," I explain.

"I didn't know you danced ballet," Kirk says with a questioning face.

"What do your parents do?" Mary asks me.

"My mom stays home, and my dad is a defense lawyer," I reply.

Mary smiles at me as she gets up from the chair.

"I must prepare the table for dinner, it will be ready to eat in ten minutes," she announces.

"Do you need any help?" I offer.

"No thanks, dear," she answers and shuts the glass door behind her.

I am unsure of how that conversation went. I don't want her to dislike me based on anything that I have said. Kirk can tell I am lost in thought.

"My grandma really likes you," he reassures as he places his hand on my knee.

I look at him and give him a halfhearted smile.

I listen to Kirk and his grandfather talk back and forth about basketball and baseball. I listen to them discuss the latest politics and argue some more about that.

We all get up and head inside to eat dinner.

"I put a big portion on your plate, Kirk," his grandma says.
"Thanks, Grandma, always trying to fatten me up." He smirks.

Kirk takes my empty wine glass from me and refills it.

"Grandma, can I pour you another glass?" he asks.
"Sure, dear." She smiles.

Kirk brings the wine glasses to the dining-room table and places them down by each of our plates. I notice again that Kirk did not pour his grandfather a glass, but I say nothing.

The dining room is situated right off the kitchen. Underneath the mahogany table is a large detailed red area rug. They have upholstered cream chairs around the table, eight of them. The whole house is decorated so beautifully.

The four of us sit at the end closest to the kitchen. His grandma didn't set a plate at the head of the table, just four seats across from each other.

"Did you decorate this whole house?" I ask Mary.
"I did." She smiles.
"Wow, you have amazing taste," I compliment.
"This is our biggest house to date. It's my dream house, we've spent the last couple years fixing everything to suit us perfectly." She smiles.

"When did you move in?" I ask.

"We moved in three years ago, just after Tory retired," she replies.

"It's really a beautiful house," I compliment again.

"Thank you," she accepts with a shy grin.

The lasagna was tasty. She is like a miracle worker with all her skills in this house. A great cook, a talented design sense, and her house is spotless. No wonder she could never have a full-time job.

Throughout dinner, the conversation was mainly about the shop and his grandfather giving him advice.

"I don't understand for the life of me why you aren't interested in taking up a job in corporate," his grandfather snarls.

"The corporate life is not me," Kirk answers.

"Look at your father, Kirk. He is very successful, and he doesn't have a problem working in corporate," Tory fires back.

"My dad is an asshole," Kirk blurts out with a sarcastic smile.

The table goes quiet, and I look down at my plate trying to avoid any involvement in this conversation whatsoever.

"You know, Kirk, I went with your father yesterday to help him pick out a Ferrari," his grandfather says.

"Good for him, hopefully that Ferrari loves him and treats him just as well as a perfectly good family," Kirk says sarcastically again.

"He asked a lot about you, you're his son. This conflict has gone on too long. You have made your point loud and clear. He knows he's been an absent father," he continues.

"Now, now," Mary chirps in.

I look at Kirk, and he also has his head down looking at his plate of his barely touched lasagna. I can tell this is a sore subject.

"Can we talk about something else?" Mary asks.

"Mary, don't protect him from his problems. We have given you everything you want and it kills your grandmother and I that you and Chase want nothing to do with your father," Tory states.

"He made a choice! He makes no effort with either of us! You know Chase had his first child almost five months ago. My dad didn't even call to congratulate him! What kind of father fucks up that badly?" Kirk raises his voice.

Another wave of silence fills the dining room. I take a large sip of my wine.

"I agree with your grandfather, Kurtis. You need some common ground with your father. You only have one, and Grandfather and I are not getting any younger," she says.

"I'll think about it," Kirk replies.

Dinner finishes, and Kirk leaves the table right away without clearing his plate. I stand up, take my plate in my hands, and walk toward the kitchen.

"Veronica, dear, you just leave your plate right there, I will take care of it." She smiles.

"Are you sure?" I ask.

"I am very sure. Go along now," she says.

I search for Kirk. I find him in the spare room we are occupying tonight.

"Are you okay?" I ask him.

"I'm fine," he replies.

"Should we just go do something?" I ask awkwardly.

"This argument will blow over in a few minutes, and we usually play blackjack on the dining-room table. My grandpa just needs some time to cool off before I face him again," he explains.

Kirk opens the neatly made bed and climbs in.

"Come," he signals.

I crawl in beside Kirk and place my head on his chest. I'm sure the drama with his dad is hard for him to handle. I can't imagine it. Kirk strokes my hair, and I close my eyes and breathe in his scent. I begin to drift away in a catnap. I didn't realize how tired I was until I lied in this heavenly bed.

I don't know how long I fell asleep for, but Kirk gently moves and wakes me up.

"Sleepyhead." He smiles.

He jumps out of bed, and I follow him back into the dining room. The room is clear again as if we never ate in it.

"Who's up for a challenge?" he calls loudly.

His grandma comes into the room.

"Kirk, I'm not sure that grandpa is feeling so well this evening," she says.

"What do you mean?" Kirk asks.

"I think tonight we will have to pass on cards," she says softly and walks away.

I look over at Kirk whose eyes fall to the floor. I feel terrible for him.

"All right. You and I can play," he says.
"Sure." I smile.

Kirk walks over to the cabinet in the dining room and pulls open the middle drawer. He draws out a deck of cards and walks back to the table.

"We can play whatever you want," he offers.
"Let's play 'Go Fish,'" I suggest with a big smile.
"You're on." He grins back.

After numerous games, we decide to go into the hot tub. From what we can see, his grandparents called it a night a while ago. Kirk and I throw our bathing suits back on and slip into the hot tub. It's a beautiful night with only a few stars lingering in the sky.

"Thanks for coming here with me," Kirk says as he begins to massage my shoulders.

I just smile and close my eyes to enjoy.

"Why didn't you tell me earlier that you draw and you danced ballet? Those are both wicked things, are you embarrassed about them or something?"
"No, not embarrassed. I don't know why I never mentioned it, you never asked me."
"I want to know everything about you. From now on, I want you to share everything with me. Is there anything else?"
"No . . . I like roller blading on occasion?"

Our hot tub venture doesn't last long. We are both tired and ready to get to bed. I remove my bathing suit and jump into the shower. Kirk showered off outside and went to lock up the house.

I finish in the shower and dry myself off. On goes my silk nightie, and I crawl back into the bed. There was no sign of Kirk anywhere, and before I even knew what hit me, I was out like a light.

I wake up with Kirk still passed out beside me. I gently push the covers over me and drop one foot to meet the stone floor. I drag myself out of the bed making an effort not to wake Kirk.

I changed into something more appropriate and make my way to the kitchen. The house is so big I am grateful I could find my way there.

"Good morning," I smile at Mary.

She looks like she's been up for hours already. I glance at the clock on the microwave and read nine-thirty.

"Good morning, dear. How did you sleep?" she asks.
"I hit the pillow and I was out." I laugh.

She hands me a cup of freshly squeezed orange juice.

"Kirk told me you like orange juice, but this is the real good stuff." she smiles.
"Thank you, it looks delicious," I say.
"Kirk won't be up for hours," she adds.
"Hours?" I clarify.
"Uh-huh. That boy loves his sleep." She smirks.

I was planning on giving him an extra thirty minutes before jumping up and down on the bed to wake him.

"I have brunch this morning with some ladies from my tennis club, I hope you two won't mind. Tory left early this morning for another round of golf. This is what old people do in their retirement." She laughs.

"I don't think it's a problem at all," I offer.

"It was such a pleasure to meet you, Veronica. You two seem good together—that's what he's been missing in his life," she states.

I don't say anything. She comes over to me, gives me a swift hug, and leaves me alone in the kitchen as she heads to the garage. She looks very cute in her tennis clothes. I enviously wish that for myself one day. Maybe I will take Fiona up on those tennis lessons after all.

I go back in the room and take out my phone from my bag. No texts.

I decide to wake up Kirk.

"Wake up, sleepyhead!" I yell in his ear.

He wakes up suddenly and smiles a toothy grin. He stretches out his whole body and makes a gratified loud sigh. Then, he pulls me down and buries me under his arm so I am back in bed.

"Your grandparents left already," I tell him.

"They leave every Sunday morning. They're busy retirees." He laughs.

"What's our plan then?" I ask.

"No point of sticking around here all day. We can get out of here after I shower," he suggests.

Kirk crawls out of bed and walks into the bathroom, turning on the water. I stay in bed as I wait for him to finish.

"Come!" he yells.

I go into the bathroom.

"Strip down and get in here with me," he grins.
"Do I have to?" I whine.
"Yes!" he commands.

I strip down naked and join him in the shower. Kirk shampoos his hair, making it super foamy and then reapplies shampoo to his hands and begins to wash my hair too. He gives me an amazing scalp massage, and then we stand under the water and let the shampoo rinse out of our hair. Next, Kirk squeezes body wash into his hands and begins to apply it on me. He starts at my neck and works his way down to my toes paying extra attention to my chest area.

I pick up the body wash and begin to repeat his steps starting at his neck and working my way down. The shower is a foamy hot mess. One thing leads to another, and soon we are becoming quite friendly in the shower.

"You owe me this for falling asleep on me last night," he whispers in my ear.

His whisper sends a sharp shiver down my spinal cord.

The shower is very spacious, enough room to lie down in it, so Kirk lies me down as the hot water continues to barely hit us. Kirk takes a firm grip on the tiled floor by my ears and thrusts his erection into me. I sequel with pleasure and run my hands down his chiseled back. He carries on thrusting, we make eye contact, and I close my eyes in ecstasy. Soon, Kirk pulls out and touches me between my legs vigorously until I meet my climax. He gives me a kiss and grins.

Kirk leaves the shower; I stay in to condition my hair. When I get out, he is already dried off and dressed. He is wearing white khaki shorts and a blue V-neck.

"Get dried off so we can head out." He winks.

I dry myself off, slip my underwear and bra back on, and pull up my dress. I take my leave-in conditioner and generously apply it to my hair, brushing through the tangles. Once it's smooth, it's time for deodorant and perfume spritzes.

Gathering up my things, sadness washes over me as reality hits that we are only two hours away from home.

"Ready, Freddy?" I tease.
"Ready." He winks.

We climb into the truck after Kirk locks up the front door. It seems so safe around here you would never be worried if you forgot to lock your door. I will always be amazed by his grandparent's marvelous house. They are so humble and generous.

My phone buzzes. It's ringing.
"Hi, Fio."
"How is Palm Desert? Do you think you're going to stay another night?"
"It's great. We are actually just leaving, so I'll be home soon. How are you?"
"I'm fine. I've been working like crazy lately."
"Great. Do you work tonight? Will you be home to catch up?"
"I'm waitressing tonight. Sorry, V. I know I've been a terrible friend."
"Anyways, I'll see you when I see you."

We hang up. I am surprising her at her job tonight with Kirk, Bridgette, and Konner, so I'm glad she is working.

"Still up for that dinner tonight?" I ask Kirk.
"Sure, babe," he replies.

He turns the radio up really loud, and we soar down the highway on our way home.

# Chapter Eight

When we finally get back, Kirk parks his truck on the road, and we head up to my apartment. When I walk in the door, there is a total mess. She has had a party here.

"What the fuck!" I yell.

I look around and see beer bottles; empty red Solo cups everywhere, two empty pizza boxes, and some girl's bra. I am horrified. I know this place is a shithole, but still. Where is her respect?

I look at Kirk.

"What a mess," he says, shaking his head.

"Fiona?" I yell. No response.

I am scared to turn the corner to my room. Sure enough, as I do, I find my bedroom door wide open, my bedding all over the ground, my closet doors exposed.

"What the fuck!" I repeat.

I take a deep breath in and exhale loudly.

"That's a pretty low blow," Kirk says as he enters my room.

I grab my phone and dial Fiona. No answer. How shocking!

Tears well up in my eyes. I don't even know this girl anymore.

"She would never have done this before," I cry.

"Shhhh . . . ," he whispers as he hugs me tight, "we'll clean this up."

The bathroom is a horrendous mess. Someone puked all over the wall, and the shower curtain is hanging by a thread. I stand in disbelief.

Kirk goes into the kitchen and finds a garbage bag. He begins to pick things up and throw them in; one garbage bag later and the kitchen is clear.

"You don't have to do this, Kirk," I sob.

"Listen, I know how you must be feeling right now. I'm going to clean this up and you are going to have to confront Fiona about this. This is not right. *She* is not right. She's fucking selfish, and that's been made clear," he states.

Kirk continues on in the kitchen as I clean my room. I strip my bedding and hang my clothes back up on their rack. Thankfully, no one touched my computer or any of my other personal belongings. I put my bedding in a bag with intention to wash it at Kirk's later. I don't want to know what was going on last night in my bed, or my clothes.

"Just pack up all the clothes that were on the floor too, babe," Kirk suggests.

I pick through and throw them into the bag with the bedding.

"You can wash them at my place," he offers.

Kirk begins to clean up the bathroom as I walk over and knock on Bridgette and Konner's door.

"Hi, Vero, are you okay?" Bridgette asks me and pulls me in for a hug.

"Was there a party at my place last night?" I ask.

"There was. A pretty big one," she answers.

"I'm so disappointed and mad, it is a pig pen," I explain.

"We didn't bother to knock or anything. The building appears to be fairly empty, so I don't think you'll have any fines to worry about," she offers.

Bridgette follows me into my apartment. She didn't see the worst of it; Kirk has done an amazing job cleaning this mess.

"How disrespectful," she hisses.

"So not like her," I defend.

"From what I saw, there were a lot of guys here, I mean, when we came home from getting groceries we saw her for only a moment. She's not very friendly," she says.

Kirk comes out from the bathroom.

"The good news is, it's a small space, the bad news is, I might have added to the puke on the wall," he jokes, trying really hard to lighten the mood.

"Gross! Someone puked on the wall," Bridgette repeats.

"So there was a party here?" Kirk confirms with Bridgette.

She nods and he shakes his head and rolls his eyes.

"This isn't exactly the most bangin' spot for a party," he answers.

"Where there is a will, there is a way," Bridgette says.

The apartment is back in decent condition, thanks to Kirk. I notice basically all my food has been eaten, and she mentioned not a single word to me on the phone.

"Is Konner around now?" Kirk asks Bridgette.
"Yeah, he's working," she replies.
"I was going to suggest we all pile into my truck and head to my place so Vero can clean her bedding and whatnot. We can go to dinner from my place," he offers.
"I'll go grab him, give me five minutes," she answers.

Kirk and I wait on the street, and he puts my laundry bag in the bed of his truck for me. He hugs me tight and kisses the top of my head. I am still fuming mad. How could she be so irresponsible?

Konner and Bridgette meet us at the truck, and the four of us barely can pile in. We get to Kirk's and are all finally able to move again.

Konner and Bridgette seem like a really compatible couple. He holds her hand and looks at her with that look. He adores her, you can just tell.

My phone buzzes and is ringing again. It's an unknown number.
"Hello?"
"Hi, is this Veronica White?"
"Yes it is."
"You live in an apartment building that I manage, my name is David Spring. I have several complaints from your girls' party last night. Please consider this a firm warning. If this happens again, you will be evicted. A written notice has been placed in your mailbox. You are lucky the police were not called, as far I remember, you two young ladies are underaged."

"I'm sorry, sir, but you will have to get in direct contact with Fiona. I was out of town last night and was not in the apartment."

"That doesn't matter to me, Miss White. You have a written lease stating you will follow rules. We are in no position to condone parties, please pass that message on. Good day, Miss White."

Everyone looks at me. My mouth drops open. Unbelievable! I wasn't even there and I am the one being scolded for appalling behavior.

"I guess I was wrong," Bridgette says apologetically.

I say nothing and just roll my eyes. This is a joke. I can't wait to come face-to-face with that pretty little girl and give her a piece of my mind. I dial her number and it goes straight to voicemail.

"Fiona. Call me back. This is urgent. What you did last night is disgusting. I am expecting an apology. Kirk cleaned up your whole mess so you owe him an apology too," I scold and hang up.

We get to Kirk's, and he immediately throws my things into the washing machine. I sit on the couch with a glum look on my face.

"Cheer up, Vero," Bridgette says.

I give her a halfhearted smile and turn on the TV.

"Konner, can I get you a cold one?" Kirk asks.

"Yeah, sure," he replies.

"What can I get you, girls?" Kirk asks.

"Just water is great for me," Bridgette answers.

"I'll have a beer too," I request.

Bridgette is very naturally beautiful. She has straight dark brown hair past her shoulders, nice teeth, brown eyes, and a good complexion. She is about five feet six inches, just a little shorter than me. Konner is around the same height as Kirk, maybe a little taller. He is in good shape, dark hair, dark features; he and Bridgette look good together.

I hate beer, but right now, I just need something to take off the edge. I have never been this mad at her before. She never does things like this, ever.

My phone rings. This time it's Fiona. I excuse myself and take the call on the deck.

"Stop being such a raging bitch all the time! You think you're the only one who's hurting lately? Look past yourself for once, Veronica!"

"Excuse me, Fiona? You think what you just did is acceptable? Are you kidding me? Who are you lately? I understand you are going through some things, but go to a fucking shrink and deal it the way you should! This is the wrong thing to do! We have been friends since we were seven! I think we've made a huge mistake moving in together!"

"I'm going through some stuff right now you could at least be understanding. I have always given you the same! The only mistake I have ever made was becoming friends with you! You're the most self-centered, judgmental—"

I hang up on her. She is out of her mind.

After the guys finish their beer, we are ready to go. I barely sipped mine; it was gross. I definitely don't like beer. We all put our shoes on and walk out the door.

"You have a nice place, Kirk," Bridgette smiles.

"It ain't too shabby," he replies.

"Where are we going for dinner?" Konner asks.
"We are going to Joe's," I answer.

We walk in the door at Joe's.

"Welcome to Joe's! For four?" the hostess chirps.
"Is Fiona working?" I ask bluntly.
"Fiona no longer works here, but all of our servers are great," she reassures.
"What do you mean Fiona doesn't work here?" I snarl.
"Um . . . Fiona quit her job a week ago," she replies.
"Oh, is that right?" I ask rhetorically.
"Any section is great," Kirk interrupts with an oversized grin.

I have entirely lost any appetite I may have had before I was served with that information. How can she say that to me? She regrets ever becoming friends with me? That I'm the most self-centered person?

"Kirk, I think I'm going to camp out at your place for a while until I figure out what the hell is going on with Fiona," I tell him.
"Of course," he answers.

I feel really bad for everyone at the table. It is such an awkward evening; I should have cancelled the whole thing altogether when I saw the state of my apartment.

"I'm sorry you guys," I offer.
"It's not your fault," Bridgette says.

The guys say nothing. They just sip their beers and ignore my comment. I get it, guys hate drama, but fighting with girls is nothing new to me.

When dinner is finally over, we drop Bridgette and Konner off at home. There is no sign of life coming from my apartment. I don't know if that's a good thing or a bad thing. I put this whole thing at the back of my mind and I move close to Kirk and put my head on his shoulder. He doesn't deserve to spend his Sunday evening with this, and neither do I, frankly. He puts his arm around me and begins to rub my right shoulder.

Monday morning arrives, and I am off work *again* today. I am getting so tired of that. I wake up Kirk and tell him to get up. We slept in a bit, and I know he has a big day at work with the reconstruction of that Chevy.

I go into the kitchen and pull out the egg carton from the fridge. I make Kirk eggs with two pieces of white toast. He joins me in the kitchen and gives me a kiss.

"Thank you, baby," he says as he grabs the plate.

"You're welcome." I smile.

"So today is my pal's birthday, he's turning twenty-three, so I'm going to spend the night out with the boys," he explains.

"Okay," I agree.

"You are welcome to stay here, just kick back, watch a movie, make yourself at home. The dish has a lot of great movies, just order whatever you want," he offers.

"Sure." I smile.

"Hey, if I get you to drop me off at work, you can have my truck today if you have anything you want to do," he offers.

I contemplate for a few minutes. I would love to go shopping and distract my mind in a good book.

"Okay, sure, I'll take it," I agree.

Kirk gets into the shower and changes for work. We leave the apartment about fifteen minutes later, and we drive to the shop.

"Have a great day." I smile.

"You have a great day, gorgeous," he replies and kisses me good-bye.

I drive the truck to the shopping center. I park, grab my purse, and proceed inside. There is a large Starbucks. I stand in line and wait to order myself a strawberry Frappuccino.

I decide I'm going to shop for some new clothes today. The mall has everything I need to do some serious retail therapy. I double-check that I have my parents' AmEx on me. They'd understand; at least I hope they will!

Shortly after, my phone buzzes with a text from Kirk.

-Kirk: I miss you.

I smile. He left me roughly fifteen minutes ago.

-Vero: Miss you, too, silly.

There are so many beautiful things; my arm already aches from the weight of the clothes I have thrown on my arm. I have chosen a few things I will give to Kirk. He is overly generous to me all the time; the least I can do is give back a little.

My phone rings and Bridgette's name appears on my screen.

"Hey, Bridgette!"

"Hey, girl."

"What are you up to?"

"Nothing too special, I just got home from teaching. So I just talked to Kon, he said your boyfriend has invited him out tonight on a boys' night. My eyebrow is raised."

"Apparently it's some guy's birthday, I don't really know the deal."

"If you're not doing anything, I was thinking we could do our own version of a girls' night?"

"That sounds like an amazing plan!"

"I'll call you in a few hours when their plan is more solid."

"Talk to you soon."

I phone Kirk.

"Hey, baby."

"Hey, so you invited Konner to your boys' night?"

"News spreads like wildfire."

"I'm just asking. Bridgette and I are going to have our own girls' night if that's your guy's plan."

"Yeah, I invited him. He seems like a cool guy, he likes to throw back a few cold ones. I think he'll enjoy himself."

"Great, so I will get you from work at five?"

"Come at four."

I browse at the clock on the wall, it reads one, and my day is flying by. I purchase all my new things and make my way to the mall's exit.

When I get back to Kirk's, I run the water. He has a gorgeous shower with three different facets. I turn the first one I see and wait for the water to boil warmer. On the floor is a decent shampoo, no conditioner, body wash, and face wash. I absolutely cannot shower without conditioner but luckily have one in my bag. Returning to the shower, it's toasty warm—the perfect temperature. I have a long, dragged-out shower.

After I wrap myself in a towel, I return to bed and crawl up into a ball. I doze off to an afternoon nap, Kirk's smell lingers in his bed sheets.

I wake up to my phone buzzing on the bedside table. It's Bridgette.

"Hey."

"Hey, I just saw Fiona going into you guys' apartment with another girl."

"Probably Ivory."

"They were dressed in less clothes than hookers on a busy Friday night!"

"Not surprised."

"Anyway, Konner said he's definitely going to that boys' night tonight."

"Yeah, do you know where they're going or anything?"

"No, he doesn't know either."

"Okay, well I'm getting Kirk from work in an hour, I will find it all out. I will offer to drive him to wherever it is he is going. I don't want him drinking and driving."

"Yeah, good plan."

"I'll pick you up on my way back from dropping him off."

"That would be great, see you later."

A yawn invades my face, and I stretch my body into a stiff X form.

It's time to get dressed so I can pick my adorable boyfriend up.

Four hits the clock, and I am parked outside the shop. I see Kirk locking the main door and he walks to the truck. I get out to greet him.

"Hi, babe." He smiles and hugs me.

"Hi." I grin.

"I missed you all day," he says.

"I missed you too." I smile.

"Should we go home and do something about that?" He winks.

I roll my eyes and head for the passenger door.

"How did it feel driving today?" he asks.

"It felt liberating, I guess," I answer.

"What did you do?" he asks.

"I went to the mall and shopped, I showered, napped, and cleaned a few things," I tell him.

We get to his apartment, and finally I remember to get the details of the evening ahead.

"So where are you guys going?" I ask him.

"Grabbing a burger and a few beers at a pub on Main Street, nothing crazy," he answers.

"I was thinking I could just drop you off and pick you up?" I suggest.

"If you want to," he replies.

"What did Konner say when you invited him?" I ask.

"He said he was down. What's with the interrogation?" he snaps.

"I'm not interrogating you!" I defend.

"Don't worry about Konner. By the sounds of it, his girlfriend does enough worrying for the both of you," Kirk snaps again.

"What is that supposed to mean?" I ask.

"It means, Konner said his girlfriend is constantly worrying about what he does and where he goes," Kirk tells me.

"Of course she worries, Kirk! She's engaged to him for Christ's sake!" I defend.

Kirk goes into his room and runs the shower. He makes it clear he doesn't want me to follow him. Why is he so defensive? I laid out the three new shirts I bought him on his bed, and he didn't even mention them.

He finally comes out of his room thirty minutes later and joins me to watch TV.

"Dinner's at seven," he tells me, barely looking up at me from his cell-phone screen.

"Okay," I reply coldly.

"Hey, babe? Did you buy me some shirts today?" he asks.

"Mhmm," I answer.

"I love them, thank you so much," he says as he gives me a light kiss on the cheek.

We sit in silence as the five o'clock news blares on television.

"What's the matter?" he asks.

"Nothing, just not so sure why you're being defensive. I just asked a question," I say.

Kirk doesn't say anything. I give him a questioning face.

"Sorry," he finally says and cuddles up to me.

"It's fine," I response.

"My friends are good guys, it's kind of annoying when girls get jealous," he starts.

"I am not jealous, Kirk," I glare.

"I wasn't referring to you, Vero," he answers.

Altogether, things are just not running smoothly for us tonight. I secretly wished it were seven already so I didn't have to sit here with him anymore.

I get my phone and send a text to Bridgette.

Vero: They are going to a pub. I'll get you at 7:15.

"Who are you texting?" Kirk asks.

"Bridgette," I tell him.

"So they're engaged?" he asks.

"Yes," I answer.

Did he not see her gorgeous ring? I then remember that guys don't really look for things like that. I don't know why Bridgette acts insecure toward Konner. He seems like a really nice guy, and it appears that he treats her well.

"My grandma called me today. She said you forgot some earrings there or something," he says.

I immediately reach for my earlobes, and they are bare. Dammit! I forgot my diamond studs my dad treated me with for my graduation gift. I always wanted and begged for them. I remember placing them on the bedside table before I fell asleep.

"Dammit!" I whispered.

"Don't worry, she said she will keep them safe for you," he supported.

I haven't called my mom in days, I'm sure she is losing her mind, so I go tell Kirk I need to call my mom in his room.

"Hi, Mom."

"Hi, honey!"

"How are you? Sorry I've been quiet lately."

"We've been getting so excited about our trip! I can't believe it's only a couple of weeks away!"

"You guys will have an incredible time."

"What's new with you?"

"Nothing, still just working and that."

"How was Palm Desert with Fiona?"

"Fun."

"What did you girls do? I'm shocked you had fun. There's not tons to do there."

"Uh . . . we went to the mall."

"You went on Saturday for the day?"

"Yeah, Mom. I just wanted to check in. I'm actually on my way out. Can I call you tomorrow?"

"Sure, honey. We miss you!"

"Miss you guys too."

"Bye, sweetie."

That was close! I froze when she asked me what we did there. Certainly, we wouldn't have spent the day at a mansion if it had just been Fiona and me. My parents would be beyond livid if they knew what I had really been doing there.

"How are your parents?" Kirk asks me as I sit back down.

"They seem good. My dad has surprised her with a cruise around Europe for three week in October. They are excited to leave," I explain.

"That's crazy, they'll have the time of their lives," he supports.

Finally six forty-five hits the clock and it's time to drop Kirk off at this birthday party.

"Are you all ready? You look handsome in that shirt," I compliment.

He does a model pose, and we both laugh. I laugh much harder than he does.

# Chapter Nine

I drop Kirk off, and he is only early by five minutes. He told me Konner was going to meet him there. I give him a kiss good-bye and wish him a fun night. Now, time to pick up Bridgette so we can have our own fun!

I get my phone and call her.

"Hey! I'll be there in five! I figure we can just hang out at Kirk's so I can avoid running into Fiona."

"Great, I'll see you soon!"

When I arrive, she is waiting for me outside. She gives me a wave, and I stop the truck to let her in.

"You look cute," I compliment.

"So do you," she blushes.

"Thanks! I bought these shorts and tank today. What do you feel like for dinner?" I question.

"I want to order in! Are you in the mood for that?" she asks.

"Sure, I know Kirk has like a million delivery brochures at his place." I laugh.

We get to Kirk's and we search for a Chinese place that delivers. Bridgette comes across one and calls. I hand her his address so she can give it to them. On TV, it's *The Bachelorette* for girls' night. Kirk would never sit through that with me! Bridgette joins me, and I hand her a blanket in case she's cold. Kirk always has the A/C cranked in his apartment.

There's a knock on Kirk's front door. It startles me because I wasn't expecting anyone.

"Is that the Chinese already?" I ask her doubtfully.
"No, definitely not," she answers.

I don't know if I should open his door, but do it anyways. To my surprise, there is an attractive blonde girl about twenty-five years old.

"Uh . . . Hi?" I say.
"Oh! . . . Is Kirk here?" she asks.
"Kirk's out," I answer rudely.
"Okay . . . I just wanted to return his shirt. Just tell him I found it finally in my laundry." She smiles.
"Sorry, what is your name?" I ask.
"Penny. Don't worry, he knows me," she answers.
"All right. I will . . . ," I say awkwardly as I accept the shirt.
"Thanks!" she says and walks away.

What the hell?

"Who was that?" Bridgette inquires.
"Some slut who obviously has been around this block," I growl.
"My sweet Vero, you really need some serenity in your life." She laughs.

She's right about that!

"Hey! I have an idea!" she shouts.

"What?" I ask.

"Come to one of my Bikram classes! I bet you would love it!" she suggests.

"Bik-what?" I ask confused.

"Hot yoga, Bikram hot yoga. You've never heard of it?" she laughs.

"I know what hot yoga is," I defend.

"Great! Well, I teach it Thursday nights as a karma class, meaning it's by donation, typically like five dollars. I could lend you everything you need. You might actually find some peace and relief," she suggests again.

"I'll give it a try," I commit.

She smiles a toothy grin at me.

Kirk's house phone rings, and I assume it's because the Chinese is here. I am desperately hoping it's not another whore looking for a quickie. I remember he presses nine to release the front door, so I press nine and hear a loud beeping noise.

Within minutes, there is a knock on the door. I choose to peek through the hole to make sure Penny isn't hanging around again. It's a small Asian man, so I open.

"That will be forty dollars and fifty-seven cents," he informs me.

Bridgette runs to her purse and hands him $45.00.

"Keep the change." She smiles and accepts the food from him.

I tell Bridgette to drop the food on the dining-room table, and I will get plates, forks, and knives. I open the fridge to search for something to drink. I find a few cans of pop and opt for those.

"It looks like this is all he has, hope you like Coke!" I say apologetically.

"Coke is great, don't worry. Hey, have you heard anything from Kirk?" she asks.

"No. Have you heard from Konner?" I ask.

"No," she says worried.

"Is everything okay? Kirk mentioned you might be worried about Konner going out tonight?" I snoop.

"Before we moved, I was really suspicious Konner was cheating on me. I never found anything, but since then, I've been driving myself insane about it," she admits.

"What made you think that?" I test.

"He would leave his phone out of sight, he stopped sleeping over for a few days. I just had a bad feeling about it, so finally when he did leave his phone within arm's reach, I went through it. I didn't find anything, but you know when you have that feeling," she announces.

"Why are you going to marry him then?" I ask with surprise.

"I love him way too much to ever leave him! I'm totally crazy about him," she cries.

"Trust him then!" I protest.

She smiles at me, and we both dive into our food.

"This night is exactly what I was needing," Bridgette declares.

"I know, I feel the same way," I told her.

I suggest she and I go into Kirk's hot tub. She accepts, and I rummage through my bag to dig out both my bikinis. We change, get towels, and leave for a relaxing hot tub.

I don't believe it when we arrive there. Penny is there swimming in the pool.

"Oh great," I murmur and roll my eyes.
"Just ignore her," Bridgette suggests.

The two of us head for the hot tub. I secretly wish that I were with Kirk so she would see us together. I accidently glare at her as we walk by. She didn't pay any attention to us. She was too busy attending to her glass of wine.

A few minutes after we settle into the hot tub, Penny comes in.

"Hi girls!" she cries.
"Hi," Bridgette says.

The hot tub becomes the most awkward place on the earth. I just want to disappear right then and there.

"So you're staying at Kirk's? What are you, like, his sisters or something?" she asks.

"I'm actually Kirk's girlfriend, and this is my good friend, Bridgette," I snarl.

"Kirk's girlfriend? Opps, I hope it hasn't been that way for long," she says under her breath.

"No, they've been together for a couple of weeks, but he totally adores her," Bridgette protects.

"Good for him, he deserves to be happy. It wasn't going to work out with us, that's for sure," she says.

What kind of nerve does this bitch have? Who has the audacity to say that out loud?

The hot tub goes quiet again, and my face is luckily red from the steam, so it masks my fury. Bridgette turns her back to Penny and I to look around the grounds. Penny just stares at me and says nothing.

"Did you use to date Kirk?" I pipe up.
"We didn't date, we just messed around," she tells me.

My mouth is dry, and my heart is beating fast. Why am I so upset about this? I am so jealous of this woman, and I really should not be.

"Anyways, it's been a pleasure, ladies," she says as she lifts her perfect body out of the water and heads up the stairs toward her towel. She disappears into the darkness, and I beg that's where she stays.

"Wow, that girl has nerve!" Bridgette declares.
"Can you believe that?" I ask rhetorically.
"Some girls are really disgusting," she offers.
"Yeah, they seem to have been Kirk's flavor," I agree.

I wonder to myself why Kirk is after someone like me when I meet a girl like that. He used to be involved with her. Not on a romantic level, but definitely on a physical one. I tell myself to make Kirk go to the doctor; I need to be sure he is clean before I sleep with him again. Sadly, I also realize, it would be too late at this point.

It's time to drive Bridgette home. She teaches early and needs to go to bed. I haven't heard a word from Kirk and bothering him seems like the wrong thing to do. It was so weird when I dropped him off. He was really closed off.

"Thank you so much for the ride," Bridgette says sweetly.
"My pleasure, sleep tight," I reply.

I drive away with gratification that I don't have to sleep in that repulsive building tonight. Poor Bridgette, she does.

When I get back to Kirk's, my phone buzzes. It's Kirk.
"Hey, can you come get me now?"

The urgency in his voice gets my attention immediately.

"Is everything okay?"
"Just come."

My heart drops. There are a million possibilities running through my head. Did something happen to him or Konner? Is Kirk okay? Was there a fight? Anything could have happened.

I throw my shoes back on and rush to the truck. I throw the truck in reverse, back up, and throw it back in drive. I speed off to find Kirk.

I see him waiting for me outside the pub, but I don't see any of his other friends.

"Turn off the truck," he orders as he opens the passenger door.

My heart is pounding a million beats a minute. Something is wrong.

"Are you okay?" I ask in disarray as I see his busted lip and swollen eye.
"It's Fiona," he starts.

My heart stops.

"Listen, I didn't tell you my buddy's party involved the strip club, I didn't want you to worry," he continues.

"What happened to Fiona?" I ignore him.

"At the pub, my one bud was saying how he's been sleepin' with this Fiona girl lately and that he was at that party she threw. He told me he met her at the strip joint," he answers.

"Cut to the chase, Kirk," I say.

"Well, I just didn't think much of it, she's a big girl she can make her own choices. We got to the strip club, and I kid you not, three songs in and Fiona hits the stage," he tells me.

"If you are lying to me, Kirk, this is absolutely not funny." I begin to cry.

"I'm dead serious, Veronica. Fiona has started stripping. I saw her filthy little sidekick walking around the place trying to get someone to pay for a dance," he continues.

"So what the fuck did you do? You just watched my best friend take her clothes off for you for money?" I yell.

"I got on the stage and I told her to get the fuck out of there before she even started her dance," he assures.

I look at Kirk, and I begin to ball my eyes out. What the fuck has happened to my best friend in a month? She has gone from being a stunning, free-spirited, knockout to being a shady, sneaky stripper. Kirk runs around to the driver's side and flings open the door. I cover my face, and he holds me tight as I sob in his arms.

Kirk drives us home in silence as I stare out the passenger side window. Not only has she made terrible choices for herself, she had Kirk's face punched in for getting on the stage to defend her morals. I am so lost in thought now; I don't know where to start. I close my eyes, and I wish when I open them all these terrible things will disappear into thin air.

When we get back, I clean Kirk's lip off with antiseptic I found in the bathroom. He will have a black eye in the morning. That will be a good first impression for his clients at the shop.

I can't believe Fiona hasn't even called. Of course, she knows I have heard about this by now. I am sure Konner thinks we are complete crazies, and he and Bridgette probably never want to see us again.

I think about the apartment and how badly I need to move out. I remember coming home to that horrific mess and Fiona making no attempt to fix things there either. It's so late at night by now, and I start work at nine. I am exhausted with a pounding headache.

"Thank you for defending Fiona tonight," I say to Kirk with sad eyes.

"It's nothing," he replies.

"I feel really bad that you will have to sport a black eye for the next week," I tell him.

"Don't worry about me, Vero. Seriously right now, I'm not the one who needs help," he says.

He's right. Fiona needs help. Tomorrow is a new day, and I am going to make sure I hunt her down even if I have to go into that filthy strip club and drag her out.

I tossed and turned all night. I wake up with obvious black circles around both my eyes, but not nearly as ugly or painful as what Kirk will wake up with. I notice there is blood on his pillow from his busted lip.

I get out of bed and run the shower. I stand under the water and go through the motions with my mind somewhere out in space. When I step out, I dry myself off and brush my teeth. To work, I will wear a usual sundress, as I do almost every day, and I will need some serious concealer to hide the aftermath of my night.

Kirk finally rolls out of bed. I ask him how he is feeling, and as always, he tells me he is great. I am still so incredibly annoyed and disappointed with Fiona, I don't even know where to begin.

When Kirk is ready to leave, we head to work together, and he drops me off outside the coffee shop. I give him a gentle kiss and head inside.

"Good morning, Melody," I greet.

"Morning, kid," she says.

"How was your weekend?" I ask.

"My weekend was spent here, as usual." She smiles.

"You need to take a day off here and there, you know?" I say.

"How was your weekend?" she asks.

"Well, I have a new boyfriend, so, I've been consumed with him," I tell Melody.

"A new boyfriend! What's his story?" she asks.

"His name is Kirk, and he has his own auto shop—" she interrupts me.

"Kirk Floyd?" she asks me.

I figured she probably knew him from a tune-up or something.

"Yeah," I answer.

"You know, Veronica, Kirk is Mandi's ex-boyfriend," she tells me, horrified.

I become quiet. Another thing to add to my problems!

"Oh . . . ," I reply.

"He really is an awful person, Veronica. I need you to know that," she demands.

"I see," I murmur.

Melody leaves to the back room. I am speechless and shocked. I figure I should probably quit this job now if I'm not already fired.

Melody comes back out.

"Do you have any idea what he put my daughter through in four years?" she spits.

"Honestly, I have no idea," I reply.

"He is the reason she moved away with her dad. He is the reason she hasn't had a relationship since and probably never will again!" she shouts.

This makes sense to me. This is why he has never come into the coffee shop;the reason he was so interested when he knew I was bowling with her and tried to rush me away; the purpose he is always encouraging me to get a new job. This is why his grandmother gave him an awful look when I told her where I work.

"Melody, I am truly sorry," I tell her as tears stream down my face.

"I'm going to have to let you go, Veronica, it's just a conflict of interest now. It's the same as siding with the enemy, I'm sorry," she says softly.

"I understand." I cry harder.

"Please hang your apron in the back and make your way out," she orders.

This is by far the worst twenty-four hours of my life. I leave the coffee shop, and tears continue to soak my face. I can't stand confrontation like that! It makes me shiver with nerves.

I feel I have nowhere to go, no one to call, I feel so alone. An emptiness forms in the deepest part of my stomach as I feel the urge to double over and throw up. This actually happens—I do vomit all over the road. Luckily, no one was around to see it. I choose to walk to my apartment. If Fiona is there, now is not the time to deal with her.

# Chapter Ten

When I arrive, Fiona's things are gone. She has moved out on me. She didn't leave a penny for rent, she didn't leave a note, she didn't call or text, she did nothing!

I snatch my phone from my purse, and I dial Fiona's number. I am now viciously angry with her. It goes straight to voicemail. My life is falling apart around me. Last week I would have told you I have never been happier. Now, I feel I am at my lowest ever.

I pick up my phone and dial Kirk.

"Hey."

"Kirk. We need to talk. Drop what you are doing and come see me now."

"Where are you?"

"At my apartment."

I sit on this shitty couch and wait for him to arrive. I hate this fucking apartment. I hate everything about it.

When Kirk comes, he can see I am livid.

"Kirk, give me some advice here," I start.

"Advice about what?" he asks.

"I just got fired from my job after I mentioned to Melody that I have a new boyfriend named Kirk Floyd," I tell him.

"I told you not to mix your personal life with your business life, Veronica," he blames.

"She told me Mandi is your ex-girlfriend. A girl I spent a considerably lovely evening with. A girl I could consider a friend. You knew all along I had spent time with your ex-girlfriend and you didn't say one single fucking word about it," I spit.

"Veronica, I was not about to tell you who you can and cannot spend time with. I told you she is a nice girl, I told you it's been over for a long time, why should I have had to tell you she is my ex?" he asks.

"Why would you not tell me? Do you know how foolish I feel? Do you even care?" I quiz.

"I think this is a shitty situation, and I understand you are upset. Last night threw a wrench into your life, I think you might be overreacting here," he says.

"Are you fucking serious?" I scold.

"I'm leaving, Vero. I can't do this with you right now I have a lot of work to do," he answers.

"Kirk, if you leave me like this you can bet you'll never see me again in your life. If you leave, Kirk, it's over," I cry dramatically.

"Bye, Veronica. You are being so dramatic," he shakes his head as he turns and walks away.

I freeze. Not a single thought passes through my head. Not a muscle moves. Only my eyes, as tears run down my face and land on my bare legs.

I break down and finally call my mom.

"Mom!" I cry hysterically.

"Oh my god, Veronica! What in God's name is going on?" she cries.

I tell her everything. I tell her about Kirk. I tell her about Fiona, I tell her about my job, I even tell her that Kirk just walked out on me.

"Oh, honey."

"I know. I am so upset!"

"That is a lot of drama for one little girl to take."

"What do I do?"

"This is what you do, sweetheart. If you are falling for Kirk, you release his past and chalk that one up as a bad coincidence. Think of how he felt when he found out you worked there. It sounds like you are taking this out on him, and it seems he has been nothing but good to you."

"He has been."

"That part is easy. It was just a temporary job. It sounds like he is quite smitten with you; I think he'll happily forgive your outburst. As far as Fiona goes . . . this one is tougher."

"I know. That situation is dreadful."

"She is going through a tough time in her life. Certainly a strip club is no place for a respectable young girl. I am terribly saddened by this news. You really haven't heard a word from her since this all happened?"

"She moved all her things out of the apartment and her phone is off."

"You know what, honey, I need some time to ponder. I'm going to call you back in a few hours."

"Mom, *please* don't tell Dad."

"Veronica, depending on this outcome, I may not have a choice. Take care, honey."

I can tell by my mom's tone that she is not happy. I don't blame her, she is so far away and there is really nothing she can do.

My front door opens and in walks one responsible little whore.

"Ivory?" I question.

"Oh, I had no idea you'd be here. Fiona told me you had basically moved to your boyfriend's," she explains.

"Where is Fiona? Why did she move out?" I ask.

"Um . . . she said you guys are in the middle of a huge fight. She is at my place," she answers.

I clench my teeth.

"If I write her a note, will you give it to her for me?" I test.

"Oh, . . . okay," she agrees.

I go into my room and return with a notebook and pen.

Fiona,

I love you, and I miss you. Please call me so we can talk. I know you're not going to leave your best friend high and dry. All these things can be fixed.

Love your very best friend,

V

I fold the note and hand it to Ivory.

"Ivory, you have not been innocent here. She is my best friend; this is not the life she wants. Her parents are getting a divorce and she is just lost. Please tell her how much I love her and need to see her," I beg.

She says nothing and puts the note in her pocket.

"I forgot my straightener in your bathroom . . . I was just coming to take it back," she explains.

She returns from the bathroom with her straightener in hand.

"Well, thanks," she says.
"Ivory, please tell her," I repeat.

She nods and leaves.

At this point, I have pulled myself together enough to call Kirk. It rings and rings, but he doesn't answer. I try again. Same result. This time, I leave a message.

"Kirk, you were right. I overreacted. Please call me back."

I bring myself back to a realization point. Why did I move here? What was I after? I remember I came here to change the things I didn't like about myself. Right now, I am being controlling, I am being judgmental, and worst of all, I am being difficult. I fall back into a distant memory.

It was the day of my graduation. It wasn't an option; I was having the best makeup artist in town and the best hairstylist. I knew I was being so annoying. My poor mom nearly ripped her hair out dealing with me. My dress was a gorgeous custom-made gown that I absolutely had to have. Once I was all ready, my boyfriend came to meet me at my house. I was so angry when he arrived because he had forgotten to get me a corsage. I stomped around my house, making a scene yelling at everyone. I started his graduation day off to a terrible start because I didn't have everything perfect. I had called him three times earlier in the day to make sure he wouldn't forget. The fact that he brought me a massive display of white roses that likely cost a fortune was dismissed because I didn't have a damn corsage like everyone else. My dad felt so bad for me, he went and bought me one that outdid everyone else's.

When we went to meet up with friends, I was still annoyed, and Tyson didn't want anything to do with me. He left for a majority of the pictures to talk with his buddies, and we were not in a good space. My parents were furious too because it was their only child's graduation. They only get to go to one, and I was acting like a total princess. Their pictures turned out horribly and had to buy some from the overpriced photographer I was happily smiling for.

I look back on that story now, and I have so many regrets. I don't want to do this to Kirk. I don't want him to dread my company. I want him to love me and cherish me because he truly does. Not because I have to tell him to.

My phone begins to buzz. It's Kirk.

"Hi!"

"Hi, Veronica."

"Kirk, I am so sorry! Please forgive me, I beg!"

"I would prefer to put this entire day behind us forever."

"Me too, I don't care about your past. I don't care about the job either! I just want you, that's it."

"I forgive you, babe."

"Can I see you?"

"Sure. When I'm done at five, I will come by and get you."

I was able to fix one problem, I am confident I can fix the rest. Now, I dial Bridgette.

"Hi!"

Phew! She doesn't sound like she hates me after all.

"Hi, Bridgette."

"How are you?"

"Are you home?"

"Yeah, are you?"

"Yeah, come over, I can explain things so much easier that way."

"Okay, I'll be there soon."

A few minutes later, Bridgette knocks on the door.

"Come in!" I yell.

She opens the door and shuts it behind her.

"How are you?" she asks with a questioning face.
"I have had the most exhausting twenty-four hours," I tell her.

We sit on the ramshackle couch together as I open up to her about everything. She mentioned that Konner had come home quite horrified from the whole ordeal but reassured me that they both still love us and it's not a reflection at all on our newfound friendship.

Bridgette gives me a big hug, exactly what I was aching for. She tells me to try and find my sunshine in my life always. She seems to always be right; she is a very smart person, and I appreciate her advice immensely.

"What do you want to do about Fiona, Vero?" she asks.
"I want to make everything right. I have known Fiona since I was seven years old. Her parents are divorcing, she is releasing her anger in the wrong way," I explain.
"Fiona's life is not your life. You can choose to support her or not, but you cannot change her. If she decides this is a lifestyle she likes for now, you will not be able to change her mind," Bridgette tells me.
"It's not fair!" I start to cry again.

Bridgette gives me another hug, rocks me lightly back at forth and pats my back. She is very motherly and nurturing.

Kirk calls me and tells me he is waiting for me. I make sure the front door is locked before I leave. I don't need to be robbed on top of all this.

"Hi," I mutter.

"Hi," he answers and places his hand on my left thigh.

"Have you spoken to Fiona?" he inquires.

"No. Did I tell you she moved out?" I ask.

"No! What the fuck?" he says with surprise.

"All her stuff is gone. She didn't leave a single thing, not even a note," I say sadly holding back more tears.

"What kind of person doesn't even leave their rent money behind? What a disgusting best friend! She still has responsibilities no matter how much she wants to change her life," Kirk hisses.

I explain to Kirk that Ivory came into the apartment looking for her straightener and that I gave her a note to pass to Fiona. I tell him I am desperately hoping she calls me so we can sort everything out. Things have escalated from zero to sixty in very little time, and I am not ready to lose her.

"If she doesn't return your call, Vero, are you really going to chase her?" he asks.

"I don't know what's going on . . . ," I reply.

* * *

A few days go by and I haven't heard anything from Fiona. I begin to doubt she even received my note. I need a new plan, so I decide to call Bridgette.

"Hi!"

"Hi, I need a new plan."

"Okay, how can I help?"

Together, we scheme a way so I can come face-to-face with Fiona. Bridgette suggests I go to the strip club and see for myself how bad it really is. She says I can use her ID card and that with a little dress-up fun I would get away being her easily. I decide to not tell Kirk about this.

I've been spending a lot more time at my own apartment now too. Bridgette and I cleaned up the entrance to the building, pulled some weeds, and replaced the broken terracotta pots so when we come home, we're not so appalled.

Kirk tells me his grandfather invited him back this weekend to play golf in a tournament with some of his high-rolling buddies. Apparently, it'll mean a lot to Tory. Kirk invites me, but I tell him this weekend I have made plans with Bridgette that I cannot cancel. I tell him to go without me. He is reluctant but agrees that maybe he needs to spend time with his grandfather. Kirk leaves after work on Friday and won't be home until Sunday evening.

This weekend, I am executing Project Fiona, and it's going to be so helpful that Kirk isn't around. He would not approve of my plan at all and likely try and change my mind.

I call Bridgette.
"It's go time!"

We make a total mess in my room with makeup, clothes, and shoes everywhere. We tried to make my face look as closely to Bridgette's as possible. I had to buy brown contact lenses so I pass her characteristics. I also bought a longer brown wig so I am not recognizable by Fiona. Her card has to work for me; it's the only way I will be able to get in.

"Are you absolutely sure you want to go in alone?" Bridgette confirms.

"I am sure," I answer.

"This is so funny. We did a pretty good job!" she high-fives me.

"It was a genius idea!" I proclaim.

"I hope I don't have regrets about it tomorrow," she worries out loud.

I am all dolled up with my new brown wig, high stiletto heels, and a tight black dress. I bought some ridiculously big sunglasses to wear as well. I feel totally outrageous, but I know I have to do this.

# Chapter Eleven

I fetch a cab and tell him to drop me off at Erotica Strip Club. I am sure the driver thought I was a total weirdo. I arrive and begin to sweat because my heart is beating fast and my nerves are through the roof sending jolts of adrenaline through my veins.

"ID please?" the bouncer demands.

This guy is huge. Not someone you would want to get on the bad side of. I immediately wonder if he was the one who threw Kirk out.

I hand him Bridgette's ID. He gives it a brief look and hands it back to me.
"Go in," he commands.

Whether or not he believed it was my face is a thing of the past. I put on my sunglasses as I enter the doors of the club. It's not very busy. There is a man far too old to be looking at naked underage girls. His granddaughter is probably older than Fiona.

"Cover is ten dollars!" a girl yells at me from a hole in the wall that appears to be a coat check. On the ledge of the counter are six different business-card holders for all of the owners and operators of the club. I look closer and read, "Kirk Floyd, Owner" on one of the cards. My heart drops and my eyes jump out of my head.

I hand the girl a ten-dollar bill.

"Is Kirk here tonight?" I ask her casually.
"No, I saw him a few nights ago in here, but I haven't seen him tonight," she yells to me over the blaring music.

I grab his business card and throw it into my clutch.

I take a seat in the back of the club at a table alone. A waitress approaches me right away.

"What can I get you, doll?" she shouts over the music.
"Uh . . . I'll have a . . . cranberry and vodka," I order nervously.
"That'll be ten-fifty," she replies.

What the fuck? Talk about expensive drinks! Kirk must be making a fortune here!

I hand her a twenty, and she gives me the change as she waits awkwardly for her tip. I hand her three extra dollars and she disappears.

A few minutes later, she returns with my drink. She places a napkin on the table and puts the drink on it. I remove the wedge of lime from the rim of the glass and squeeze it into my drink. I take a sip. Ouch! That's strong.

I look around, but I don't see Fiona anywhere. I don't see Ivory either, but I had heard Friday nights are a must for strippers if they want to make some good money. They have red carpets throughout the club and the bar right off to the right side. There are numerous plain black chairs, some of which are situated right along the stage. The stage is raised and is a glossy white color with a lit trim. They have the infamous gold pole from the stage to the roof, and the lights are dim. They have spotlights on the stage and a few cocktail waitresses wandering around waiting for someone to call them over.

I notice the DJ has his own booth to the right of the stage right across from the bar. It's very dark, so you can barely make out his silhouette. He has canned music playing on the speakers at a decent volume.

A group of guys sit around the front row of the stage. They are anxiously waiting and are obviously already drunk off their pints of beer. I wonder if those are Kirk's buddies. Nothing is happening. I don't see one stripper, I don't understand. Moments later, the DJ comes on the speakers through his microphone and a light show begins throughout the club.

"Next show starts at nine!" he yells.

I browse around for a clock. I really need to start wearing a watch. Bridgette told me not to take my cell phone out while I was there, it's bad etiquette and I would get thrown out. I finally find the time. It's eight fifty-five.

I nervously sip my drink as I notice one stripper silhouette appear. She isn't on the stage; she walks closer the group of guys and begins flirting with them. Her outfit leaves nothing to the imagination. She is wearing clear high heels with lights blinking in each heel, revealing black bathing suit bottoms, and a tacky neon pink bathing suit top accentuating her obvious boob job. As I peer closer at her, I realize I recognize her. It's Penny.

I swallow deeply and take another sip of my drink.

The lights come on and I hear "Candy Shop" by 50 Cent begin to play loudly. A girl walks out with the same kind of outfit as Penny. She grips the golden pole and begins to swing around on it. I doubt Fiona can do that. It's actually kind of fascinating. She has a giant tramp-stamp tattoo piece on her tanned skin with long black hair—obviously extensions. She is in shape and also has an evident boob job. Her face isn't very attractive. She has a large nose with a nose ring, skinny lips, deeply eye-lined beady eyes, and exaggerated penciled eyebrows.

She seems to know her way around the pole. She holds herself up as she swings her legs upward. Her legs grip the pole as she swirls herself around.

A few more girls follow, each stripping to their own song. I notice Ivory sitting on a guy's lap. Fiona must be around here. I will be mortified if she sees me. A lot of these girls have tattoo pieces throughout their bodies; some really interesting ones, like angel wings and various sayings. All these girls are in good shape; I can't understand how you couldn't be in these circumstances. These girls are keeping Brazilian waxing places in business. I've seen more vaginas in these last songs than I have in my eighteen years of life.

Here I am, sitting in a dirty strip club, with a dark brown wig and large sunglasses, hoping to find my best friend who is now a stripper. I pinch myself; apparently it's not just a bad dream.

Penny approaches me and I freeze.

"Can I interest you in dance, honey?" she asks.
"Uh . . . no," I answer with wide eyes.

Thank god I have sunglasses on. I decide to change my voice to make it a little higher. I have to remember to do this religiously.

She reaches for my sunglasses and rips them off my face. She leans down and puts her hands on my thighs and looks deep into my eyes.

"Are those your real eyes?" she asks.
"Yes," I lie.
"What are you doing here?" she asks again.
"Uh . . . I'm thinking about getting into the business," I answer.

I don't know where that answer came from, but she seems to buy it. She releases my legs, stands up, and puts my glasses on the table by my drink.

"No need to be embarrassed," she says.
"I'm not embarrassed," I lie again.

She grins at me.

"I'll be back," she smirks and glides away.

Oh, great!

I look back over to where I had seen Ivory previously. Ah-ha! I spot Fiona. She too has taken a seat on a guy's lap. She has a big smile on her face as she teases him running her hand down his back.

I wish I knew who these guys were.

She looks . . . happy. She is dressed in a red full-piece bathing suit with two deep cutouts on their side of her waist.

She has those hideous clear light-up heels on her feet and her long hair is down grazing her lower back. She doesn't have any new tattoos that are visible . . . yet. I also have noticed a couple of these girls have jewelry on their lady parts. I cringe to think how painful that would have been to get pierced.

I've been so sheltered my whole life, now I understand why. I need to get out of here before that crazy Penny comes back and harasses me again.

I stand up to leave, and as I do, I hear Penny.

"Where do you think you're going?" she snarls with her hands firmly on her hips.

"Fresh air," I lie.

"I just spoke to my boss. He said you can come down to the dressing room, see what it's like down there," she explains.

"Oh," I answer.

"Come on," she commands.

"Really, I don't have time tonight, but thank you," I lie and walk to the door.

By boss, did she mean Kirk?

Penny grabs my arm and pulls me toward her. She keeps her grip and pulls harder, leading us down a mystery staircase into a grungy dressing room. In the room, there are three girls standing around fixing their hair and makeup.

"What's your name?" she inquires.

"Uh . . . Bianca," I lie.

She gets the girls attention and introduces me to Star, Sparkle, and Sugar. Obviously their stage names, as I highly doubt anyone would name their daughter Sparkle.

Penny tells me her stage name is Million, insinuating she is worth a million bucks.

Mhmm . . . I think Penny is a more appropriate name, insinuating she's actually worth a penny. Her parents figured that out right away.

She goes on to tell me the other girls are up in the audience getting friendly with all the clients. She tells me you can make a thousand dollars a night if you attract the right guy.

"So how do I, like, become a stripper?" I ask awkwardly.

"We don't call ourselves strippers! We are dancers!" she snaps.

Strippers, dancers, whores, it's entirely the same thing.

"I can give you our boss's number. His name is Kirk. He's a really nice guy, but you might need to sleep with him before he gives you a chance," Penny explains.

"Oh, I grabbed his business card when I walked in," I say as I wave the card.

"He's totally sexy though, so that helps," Penny adds.

I can hear the music get loud again as the DJ makes another announcement.

"Come, we can watch the dance together," she suggests as she grabs my arm again.

I basically never wear heels, my feet are throbbing and all these stairs aren't helping. She is treating me like a rag doll.

I can see Ivory take the stage, and I do everything in my power to avoid having to watch this.

"What's her deal?" I ask Penny.

"She's been around for a while now, she sells if you ever need," Penny answers.

"What does she sell?" I ask.

"She sells pretty much everything," she answers casually.

"Did she have to sleep with the boss too?" I inquire.

"She's definitely been with Kirk," Penny confirms.

I just want to cry. I want to leave; I have had more than enough of this.

"We have a new dancer though, and she hasn't slept with Kirk. I think he hates her. There was a lot of drama here this week. She got thrown off the stage. I don't think she was cleared by Kirk yet," Penny says.

"That's nice," I reply coldly.

"If that's what your biggest worry is, don't sweat it. I met his pathetic, jealous girlfriend. It has to be serious because he never lets girls stay at his place. Ah, this is why I never drink rum! I can never keep anything to myself!" she explains.

"Yeah, I know that already," I mutter under my breath.

"What?" she asked confused.

"Honestly, I really have to head out. Thank you for everything, I'm going to call Kirk tomorrow," I lie.

"Tell him Penny helped you out." She winks.

I take one last glance at Fiona. I can't believe how happy she is. This is like a sick little Girl Scout Club they have in here. There is someone behind this operation, and it's Kirk Floyd.

I rip off my painful high heels and walk barefoot all the way to my apartment. This doesn't make any sense to me. Why? After everything I have been through, why is Fiona the one who seems to be happy? I have never done anything wrong! I am a law-abiding citizen. I am a good friend, and a loving daughter. It isn't fair! Why do I now have the most appalling boyfriend of them all! I knew there was a reason I was so hesitant at first! Fiona told me she had run him by Ivory, and now I found out she's also been in his bed! What a horror story!

# Chapter Twelve

I finally stumble home and cannot wait to put my feet up. I know Bridgette is waiting patiently to hear me open my door. One minute after I'm in, she comes.

"How did it go?" she asks excitedly.
"It was an experience," I answer.

After I explain the whole story to her, she sits across from me with her mouth wideopen.

"So what are you going to do?" she asks with intrigue.
"For once, I'm going to be rational and try to do this in a mature manner. I will get to the bottom of this, but not the way I would normally," I explain.
"Good plan," she smirks, and we high-five.
"I need to figure out why I'm here. I must have come for a reason," I admit.
"I think you're right." She smiles.

I grab two bowls from the cabinet and dish out two generous doses of vanilla ice-cream into each. I hand one to Bridgette and keep the other for myself.

"Thank you!" she says.
"You're welcome." I smile.

"What are you going to do about Kirk?" Bridgette inquires.

"I'm not going to do anything. I think my best bet is to go along with this whole thing, see how it turns out," I admit.

"You aren't telling me you are going to keep this alterego going?" she confirms.

"Bianca is the new Vero," I laugh.

"No way! Really?" she asks.

"Why not? I will never know the truth until I see it for myself," I respond.

"I sense trouble," Bridgette says.

"Me too." I smirk.

Bridgette leaves, and I promise I will attend her class in the morning. She tells me she will meet me at eight-thirty tomorrow and we will walk there together. She said the studio is only a fifteen-minute walk away.

The thing that's great about Bridgette, something I really admire, she is not judgmental at all. She is someone you could say anything to, and she doesn't push her opinion on you. She nods and seems to be supportive. I love that. I am never afraid she is going to leave and talk to someone about how much she can't stand my stupid decisions.

I had two missed calls and three text messages from Kirk when I looked at my phone.

-Kirk: Hey, baby. I'm at dinner. I'll call you in an hour.

-Kirk: Babe?

-Kirk: Call me back!

I didn't reply or return his call. I will tomorrow, and I'll tell him I crashed really early. I am not dealing with him right now. Who could blame me?

The alarm clock goes off at eight, and it's time to get my act together for this suspicious hot yoga class. I wear spandex black shorts and a blue Lululemon sports bra. I toss a sweatshirt on and walk to the bathroom to brush my teeth. I filled up my water bottle and ate a banana just in time to meet Bridgette.

"Are you ready for this?" she teases.

"As ready as I ever will be!" I laugh.

"You have a ballet background, you have to be flexible for that!" she says.

In the yoga room, I lie a mat and towel down just as I was instructed. Bridgette told me to lie on my back with my palms facing up and to relax and breathe. It's not as hot as I feared, and I find I am able to relax easily. Just as I found myself dozing off into a sleep, Bridgette begins to talk.

"Good morning, everyone, please find yourselves and come to the tops of your mats in a cross-legged position," she orders delicately.

Everyone in the class collectively does as they are told. I watch and follow.

"Is this anyone's first class?" she asks.

I raise my hand, and so do a couple other people.

"Marvelous, please practice at your own pace. This is not a race but rather an exercise to explore the capabilities of our bodies. If at any point a position is painful or seems unreachable, step back to your comfort. You may feel free to take a break at any time," she educates.

After five minutes, I began to really sweat. The room became progressively hotter, and the people around me seemed to be sweating the same. I am constantly peering around the room in amazement. I know it's an incredible workout, but damn, how long is this class again?

Time goes by about as fast as a slug crossing a dry road on a good day. I can't keep my sweaty hair from sticking to my face. My spandex shorts are completely drenched in sweat, and I now know it is possible to pull a muscle in your vagina. Ballet really is nothing like this.

I opt to lie back down because my feelings are overpowering me and I cannot hold my concentration. Last night's events are replaying like a bad movie through my memory. I peer at the old man beside me who is wearing extremely revealing shorts. I can't help but judge how badly he needs a full body wax. The thought makes me laugh out loud, and I am immediately humiliated by all the glares directed toward me.

I stand back up in effort to join the rest of the yogis and gracefully reposition my thong underwear that has travelled way too far upward. Some people in this room belong at the Cirque de Soleil—they are beyond flexible.

Bridgette tells us we are moving to the floor sequence. We shift into a move that would replicate a woman giving birth, and I am convinced it probably feels the same too.

Why did I agree to this? My skin is melting off my body, and I've easily sweated off ten pounds I did not need to lose. This heat is like nothing I have experienced before. My head is dizzy, and I am truly exhausted mind, body, and soul.

"That concludes our practice today, may you live the rest of your day in peace and clarity. Namaste," she praises and bows her head.

"Namaste," the class repeats.

I meet with Bridgette inside the changing room.

"You did great!" she applauses with a quiet, gentle clap.

"My favorite part of that ninety minutes was the Namaste," I tease.

"The first class will always be the hardest," she claims.

"First and only class!" My cherry-red-tomato face replies.

"Once the benefits soak in, you will feel renewed and you'll be back." She grins.

She and I decide on a café close by for a light lunch. She explains to me the benefits of practicing on a regular basis and tells me her boss mentioned she is looking for someone to work at the reception. She told her boss I would be perfect for the job.

"Would you be interested in something like that?" Bridgette asks.

"Sure, thank you so much for that," I reply.

"Great, so I'll call her later and tell her you're interested." She smiles.

Tonight, it will be me, myself, and I. Bridgette and Konner are going for dinner together, and I have no other friends to call.

I spend my evening curled up in bed and finally opt to call back Kirk who has been sending frantic texts to me all day.

"Hello?"

"Hi."

"What the fuck has been going on with you these last couple of days?"

"I've been busy with Bridgette."

"Too busy to call or text your boyfriend back?"

"I'm sorry, Kirk. I thought the space will only do us good."

"What did you do today?"

"I went to my first hot yoga class and had lunch with Bridgette. Now, I'm just at home in bed."

"I miss you, I wish I were there."

"How is the tournament?"

"Typical. I've golfed like shit and embarrassed myself, but it's been good."

"Enjoying your grandpa?"

"Yeah, he's chill. I'll be back tomorrow at five. I'm coming over as soon as I'm back."

"I'll be waiting. Sweet dreams."

"Good night, babe."

It's going to be hard to act like nothing's wrong after that eventful Friday night. I am falling in love with Kirk. I want there to be a plausible explanation about all of this. I don't want to feel foolish thinking this could all be a misunderstanding, but I need to find out for good.

I decide to call Kirk back, but as Bianca, and I press *67 so my number is blocked.

"Kirk Floyd speaking."

"Hi, my name is Bianca, I spoke to Penny last night at your club."

"What can I do for you?"

"I think I want to start dancing."

"Okay. Did Penny give you her contact number?"

"No, she told me to call you."

"Next time you're at the club, tell Hans, he's the door man, that I said it's fine for you to go in. I'll get in touch with Penny so she can help you through this process. I'm on vacation right now."

"Great, thanks."

"Take care."

He wasn't very friendly, and he definitely didn't make it sound like he was interested in me. He sounded so professional and serious on the phone, that's totally not the Kirk I know.

I lie in bed in my completely soundless apartment. I don't know if this is all a good idea, but this is the only way I can see Fiona, and I can get down to the bottom of what Kirk's involvement really is with this club.

With every dramatic situation in the past, I have always reacted irrationally and on impulse. It has been extremely difficult for me to hold my tongue and carry on as if nothing is wrong these last couple of days. It would be easiest for me to just freak out, break up with him, freak out at Fiona as well, but I know I would be left single and best friendless. I don't want to do this.

I have to make sure Kirk never finds what I am doing at the club. Even if we break up and I never see him again, I can't do this to my self-esteem. I will have to hide all the evidence of my double-life and I will need solid alibies. I need to find something that's going to mask this so Kirk does not get suspicious.

I drift off into a deep sleep after my mind is tired of processing all my thoughts. Tomorrow I will have to face Kirk and act as I always have. Tomorrow is the first day of the new Veronica White.

Bridgette tells me her boss would like to meet me for an informal interview. She tells me I will not need my resume as Bridgette has a great reputation and her boss trusts her judgment. I meet them both at the studio at twelve o'clock.

After our meeting, we agree I would start work Tuesday morning. The job is a reception-type requirement, which will include signing members into their classes, selling packages, and sending promotion e-mails out on a regular basis. It seems straightforward, and I receive a decent hourly wage as well as free classes whenever I wish.

The studio is very clean and tranquil. The walls are a chocolate brown throughout, and the reception area has two brown modern chairs with orange pillows on each one. They have a dark wood table in between and a giant fish tank. Inside, they have beautiful exotic angelfish.

The change rooms are also extremely clean. They have long light wooden benches with plenty of lockers. They have a separate area where there are showers, toilets, and sinks.

The actual practice room is a typical dance studio minus the bar. There are mirrors on the walls without windows, wood floors, and a platform in the front of the room for the instructors to teach on.

I leave Bridgette at the studio because she has to teach, so I go home and prepare myself for my meeting with Kirk. When five hits the clock, I am ready for him.

"Come in." I smile as I answer the door.

Kirk gives me a giant hug and plants a big kiss on my lips.

"God, I missed you," he admits.

"I missed you too," I reply.

"How was your day?" he asks as he shifts his baseball cap backward.

"It was great. I actually got a job at the Bikram studio Bridgette teaches at," I say.

"That's great news, hun. Doing what?" he asks.

"Reception." I smile.

"I'm just going to be straight up. I have no idea what Bikram is," he admits.

"Hot yoga," I chuckle.

"Hot yoga. It sounds awfully hard. How was your first class?" he questions.

"It was hard, you would hate it," I reply.

Kirk and I watched a movie on my awful TV. He made plenty of effort to get in my pants, so I finally had to say something.

"Kirk, when was the last time you got tested for an STD?" I ask boldly.

"What the fuck kind of question is that?" he snaps.

"I'm being serious. We never talked about it, and now since we obviously have sex, it's something I need to ask," I explain.

"I don't have an STD, Veronica," he snaps again.

"I didn't say that, I asked when you last got checked," I insist.

"I have a physical done every single year, for your information, my last one was done about two months ago, and I am clean," he informs.

"I would like you to get checked again," I declare.

"Great, and while I'm there, you can get the nice doctor to write you up a prescription for birth control, oh, and you can get a test too," he snarls.

"Fine," I agree.

I have nothing to hide, but I can't say the same for him.

"We can go tomorrow," I suggest.

"Fine," he agrees.

We sit in the waiting room of the doctor's office. Kirk seems to be fine with this, his mood is pleasant, but I am a little nervous.

"Kirk Floyd, Veronica White," the nurse calls as she looks at us.

Kirk and I rise from our seats and follow the nurse.

"The doctor will be in shortly. Make yourselves comfortable." She grins and closes the door behind her.

The clinic has patient rooms just the same as any regular doctor's office, disturbing posters on the wall, a box of Kleenex, and that weird scent of rubber and orange fragrance lingering in the air.

"Stop bouncing your leg," Kirk orders.
"Sorry, I'm nervous," I admit.

We sit in awkward silence as we wait for the doctor to come in.

"Good afternoon, I'm Doctor Pine," she introduces.
"Hi," Kirk says,
"What can I do for you two today?" she asks sweetly.
"My girlfriend here is requesting I have an STD check since we just started dating and we now have sex," Kirk explains.
"Must I remind the two of you the importance of protection?" she lectures.
"No," I answer and shake my head.
"I think it's only fair you check Veronica for any as well," Kirk explains.
"Kirk has also suggested that I be put on a birth control pill," I add.
"Well, we should get started then," she informs.

Doctor Pine puts on her glasses and writes down something in each of our files. She is a middle-aged, white woman with reddish hair and pale skin.

"I have to request I complete each examination privately," she instructs.

"I'll wait out there," I volunteer as I stand up and head for the door.

Kirk walks out of the doctor's office about ten minutes later. He tells me it's my turn and I get up and make my way back.

"Now, Veronica, birth control is a big decision," Doctor Pine starts.

"I was on birth control in high school," I tell her.

"Do you remember which one?" she inquires.

"I believe it was Alesse," I answer.

"If you are comfortable with that, I will write you the same prescription," she offers.

"That is fine with me," I agree.

"You are aware that birth control does not protect you from sexual transmitted infections and should be taken at the same time every day to ensure effectiveness," the doctor educates.

"Yes," I nod.

"Sit up here on the bed and allow me to take your blood pressure," she orders.

I sit and offer my arm to her as she takes my blood pressure.

"Excellent, everything looks good. I am going to leave this gown here for you to change into. I will have to perform a pap test before I allow you to leave with this prescription. I will come back in a few minutes, I will knock first," she advises.

Once she leaves, I strip off my clothes, leaving only my bra on. I slip the disposable gown up over my head and lie flat on the bed staring up at the ceiling. This is not my first pap test, but they are never comfortable no matter how many times you get them, I've been told. I am grateful we were appointed a female doctor. I would feel uneasy if I had a male doctor performing this.

# Chapter Thirteen

I lie on the bed waiting impatiently just wanting to get this over with. There is a light knock on the door.

"Come in," I allow.

"Great, is this your first pap test?" she asks.

"No, my second," I admit.

"This shouldn't be very different from the first one, sweetie. Place your feet here on the stirrups, and shift your backside as close to the edge of the table that you can," she instructs.

I do as I am told and I can feel my legs beginning to tremble. This happened to me the last time too.

"Relax your legs, sweetie, I won't hurt you," she reassures me through her facemask as I hear her snap on her rubber gloves.

A bright light shines down over my lady parts as Doctor Pine observes.

"Try and open wider for me," she requests.

I widen my legs.

"You will hear a quick snapping noise, don't be alarmed," she warns.

I lie there in discomfort as she continues to complete my pap test. The room is cold, and I notice goose bumps forming on both my arms. I start to shiver and cannot control it.

"I am going to a do a smear today too, Veronica. This might pinch, but it is rapidly over," she warns again.

The pinching sensation makes me jump as it startles me.

"I know, it's a bit shocking. Don't worry, we are finished. You can close your legs now," she assures.

She removes her gloves and mask and walks over to the sink to wash her hands. I sit up with my legs tightly closed and wait for her to take a seat on her chair. I think it's impossible not to feel violated after that.

"Everything looks healthy," she explains.

"That's good," I answer.

"I can't stress the importance of the consistency of your pill, Veronica. Young love can be blind, I just don't want to see you in here two months' time needing a pregnancy test because your pill wasn't effective," she commands.

"Yes, I understand. I don't want that either," I agree.

"Good. Here you go, you can pick this up at any drugstore," she explains as she hands me my prescription.

"Thank you," I accept.

"If there is anything that I am worried about, I will have one of the nurses give you a call. By the way, good for you for taking your sexual health seriously and having Kirk take a test. Too many girls don't do this," she adds as she smiles and leaves the room.

I put my clothes back on and leave the gown on the bed for the nurse to throw away. I glance in the mirror and fix my hair. I exit the room and find Kirk waiting.

"Let's go," I order as I smile to the girl at the reception desk.

Kirk follows me out the door, and we walk to the truck.

"How did it go?" he asks.
"Fine, she said I look healthy. I need to go to a drugstore and pick up this prescription for birth control," I tell him.
"Sure. So she said she'll call if something's off," he says.

I stare out the window as we drive down the road. I doubt the drugstore will be far; there is always a Walgreens close by.

We arrive at the drugstore minutes later and both get out of the truck. Kirk meets me and grabs my hand. We walk to the pharmacy section of the store, and I stroll to the drop-off counter right away. She tells me it will take roughly thirty minutes, so Kirk and I decide to have an ice-cream next door while we wait.

"I will have the Rocky Road one, please," I smile.
"I will have the Phishfood one," Kirk orders to the girl at Ben & Jerry's.

He pays and brings the ice-cream to our table.

"Do you feel better now that we went and did those tests?" he asks.
"I guess I do, but I'll feel even better if she never calls," I state.
"She won't call," he reassures.

We sit there for a good half an hour, and then we return to pick up my prescription.

"The total today will be fifty-four dollars and seventy cents for a three month fill of prescription," she informs.

"Here," Kirk says as he hands her his credit card.

"Kirk, you don't have to pay for it," I state shyly.

"It's nothing," he answers.

"So when these are empty, simply come back to get a refill. Your doctor has prescribed you a year, so you'll be good for a while. Do you have any questions about the medication?" she asks.

"No, that's great. Thanks." I smile.

Kirk picks up a few other things while we are there.

"I really need to remember to take these every day," I tell him.

"Fuckin' rights you do," he replies as he picks out toothpaste.

At the register, Kirk has toothpaste, a pack of Trident gum, deodorant, and vitamin water.

"Do you need anything?" he asks.

"No, I'm good," I answer.

Kirk tells me we are going to do dinner at his apartment tonight and later he wants to go to the beach and listen to the waves. I tell him I have work in the morning and I need to have a decent sleep. He asks me if I have seen or heard from Fiona. I lie and tell him I haven't seen or heard a thing from her.

Kirk parks his truck outside of the liquor store. I wait in the truck, as I am obviously not allowed to go inside.

"Do you feel like wine tonight?" he asks.

"Sure," I answer.

Kirk returns to the truck with a twelve-pack of beer and a brown paper bag with a bottle of wine inside. He looks really cute today with his flip-flops, white khaki shorts, and green beater. He is going through a phase of wearing baseball caps everywhere, which is a shame because he has such nice hair. He looks like he's walking off an Abercrombie & Fitch campaign, except a tattooed version considering I have never seen an Abercrombie & Fitch model with any tattoos.

He throws the beer in the bed of the truck and hands me the bottle of wine. I pull the bottle out of the bag and look at it—it's Sauvignon Blanc, whatever that means.

"Hey, hey, easy with that bottle, little missy. You know I can get a fine for buying alcohol for minors," he teases.

"When will I meet your friends?" I ask Kirk.

"Whenever the opportunity arises," he answers.

"I feel like eating sour candies," I express.

"All right, let's get some candy at the next gas station," he suggests.

As promised, we get candy at the next gas station and Kirk fills up his truck while we are there. His phone rings in the cup holder. He doesn't answer because he can't hear it ringing. I glance at the screen. It's Penny.

Kirk climbs back into the truck.

"You missed a call from some girl named Penny," I tell him casually.

"What? You didn't answer it, did you?" he panics.

"No, why would I do that?" I reassure.

"I'm just asking. Man, that chick's crazy," he mutters.
"Who is she?" I dig, acting oblivious.
"She's my neighbor. She's annoying, she always asks to borrow shit," he tells me.

*Like what? Condoms*? I think to myself. Actually, she probably doesn't use them.

I decide this is not the time to tell Kirk I have met Penny, so I change the subject. He never brought up the folded shirt I left on the dining-room table, and I assume she never told him she met me.

For dinner, we eat a delicious salmon salad that Kirk threw together.
"I assume we won't be bangin' again until you feel confident she's not calling?" Kirk confirms.
"Preferably," I answer.

*Preferably not until I figure you out*, I think to myself.

Kirk packs up the blanket and puts on his flip-flops. Time to go to the beach.

When we get to our spot, we sit in silence and listen to the waves crash.

"It's been a crazy month," Kirk exhales and wraps his arm around me.
"It has been pretty crazy," I downplay.

Kirk gives my cheek a big kiss as he pulls me in closer to him. I could never get bored of his scent. I close my eyes and wish things were simple again. Things are always way easier when you are in the dark, but that is no way to live.

We continue to sit on the beach, the moon is almost full, and it's making quite an impression on the calm black ocean. It's a very starry night without a cloud in the sky. A cool breeze picks up and gets right under our skin, causing me to quickly shiver.

"I'm tired," I yawn.
"You want to get out of here already?" Kirk asks.
"Yeah, take me home," I order sweetly, baring a grin.
"Why home?" he asks.
"I need a good night's sleep, Kirk," I tell him.

We climb up over the logs and rocks to reach the truck. We soon see that Kirk's truck has been completely vandalized. How is this even possible? We were probably at the beach for a maximum of thirty minutes and we didn't hear a sound!

"What the fuck!" Kirk yells and he throws his arm into the air in disbelief.
"Oh my god!" I screech, putting my hands over my mouth.

On the hood of the car, someone has spray-painted a big "fuck you" in pink. On the driver's side window, it has been smashed but not broken. Around the cracks are bright red lipstick kiss marks. On the passenger side window, there is also a gigantic smash with the words "he is not who you think" in the same red lipstick.

This sends a shiver down my spine. I am completely creeped out and utterly terrified.

I look at Kirk with petrified eyes. He throws his baseball hat on the ground in frustration and kicks the side of his truck with his right foot. Kirk lets out a loud grunt as he uses his hands to grip the back of his neck.

"Get in," he orders.

I open the passenger door. It's lucky whoever did this didn't smash in the windshield too. The truck is still drivable, but it's certainly not pretty. Clearly, a girl did this. At this point, I'm not even sure I could guess.

We drive in silence all the way to Kirk's. I'm obviously not going home tonight, which I am frankly relieved about now.

Kirk locks his truck and shakes his head.

"Who do you think did that?" I finally ask.
"I have no fucking idea," he answers heated.
"It was obviously a girl," I state.
"Obviously," he repeats rudely.

A weird feeling comes over me. Would Fiona have done this? Could she still be humiliated about the other night, so much that she would destroy his truck over it? Someone obviously had been watching us to know we would be at the beach for a while and that I was with Kirk so they could get their message across with the passenger-window comment.

Whoever that stupid bitch may be, she doesn't know I am onto Kirk already. This is a step too far; this is just malicious.

Kirk calls one of his buddies to tell him what happened. He steps out to the deck and closes the door to have a more private conversation. I know it's because he is talking about the club and doesn't want me to hear.

Kirk comes back inside.

"My windows will be fixed in the morning and so will that nice gesture across the hood," he informs me.

"That's good news," I answer from the couch.

I wrapped myself tightly in a blanket to add some warmth to my body; I'm still freezing from the beach.

"Don't worry about that little display, okay?" he says with his hands on my bended knees.

"Okay," I answer.

"Some girls in this city are really fucking crazy, but it never goes further than this. Don't be afraid or anything, okay?" he says again.

"Okay," I repeat.

He kisses my forehead and walks off to his room. I follow him still wrapped in his large grey flannel blanket.

"Kirk, who punched you at that strip club?" I inquire.

"Some drunk idiot," he replies.

"So a bouncer didn't throw you out?" I ask.

"No," he replies.

"Why not?" I probe.

"I don't know, maybe he wasn't watching," Kirk lies.

He is lucky. His swollen eye never turned black, and with some lip treatment, his cut healed up in only a couple of days.

I change into my pajamas and brush my teeth. I now have a permanent set of pajamas, a toothbrush, and hair conditioner at Kirk's.

He has a shower while I get into bed and turn on the TV. I decide to watch a rerun episode of *Modern Family* to lighten the mood. This situation just continues to get worse with no improvement.

Kirk gets out of the shower and crawls into bed with me in his traditional Calvin Klein underwear. He smells delicious from his shower. He lies on his side facing me so I turn into him and breathe in. I have a feeling my whole sex clause probably won't stand a chance tonight. I was right, but dammit! I tried hard to resist him. After all, he is still my boyfriend.

I run my hand along his abs. I can feel him looking at me intensely. He drops the straps off my silk nightie and begins to kiss along my collarbone and then up my neck to meet my lips. Kirk climbs over on top of me and begins to pull down my clothing until it's off completely. I shiver with desire as I look vulnerably up at Kirk. He starts to kiss my neck again and begins to make his way all down to my sweet spot. I can't watch. I throw back my head and tightened my grip in his wet hair.

Once Kirk is finished, he removes his boxers and reaches over to his bedside table to find a condom. He unwraps it swiftly and slides it over his erection. Kirk lies down beside me and reaches over to pull me up over on top of him. I sit and slowly allow him inside of me.

I lie on my stomach naked in Kirk's bed with my arms stretched over my head under my pillow. Kirk tickles my back gently with his fingertips. My eyes are closed, but I can just barely peek at him through my lashes.

"I love you," Kirk mouths silently as he plants a kiss on my back. He thinks I didn't see.

For the last thirty minutes, nothing else in the world existed. Right now, I just want to sleep. I think Kirk feels the same because he switched off the TV, and we both fell fast asleep.

# Chapter Fourteen

Kirk whips me to work in the ultra-embarrassing piece of art his truck was turned into last night. I'm happy no one knows me in this city today, but I am sure Kirk will be getting calls about it throughout the day. I managed to Windex off the lipstick on each window, but the hood of the truck will need a paint job.

Kirk said his truck will be out of commission all day, but he should have it back tonight because his friend is doing him a favor.

I give Kirk a kiss and I hurry into the studio.

"Hi," I smile to Zelda, the owner of the studio.
"Shall we get started?" she asks.

The five-hour shift from nine to two consisted of computer-program familiarity, package knowledge, promotional e-mail protocols, and class-schedule expertise. This job is much more stimulating than pouring various coffees.

After work, Bridgette is able to talk me into class number two. I follow the same steps, except today the room seems intolerably hot right from the start. I lie back down on my mat, close my eyes, and all I can think about is someone following

Kirk and I to our spot. Who would do something like that? It's so creepy and eerie. I also can't believe we didn't hear anything, but now that I think about it further, the waves where crashing a lot last night, and we do walk down quite a few rocks to reach the sand.

"Now class, please find your center and meet me at the front of your mats. We will do a short breathing exercise to bring heat into our builds. At this time, release all your worries of the day. Know that you are safe here. Close your eyes as we unite in ohm three times," Bridgette educates.

Damn, she is good at this.

I hear the entire class fill their lungs with air, and in unison, everyone releases a dragged-out ohm sound. It is surprisingly powerful as you can feel the energy in the room ignite. I peer over to Bridgette who is participating with closed, still eyes.

"Open your eyes and meet in a standing pose, palms facing forward," Bridgette said.

The class drags on as we shift from pose to pose. My muscles ache and my balance is failing me miserably today. I can't concentrate to save my life. Bridgette looks at me and gives me a smirk. Child's pose is my favorite today.

The class ends after centuries go by. Maybe not centuries, but it was a long time.

I don't see the light at the end of the tunnel with this hobby for me. It takes a lot of physical stamina and determination. I do feel wonderful after the class, though.

I wash my face in the bathroom with cold water immediately as I enter the changing room. I need to remember shampoo and conditioner next time so I can shower. That whole sweat-drenched-clothes-sticking-to-me deal is not pleasant.

"How do you feel?" Bridgette whispers.

"I have too much on my mind lately, I just can't concentrate," I admit.

"This is a therapeutic practice, you just need to find it," she answers as she squeezes both my shoulders.

Bridgette and I change our clothes and decide to get a smoothie. I tell her everything that happened last night.

"I should cancel our cable. I don't even need to watch reality TV anymore." She laughs.

"It's not funny." I roll my eyes and sigh.

It's a sunny day and we sit outside on steel deck furniture under a red sun umbrella. My mango smoothie is delicious, so revitalizing. Bridgette asks me how my first day went and how I like the studio. I tell her it's great and thank her again for thinking of me. She really saved my ass.

I tell her I am going to advise Kirk that I work late on Friday, and then will do a late hot yoga class with her so I won't see him Friday night.

"I just hope for you that your lies don't get tangled," she says.

"They won't," I say optimistically.

On Friday night, I am going to go back to the strip club, and I hope Kirk goes too. I don't see why he wouldn't if he thinks I am trapped in a human torture chamber.

I plan to come face-to-face with both Kirk and Fiona but through the eyes of someone either of them think they know.

* * *

Friday night arrives finally; I've been itching all week for this. Kirk fixed his truck so there is no evidence of the vandalism. I'm not sure how much money that set him back, but I remember that money isn't really an object for him.

He bought my story about the hot yoga. I made the story sound so genuine by complaining that I would rather be spending that time with him but have made a new commitment I need to stick to. That's kind of true.

Bridgette meets me at my apartment at seven. She brings me leftovers of their dinner on a tin-foil-wrapped paper plate. Steak, mixed green salad, and potatoes was on the menu. Bridgette is a vegetarian, so she obviously ate something else.

"Isn't it hard for you to cook meat when you don't eat it?" I ask her.

"If I didn't cook meat for Konner, that would be grounds for divorce." She laughs.

My disguise is much easier to put together tonight. We put on my wig, makeup, and Bridgette lends me a sexy red dress she wore to her twenty-first birthday last year. I choose to wear the same heels as last time. Plain black stilettos, they go with everything. I also have on my Victoria's Secret push up, giving me a fake boob job for the night. I never wear this bra; I hate attention to my chest.

I glance in the mirror. Even I don't recognize myself. Bridgette brings me a shot of tequila from her and Konner's booze stash. She hands me one and keeps one for herself.

"Good luck tonight!" she cheers as we both throw back the shot.

I leave in a cab and direct him to Erotica. The streets are unobtrusive tonight, specifically around the neighborhood of the club. The streetlights are sparse as you approach. One streetlight flickers as it's coming to the end of its life. Above Erotica is a rundown apartment building—I would say only four apartments. The building is black and spooky with a rusty old sign reading "Erotica." After seeing his grandparents' taste, I am sure they have nothing to do with this. Kirk does not take care of this building at all.

I imagine all the ashamed married men coming and going out of this place. Probably having wives and kids at home, falling asleep wondering where he is. Why are men fascinated by the thought of kinky sex? They become so spellbound they will leave their families to sit alone in a grungy strip bar, giving their eyes a feast of what they are longing for.

The bigger problem to me is the self-esteem of these girls dancing—they are someone's daughter. Why can't they find a normal job like the rest of us moral-enriched females? How do they get on that stage night after night putting on a show for men they don't know nor want to? There are women who can't even strip in the privacy of their own home for their husbands.

These are things I will never understand, especially now that my boyfriend is a guy they are entertaining, and he's also the one giving them their paycheck.

The cab drops me outside; there is a line this time. I boldly walk up to Hans and tell him Kirk sent me. He shoos me in and doesn't ask me for ID. That was easier than I was expecting. Hans follows me in.

"This lady can go through," he instructs to the girl at coat check.

She nods at him, and he returns out the door.

I feel my heart somewhere in my throat as I spot Kirk sitting at a table alone with what looks like rye on the rocks in his hand. He swirls the glass around and stares at it intensely. I want to know what he's thinking about.

He looks up and spots me. I pray to God he doesn't recognize me. *Please don't recognize me!* I repeat to myself.

He waves me over to him. I manage to pull myself together and find my inner buoyancy. Tonight I am Bianca; I have to act confident and witty. I can do this.

"You must be Bianca," Kirk says.
"Yes." I nod.
"Certainly you will need to come up with a cover name, but I'll leave that to you," he answers.

He looks at me penetratingly.

"No problem." I smile.
"How old are you?" he asks.
"Twenty-two," I lie.
"That'll make you one of the oldest ones," he answers.

*Dammit! Why did I say that?* I scold myself.

I cross my legs and look back at him.

"It's freaky how much you resemble my girlfriend," he says.

I freeze. Oh no.

"Really?" I ask nervously.

"My girlfriend's gorgeous, so take it as a compliment, it's just weird," he replies.

I don't say anything; I just turn my head hoping there will be an escape soon.

"I'll get Penny. Wait here. She will take you on for the night," he explains.

Kirk gets up from the table and grabs the attention of a waitress. He points at me and walks down the mystery staircase. I cringe because he's going to the dressing room; I know those girls are nothing but hungry for him.

"Drink's on the house," the waitress smiles at me.
"I'll have a cranberry and vodka. Make it a double," I order.

She doesn't take long to deliver my drink. She is not the same one I had last time. I reach into my clutch to give her a tip, but she just places down my drink and vanishes.

I quickly take a large sip, moving my straw to the side. I need this right now—liquid courage.

A few minutes pass and Penny appears out of nowhere. She is not in stripper clothes yet; I assume she maybe had just arrived shortly before.

"Nice to see you again, Bianca," she says.

I stand up to greet her. Uh-oh, head rush.

"Follow me," she orders.

Down the staircase we go. Kirk is not there. He somehow has left my radar.

"You won't be dancing tonight," Penny explains.

I hadn't even thought about that. *Thank god!*

"You will have to watch and act the part on the floor though. Later next week, you will have an audition in front of Kirk, Hans, and Jeff. They will decide if you are in or if you are out," she explains.

I nod in understanding.

"Good," she taunts.

She seems to be in a bad mood tonight.

I take a seat in one of the high chairs situated in front of the mirrors. It reminds me of the room we used in high school for drama plays—the round bright lights bordering the mirrors and the ledge full of various makeup brands and items.

"Help yourself to whatever you need," Sugar smiles at me.

Ew! They all share the same makeup. How unhygienic. I'm not confident you can't get an STD from that. In this room, anything's possible.

# Chapter Fifteen

She studies me as I pick up an eye shadow, swipe the black color with my finger, and begin applying.

"No, no!" she orders.

I stop and look at her.

"Let me do it," she offers.

She takes the makeup from me and grabs a filthy eye-shadow brush.

"Close your eyes," she orders again.

I do as she says and can feel her piling on the shadow like it's going out of style. I'm afraid to open my eyes, and these contacts are not comfortable. She begins to lightly pencil in my already thick eyebrows.

I open my eyes and find them bloodshot red and beginning to water. I can barely see my reflection in the mirror. Surprisingly, it doesn't look awful.

"Your eyes are so red! What's wrong with them?" she asks intrigued.

"Uh . . . before I came, I smoked a huge joint," I lie.

She nods and smiles in a trance.

"Cool," she answers, fascinated.

I hope that lie doesn't come back to haunt me.

She returns with a red lipstick and begins to lather it on my lips. Yep, I definitely look like a hooker now.

"Where is Kirk?" I ask.
"Probably in the office, he is a bad space tonight," she tells me.

In walks Fiona and Ivory, hand-in-hand like the best of friends. They are not in their "uniforms" yet either. I hear Ivory talking about how busy it is tonight and how it'll be a good idea to work the floor as much as they can. Maybe they're lesbians now—nothing surprises me anymore.

Fiona looks beautiful as ever. She hasn't put any makeup on yet, and even in sweat pants, she stands out. She has a big smile on as they begin to make-up each other's faces. We used to do that.

"What are you staring at?" Sugar asks.
"Nothing, I'm trying to decide what to wear," I lie again.
"Come with me to the closet! I'll help you!" she shrieks and skips to a closed door.

Inside the walk-in closet are several pieces of stripper clothes. Everything from thongs to nipple tassels.

"We all help add to it." Sugar smiles.
"Oh!" I reply.

"This totally suits you!" she suggests as she hands me a one-piece bathing suit, almost an exact replica to the one Fiona wore last week, only black. "You're new, you don't want to show everything off in the first go." She winks.

Luckily, it looks like I can manage my push up bra in this. That's important in a room full of silicone.

"Sure," I agree.

Sugar also hands me those awful clear heels and tells me everyone keeps their personals in a locker in the dressing room. She ushers me to the locker, and I toss my clutch in.

I assume I just strip down right there because I don't see a dressing area anywhere and this would definitely not be a place to act shy.

I begin to change into my costume, ensuring my wig doesn't move a millimeter. I have success. I return to the locker and add my dress, panties, and shoes to the pile. I hope no one steals Bridgette's dress.

Sugar takes my hand as we make our way up the stairwell. I guess she will be my escort tonight, as I don't see Penny anywhere.

I look around the room and see Kirk at a VIP booth a little further from the stage. He is surrounded by a group of guys. He still has that rye on the rocks in his hand as he engages in a deep conversation.

Sugar notices me watching him.

"We don't go to the VIP booths unless we are invited," she explains.

That makes me kind of relieved. We take a seat by a group of disgusting men that are old enough to be my dad. Sugar begins to flirt with them, and I just cannot do it to myself. I sit in silence and peer around the room.

A show begins and the song "Birthday Sex" by Jeremih fills the speakers.

"Give it up for Sparkle!" the DJ shouts, and everyone begins cheering and whistling. She opens her dance by circling the stage. She attempts to make eye contact with every single man in the room. Eventually, she meets the pole and begins to grind her ass up and down along it.

I try to keep my eye on Kirk without making it obvious. I look around for a waitress to order another drink. I feel so self-conscious in this outfit I am constantly tugging and pulling here and there.

It feels like a bad talent show, but with someone's dirty perverted grandpa in the audience with girls in less than half the clothing.

The night carries on this way. I never saw Penny again. I knew it was time to call it a night. I change back into Bridgette's dress and pick up my clutch. At least they're honest when it comes to leaving everyone's stuff in the same pile.

I hail a cab and walk toward it.

"Bianca!" I hear Kirk yell.

I turn around and face him.

"How did it go tonight?" he asks.
"Oh, it was great," I answer as I pull down my dress.

"So see you soon?" he inquires.

"Sure," I answer and duck into the cab.

Bridgette must have crashed early because she doesn't come to the door when I get home.

I wash off the makeup that identifies my new alter ego. I am more than happy to remove those itchy contacts and put them safely back into their place.

I hide Bianca's traits in a box under my bed and hang Bridgette's dress in my closet. It's time to get some sleep because tomorrow I have to find an alibi to keep me away from Kirk again.

My parents leave this morning for their trip to Europe. I call to wish them safety.

"Vero!"

"Hi, Mom, are you excited to leave today?"

"I need to speak with you. I was looking over your phone bill briefly and noticed you received a long distance call from Fiona two Sundays ago. You told me you only went for the day?"

"So much has happened since then, I can't follow along right now."

"Veronica Naomi White, tell me the truth."

"Fine! I was with Kirk! I went to meet his grandparents who live in a prestigious gated community in Palm Desert!"

"I am so disappointed with you, young lady. You know how I feel about liars!"

"I'm sorry, Mom."

"Thank you for calling. Our flight leaves in three hours, I must run. I'll be in touch. I love you."

"Love you too."

I didn't even think about that when I received the call from Fiona. I should have known better.

I call Kirk.

"Good morning."

"Good morning, Kirk. How are you?"

"I'm all right, how are you?"

"I'm good, I slept well. What did you do last night?"

"I hung out with some buddies. Do you want to go for lunch?"

"I would love to, but I'm working at twelve. I'm working the long shift again, and later we are going to this girl's house to watch a work movie on Gandhi,"

"A movie about Gandhi? Really?"

"Really. I've got to go, I'll call you later."

What does Gandhi have to do with anything? Jeeze, I have become quite the liar. I have to make progress tonight. Soon enough, I will be forced on that stage, and I refuse to put myself in that position.

I do work today from twelve to eight. I wasn't lying about that part. I hope my undercover investigation doesn't end up pushing Kirk away from me. I just don't want to give anything away. The less time I spend with him right now, the better off we'll be.

# Chapter Sixteen

After work, Bridgette meets me at my apartment again to help me prepare myself.

"I hope you don't lose your own identity with all this dress up," she sighs.

"I won't," I dismiss.

"You do know you're playing with fire, right?" she asks rhetorically.

I ignore her as I begin my makeup application. Tonight, I am wearing a tight blue dress with cream peep-toe heels.

We fasten down my wig. I shake my head side-to-side, up and down, and it doesn't move at all. Success!

Bridgette and I begin laughing so hard at all the bobby pins we have utilized in order for this wig to stay put. We laugh at the scenario of it falling off in front of everyone and how mortified I would be.

She wishes me well and off I go for another night of stripper insanity.

When I arrive this time, I don't need to say anything to Hans; he waves me through the line. Tonight is packed with guys; it appears there's a bachelor party.

I find Kirk right away again. He has the same drink and is sitting at the same table.

"Hi, Kirk." I wave.

He waves back at me and signals me over.

He and I talk for quite a while. We get friendly as he talks about the club and how he is desperately trying to sell it. We talk about a lot of things, things Kirk doesn't share with me, ever. He has drinks sent over every time I was running low. My head becomes dizzy, but my confidence is at an all-time high. I drunkenly reach my hand over to Kirk's lap and place it in the middle of his thigh.

Kirk looks at me and immediately takes a firm hold of my wrist. He throws my arm back at me.

"This won't be happening," he says powerfully.

I speedily move my hand away.

"Sorry," I murmur, humiliated.

He orders another double rye on the rocks. He gets up from the table and walks away.

I make my walk down the stairwell into the changing room. On my approach, I hear a voice I recognize well.

"I fucking hate Kirk, did you see his truck? He fixed it completely!" Ivory yells.

"So you really want me to come on to him?" Fiona asks.

"If he really likes your friend, we need to make sure we destroy that. What the fuck happened there anyways? He hates having girlfriends!" Ivory says.

"Okay," Fiona agrees like a pathetic brainwashed idiot.

I freeze and continue to listen as they change the subject. Ah-ha! They were the ones who destroyed Kirk's truck! I knew it! How will I be able to tell Kirk what I heard? He can never know I've been here.

"There you are, Bianca," Sugar says and she looks down on me from the stairwell.

I smile innocently at her and quickly pretend I was adjusting my shoe.

"Penny's not coming tonight, so you're in," she tells me.

I look at her with wide eyes. She has got to be kidding me.

"Kirk's orders." She smiles.

"Are you serious?" I ask.

"It's a full house tonight, so you better get moving," she says and walks away.

*Fuck!*

Ivory overhears Sugar and comes around to meet me.

"Don't be nervous, you'll be fine," Ivory reassures.

Fiona looks intensely at me. I look down and head toward the makeup stations. I am about to make sure my face is completely unrecognizable.

Applying a fair amount of foundation to my face, I add blush and powder. I find the black eyeliner and rim my eyes generously. Red lipstick fills my lips as I smear a lavish amount and I head to the closet.

I have no indication of what I am doing! I look absurd!

I try and copy an outfit like what Penny wore the first night I was here. I choose pink booty shorts and a matching bikini top that ties around my neck. I slip on clear heels and make my way to find Sugar.

Bridgette was right, I am playing with fire, and I don't want to get burned.

"Sugar, do I have to take everything off?" I ask her in a panic.

"If you give a good show, you can get away with taking off just your top," she says.

"What's my stage name?" I panic again.

"I'll call you, Diamond. Here, drink this and just relax," she orders as she exits.

I take a swig of the glass and return to the mirror to examine again. I accidently drop an eye shadow onto the black floor and it crumbles all over. I leave it for someone else to deal with.

Kirk comes into the dressing room. We are alone. I look at him awkwardly. He looks wasted and doesn't notice the eye shadow as he walks right through it.

"Are you sure you want me to do this?" I ask him hoping he changes his mind.

"You'll be fine," he mumbles walking toward me.

I am damn lucky I have no tattoos or piercing that would out me in this moment. The only tattoo I would get away with is one directly inside my vagina!

"You look good," he slurs.

I begin to feel extremely lightheaded. My limbs become weak and I am dizzy, much dizzier than I was before. I lunge for Kirk's face, throwing myself at him, trapping him in a kiss. I force my tongue into his mouth, and he doesn't deny me. Before I know it, Kirk and I are in a steaming hot make-out right in the middle of the dressing room. He inches us toward the closet door, not releasing me at all.

He manages to open it, and he throws us inside, slamming the door closed. The closet is dark and fiery as I feel Kirk undo my bikini top. He begins roughly fondling me as he moves his mouth to one of my breasts. I become wet and extremely turned on. Kirk begins to undo the zipper on his jeans; he reaches for his wallet and pulls out a foiled package. His jeans drop to the ground and his underwear follows.

He pushes my head down, indicating he wanted me to go down on him. After only a few seconds, he lets out a frustrated grunt. Kirk undoes my shorts and pulls them down as I kick off the clear heels. I see them light up as I do so. I am completely naked. The wig glues to my back; I am sticky from desire.

I reach for his package, but he pushes me off to roll the condom on. He lifts me up so I rest on his bended thighs. I wrap my arms around his neck as he enters me. Kirk pushes me harshly against the free wall of the closet. This is so wrong.

We continue to have hot, desirable sex as I dig my black painted nails into the back of his shirt. I moan loudly and Kirk thrusts hard.

The door to the closet opens, and I see Fiona—we are caught red-handed.

She flicks the light on and stands with her hands on each of her hips.

"You're nauseating, Kirk," she spits.

He lets me down and quickly pulls up his pants. He zips them up and rushes out of the closet up the stairs.

What have I just done? I begin to dress myself in my barely-there outfit.

"I was looking for you. You're up next, so you might want to clean yourself up," she spits at me.

"I'm not going," I say to her.

"This is a very ugly world for the ones who don't cooperate. It looks to me like you already understand that," she hisses.

"Those who live in glass houses should never throw stones," I fire back.

Fiona just looks at me as her eyes narrow in.

"What did you just say to me, you gross slut?" she hisses again.

"What I meant is, mind your own fucking business," I throw at her.

She shakes her head and leaves the room. I stand there in complete humiliation. What a fool I am.

The music goes quiet, and I hear the DJ say, "Give it up for Diamond!"

I walk out completely drunk and senseless. The spotlight blocks my vision, and I stick my hand out and cover it. I hear people applauding and the song "Seduction" by Eminem comes on loudly.

I walk out blind and pray I don't fall over. My stomach turns, and I know I am going to be sick. I turn around, kick off my shoes, and run off the stage. I push everyone in my direction away from me as I rush to the bathroom. I kick the nearest stall open and throw up in the toilet.

I sit on the floor. I feel so sick, and my sight continues to spin like crazy. I can't steady it. This is like nothing I felt before.

Sugar runs into the bathroom and finds me.

"What the fuck just happened?" she shrieks.

I say nothing and continue to puke.

"What was in that drink?" I manage to spit.

"It was just a strong drink I had made for you! I figured you were into drugs, I was just trying to help!" she defends.

"Well, you didn't!" I scream.

She runs out of the bathroom in a tiff. I manage to pick my pathetic self up off the ground and find my clothes. I change as fast as I possibly can and get the fuck out of there.

In the cab, the driver has to pull over twice for me to vomit. He charges me an extra ten-dollar inconvenience fee.

I fall asleep on my bathroom floor.

Sunday morning brightly wakes me up, and I feel worse than death. I strip off my dress and run the shower. I sit as the warm water hammers over my head. I begin to cry. How will I ever get myself out of this mess? I set Kirk up. I set myself up. I am awful.

After my long shower, I dig around my clutch for my phone. I call Kirk.

"Hi, babe."

"Hi, how are you?"

"I'm decent, how are you?"

"I don't know what has come over me this morning, I feel like I have the flu."

"Do you need anything?"

"Some PeptoBismol and Gatorade."

"Sure."

I look around everywhere to make sure there is no evidence of my night. I find a trail of my two heels, club dress, wig, bra, and panties spread out on the kitchen floor. I pick everything up and put my comfortable flannel pajamas on. I crawl into my bed and close my eyes trying my best to make this all go away.

Kirk wakes me up. I see a gigantic flower vase with beautiful white lilies in one arm and a Walgreens bag in his other hand.

"Wow," I say sitting up.

He is guilty. I recognize this behavior.

He places the lilies on my desk and hands me the PeptoBismol with purple Gatorade. I pop the medicine open and give myself a hefty dose. I take a good chunk out of the Gatorade bottle too.

"Could you also bring me some Advil? Above the fridge is the medicine basket," I ask.

"Sure." He smiles as he leaves the room to retrieve the Advil.

Kirk pushes his way in so he's lying beside me on my tiny single bed.

"Are you ever going to tell me what the story is with lilies?" he asks.

"My mom always bought me lilies for my room. She told me they are beautiful and every morning when you wake up, you should see something like that to inspire you through your days," I clarify.

I open up the Gatorade bottle and pop two Advils into my mouth. I close my eyes and fill my mouth with the juice and swallow. Everything hurts today.

He kisses the top of my head and strokes my cheek with his pointer finger.

"Before I moved here, my mom bought me fake ones so I would still have them every day. She knew I wouldn't buy fresh ones every week," I explain.

"I'll make sure you have real ones." He smiles.

I choose not to ask Kirk to elaborate on what he did last night. I don't want to hear his version of a lie. I close my eyes, and he continues to play with my hair until I really fall asleep.

I wake up to Kirk on the phone in my living room.

"Shut the fuck up, Ivory!" I hear him yell into the phone. "I will fire your ass in one second. I love Vero. I don't know what the fuck happened last night. That girl has a strikingly similar appearance to my girlfriend. I regret it a hundred percent and I don't want her back in the club!" he yells again. "You tell your friend if she wants to keep her job, she's going to keep her trap closed. I don't want to fuck you little sluts anymore. I'm over it! It will never happen again, that is a guarantee! I am selling that shithole, believe me—and none of you whores will have a job!" he spits in the phone before he hangs up.

I close my eyes tight. I don't want him to know I heard that.

He instantly returns to my room to see if he woke me. He sits on the end of my bed and shakes me awake.

"I'm going out for a bit. You can stay at my place tonight, I'll take care of you," he explains.

"Okay." I yawn.

He leaves and at the same time Bridgette comes through the door. She hurries into my room.

"What's wrong? I haven't heard from you?" she inquires in a worried tone.

"Is Kirk gone?" I ask.

"Yes," she answers.

"I had the most outrageous evening," I begin.

She looks at me with a scheming fire in her eyes.

"Kirk cheated on me, with me," I explain.

"Oh no!" she says as she puts her hands over her mouth.

# Chapter Seventeen

I tell her all about it. How Fiona walked in and we had some evil words, my drink was drugged, how I went on stage and ran off—the whole story.

"Tell me you are done with this now!" she shrieks.

"For sure. I wish I never did it in the first place!" I defend.

"This is quite the story . . . so Fiona walked in on your boyfriend cheating on you, with you?" she clarifies.

"Yes, after I heard them admit they were the ones who damaged Kirk's truck," I add.

"Unbelievable!" she shrieks again.

Bridgette leaves to go for a stroll on the beach with Konner. I still have a pulsing headache, and nothing seems to be working. I haven't been this ill in a long time.

Kirk picks me up, and I can barely make it around my place to gather up a bag. The PeptoBismol gets tossed in, with fresh pajamas and clothes for tomorrow.

"How are you feeling?" Kirk asks as I climb in.

"Still very sick," I tell him.

The motion from the car is not pleasing my stomach at all. I can't wait to be lying back on a couch.

I aim for his leather couch right away, making myself a comfortable little bed, and I switch on the TV. *Extreme Home Makeover* catches my eye, and I continue to watch it as Kirk changes into some sweat pants.

Imagine I had to work at the studio today? Yeah right, I would have been calling in sick for sure.

He joins me a little later and cuddles up to me. I am skipping dinner tonight, but I don't suspect he will. I assume he will order something if I know him at all.

"What will you eat for dinner?" I ask, but my stomach does not agree with my question.

"I'll order in, I've been going to the gym lately, I'll treat myself." He smirks.

I knew it.

It's seven-thirty already. I am grateful time is passing by quickly; I just want this day to end. *I am never drinking again!*

He decides to order meat lovers' pizza and devours almost the whole thing in front of me. The smell alone was enough to make me want to puke.

I sip my water and try desperately to keep down the little food that my stomach has. I don't want to start gagging again. My throat aches from all the acid. My body is sore and weak.

Kirk carries me to his bed after I fall asleep watching TV. I wake up, but I don't open my eyes. It feels great to not have to walk. He opens the covers and drops me into bed, tucking me in lightly.

He returns to the TV area and switches it to ESPN. I can hear the commentator enthusiastically explain the highlights of a game. I hear him crack open what I assume is a beer, but could also be a can of Coke.

The front door has an explosive knock. I can hear a girl yelling something, but I can't quite make it out. I hear Kirk rush to the door and open it.

"What the fuck are you doing here?" he says in an angry voice.

Kirk shuts the door behind him. I use all my might to push myself out of bed and run to the door. I peer through the hole and see Kirk and Penny arguing.

"I didn't touch your truck, Kirk!" she yells at him.

"Sure you didn't!" he hisses back.

"I didn't! There are *a lot* of people who don't like you, Kirk Floyd! I've always been good to you! I didn't do this!" she yells back.

"Can you keep your fucking voice down? My girlfriend is trying to sleep!" he hisses again.

"Your stupid girlfriend is the reason this has all happened, don't you understand that? We were fine before she came along! You are different since you met her! You're a total asshole! Stop making irrational choices, Kirk! Stop trying to be a good guy—you are *not* a good guy!" she shrieks.

"I'm done with the club. I'm days away from shutting it down. It's not doing anyone *any* good! You are not getting your job back, *so stop asking!*" he roars.

Penny stands in front of Kirk and slaps him hard across the face. It is difficult to stand and watch, as I would love to do the same to her right now.

"Go have another drink, Penny. You're quite obviously hammered. You better hope I don't see you again. I will have my lawyer draft up a charming restraining order and you will have to move your dream condo to the other side of town!" he snarls.

I run back to the bedroom before Kirk notices me there. I can tell that conversation is coming to an end. I nestle back into bed so he would never know I had left. I have mixed emotions about that discussion. I feel sorry for Penny because she lost her job, thanks to Ivory and Fiona, but I am satisfied that she and Kirk will never speak again.

Was she right when she said Kirk had changed since he met me?

Kirk closes the door softly behind him. Much softer than you would expect from someone who is spitting angry. I hear him open the freezer and take out what I assume is an ice pack, probably trying to numb the pain from that slap. She seemed to have hit him pretty hard for a petite girl.

I close my eyes because I can hear him walking toward the bedroom. I peek at him through my lashes and can see him poke his head inside. He doesn't appear concerned. He does have an ice pack wrapped in a dishcloth situated on his left cheek. He shuts the bedroom door and returns to the TV.

I can hear him on his cell phone only seconds later.

"Dad, it's Kirk. I'm done with Erotica. You can't make me cover this up for you forever. You have three days to make a plan for it before I officially resign and hand it over to Grandpa."

Kirk shuts his TV off and joins me in bed. He gently lifts the covers over so he has enough room to get in. He lightly strokes my face with his pointer finger and kisses my forehead. I can tell Kirk adores me, and that feels great, even if we are stuck in a nasty dilemma.

I have work this morning. Zelda and I agreed I would have Sundays and Wednesdays off. Those are the two slowest days at the studio, and she can handle it herself. I feel way better today. I completely passed out last night and woke up feeling great.

Kirk and I jump in the shower together. I feel like I have been neglecting my boyfriend a lot lately. I know he is more sexual than he will admit to me. I just saw it for myself on the weekend. I think he is trying to play it down so he doesn't intimidate me. I know I need to step up my game in this department if I want to make him happy.

He shows no interest in having any of me this morning. When we got out of the shower, I tried harder to let him know I wanted him. I quickly dried myself off and went straight back to bed. I lied on my side so Kirk could see me and rested my head on my prompted up arm. I signaled him over with my right pointer finger.

"I'm not done with you yet." I wink.

Kirk looked shocked as his mouth drops open. He drops his towel that was wrapped around his waist, runs toward me, and jumps to my side. I wrestle with him, finally landing a straddling position. I bend down and kiss him. He pushes me back up and grabs a hold of both my breasts with each of his hands. I slide down toward his knees so I can take him in my mouth. He doesn't let me suck for long as he watches me in a trance. Once it is lubricated enough, I sit on him. He grips my hips and thrusts upward as I moan intensely.

"You're so tight," he whispers.

He is aggravated lately, but I don't mind him finding a release on me in this way. He grunts as I meet his thrusts with my own. Kirk throws me to the side and instantly makes his way through my legs. He keeps thrusting deep as I whimper with pleasure. I feel my body electrified as I aggressively tug on his hair. I reach my point of no return and feel my body vibrating. He too lets go of a grunt as he releases.

We lie in bed, panting as both of our hearts race. I hope Kirk felt as much satisfaction as I just did.

I stand up and clean myself off. Kirk flashes me a toothy grin as he gets up and slaps my ass while giving me a kiss.

I hop back into the shower and hear Kirk call after me, "I love you." I pretend not to hear him over the sudden gush of running water.

"What?" I yell.
"Nothing," he replies.

I'm not ready for those three tender little words yet, even if I feel the same.

I get to work, and Zelda has laid out a list of things that need to get done today. This is the easiest way for me to work. Hand me a list and let me get through it on my own pace. She is nowhere to be seen, but she often participates in classes. She is in amazing shape for fifty something.

We are strictly forbidden to have our cell phones out at work, but thankfully, this job goes by fast and I don't even notice. I have been wondering throughout the day how my parents are enjoying their European rendezvous and I am instantly jealous that they are probably on a Spanish beach somewhere.

I hope by the next time my mom and I talk, she will have forgotten all about that phone bill incident and we will never have to talk about it again. My mind then brings me a face I used to know so well—Fiona.

She saw Kirk technically cheating on me, and she felt no need to even say anything about it. I still feel that if it were the other way around, I would at least tell her. She seems happy, yet she is doing something so degrading to her body and her self-worth. I don't understand at all.

When I am done with work, I give myself an invisible pat on the back for finishing everything on the list. I take out my phone to call Kirk and tell him to pick me up now. As I take it out of my bag, I notice it is ringing. An unknown number with a lot of numbers appears on my caller ID.

"Hello?"

"Vero? It's Jordan!"

"Jordan! How are you?"

"I'm great. I am in Rome! I have tried several times to call Fiona."

"Never got through?"

"No! How is she? What's wrong with her phone?"

"She's been busy."

"Shame! I miss her! I need to talk to her desperately! Listen, I have to go. Eduardo is paying for this. Please tell her I am looking for her! Miss you!"

"I miss you too, have fun!"

"Check out my Facebook pictures if you want to be jealous! Ciao!"

That girl is crazy. Always living large, that's for sure.

I call Kirk.
"Are you ready?"
"Yeah."

I wait patiently for Kirk to come and pick me up from work. I sit on a nearby bench and begin to reflect on my Saturday night. Should I be mad that Kirk didn't push me away when I came on to him? I am so confused as to what to do about Kirk now. Our relationship is in a good place, but I can't forget the dark side he lives.

Kirk finally pulls up to the studio and I get in the truck.

"What is the plan for Bridgette's birthday?" Kirk asks me.
"Definitely not the strip club," I tease.
"No kidding," he says sarcastically.
"How did you know about her birthday?"
"Konner told me."

It seems like Konner and Kirk are developing their own friendship behind Bridgette and my back. I wonder if Konner knows about Kirk's involvement with the strip club. It's not a secret to any of us, but Kirk doesn't know that.

"I could throw her a party at my place," Kirk suggests.
"She and I just moved here, we don't have enough friends to fill a party," I explain.
"It's a good way to meet people," Kirk answers.
"She's not like that, Kirk. She is very simple, I think she would prefer a casual bonfire on the beach with birthday cake and maybe a few drinks," I educate.

“That’s easy enough to do,” he responses.

Bridgette has been an amazing friend to me over the last few weeks. I would be lost without her. She should have a simply flawless twenty-second birthday. She is a beautiful person inside and out, and I am going to make sure her birthday treats her how she deserves.

“Which day is it anyway?” Kirk inquires.
“Saturday,” I answer.

On Saturday, I am off work at two; I have booked Bridgette and me a pedicure each at a local day spa. My feet need some TLC after I walked home barefoot in them. It’s the perfect birthday gift for two girlfriends.

“My grandparents are coming tonight,” Kirk tells me.
“What? Is your place clean?” I panic.
“Yeah, the maid came today, it’s spotless,” he explains.
“You didn’t tell me you have a maid,” I point out.
“I don’t have a maid. I occasionally hire one to pick up my slack.” He smirks.
“I have a feeling she only ever comes when your grandparents are coming to town,” I explain.
“She only ever comes when my grandparents are coming to town, or the day after I throw a party. I used to throw a lot of parties,” Kirk clarifies.

We arrive at Kirk’s, and just as he said, his place is spotless. The carpets are in showroom condition, the couches have all been fluffed, and his bed is flawlessly made. She did a nice job. His place looks great.

“I don’t want to sit anywhere. I don’t want to mess anything up.” I laugh.

"The trick is living in the apartment for a few hours before they arrive. This way, they never know I hired a maid because not everything looks impeccable," he teaches.

"You're like a con artist," I tease.

# Chapter Eighteen

I take a seat reluctantly on the couch. He frowns at me insinuating I can sit comfortably as I please and not to worry about the maid's work.

"Are you going to make dinner for your grandparents?" I ask.

"No, Vero, you are." He smiles.

"What? Me?" I confirm.

"Yes, you." He laughs.

I look at him with wide eyes. I don't want to make dinner for his grandparents! Especially after her homemade lasagna; I could never make anything from scratch that compares to that!

"What are you expecting me to make?" I ask with a frown.

"Whatever you want to make! We will go to the grocery store in a bit," he tells me.

Talk about pressure! The only things I am good at making are spaghetti, cupcakes, and the occasional chocolate cake for birthdays.

"Let's hit the pool," Kirk suggests.

"What time are your grandparents coming? I will need some time to prepare dinner. I don't want this to be unorganized, Kirk!" I scold.

"They said they'll leave the desert after my grandma's hair appointment, which finishes at five," he enlightens.

The clock reads three. I guess we do have enough time to have some fun in the water. We get on our suits and head to the pool. It's a hot day today, so it won't be hard to get in. Kirk's pool isn't the warmest one I've ever been in.

It's five o'clock, and I beg Kirk to take me to the grocery store.

"Stop stressing about this! They won't care if you put McDonalds on their plates. Just as long as you picked it," he attempts to reassure.

"You are crazy if you think I am buying McDonalds for your grandparents!" I laugh and playfully punch him in the arm.

He finally agrees to take me, and he makes me promise I will not try and overdo this meal. I tell him since I am good at making spaghetti, that's what we are having. If it isn't broken, don't try to fix it.

"Great, they love Italian food," he replies.

At the grocery store, I buy spaghetti noodles, ground beef, tomato paste, tomato sauce, canned tomatoes, basil leaves, garlic, garlic bread, and fixings for a salad.

It is so intimidating making dinner for a woman like Mary. I know no matter how good (or bad) this spaghetti turns out, she could make it better.

"I can see it in your eyes that you're stressing about this. Forget it! I regret asking you. I thought it would just be fun," he scolds.

I ignore him and his hissy fit.

When we get back to the apartment, I get to cooking straight away. Kirk had picked up his grandma a nice bottle of wine earlier in the day.

"Doesn't your grandpa drink?" I ask Kirk.
"No, he stopped drinking a while ago," he tells me.

That's good to know. I instantly wonder if his grandfather knows about the strip club.

A couple of hours pass and we can expect his grandparents at any moment. I stress working around the kitchen stirring this and tasting that. I want this dinner to be perfect. I am sure they want Kirk's girlfriend to be domesticated just like his grandmother.

They enter through the door with each of their small suitcases and a vase of assorted flowers similar to the one that was on their kitchen island.

We both rush to the door to help them with their things. His grandma hands me the vase of flowers. I place them down and return back to give them each a hug.

"It's nice to see you again, Vero," Tory says.

I wonder if he was convinced he never would.

"So nice to see you, dear," Mary gushes.

They give Kirk a warm greeting and disappear into the guest room together.

"Don't worry, they will love your dinner," Kirk says as he kisses me.

"How hard is it for a lady to get a glass of wine around here?" Mary teases.

"Not hard at all," Kirk answers as he hands her a glass of wine.

He had already prepared it before she even asked. Such a nice grandson!

Tory lights a cigar, and Mary immediately scolds him and shoos him to the deck. Kirk meets him out there after he cracks a beer for himself. Tory seems to always try and get away with smoking inside the house; it's entertaining.

"What's for dinner, dear? I heard you are making something delicious," Mary smiles.

"Oh, I can only hope it's delicious. I am not much of a cook. Especially compared to you!" I say honestly.

"Nonsense. The only way you get better at anything in life is with practice," she says.

Mary is so kind. I am sure even if it tastes horrible, she will grin through it.

"It's basically ready, so whenever you want, we can start," I suggest.

"Marvelous. I know Kirk's grandfather is hungry," she answers.

She steps onto the deck and gathers the boys. I watch Tory put out his cigar before he comes back inside.

"The place looks good, son," Tory grins.
"I'm taking good care of it," Kirk boasts.

He means the maid is taking good care of it.

"I always try and picture my grandson battling it out with a vacuum cleaner, but it seems he really does. Every time we come, it's spotless! You're such a good boy, Kurtis," she expresses.

I smile and stop myself from rolling my eyes. Kirk and his vacuum are definitely not friends.

I set the dining room table, and we all take a seat. Kirk tops off his grandmother's glass of wine and brings me one. I hesitate, remembering my Sunday. I still hate alcohol.

"Vero has been feeling under the weather, Grandma," Kirk tells her.
"Oh no, what's the matter, dear?" she asks, concerned.
"I think just the common flu," I say as I shift in my chair.

Mary rises from the table to retrieve a tall glass of water for her husband. I have a huge problem lying to Kirk's grandmother. I feel so guilty I am sure my face is obviously red.

"Lots of ginger ale," she suggests when she returns.
"Give her some Jack Daniels, son. That'll clear it up," Tory adds.

That brings me back to Kirk and his rye on the rocks this weekend; must be a learnt behavior.

I bring a bowl of noodles and a bowl of sauce to the table. Next, I place the salad down and the plate of garlic bread.

Everyone helps themselves to fairly generous portions. I hold my breath as his grandmother takes her first bite.

"Excellent." She smiles genuinely.

"You can breathe now, Vero," Kirk teases.

"Very good, dear," Tory adds.

Hallelujah!

"How is the coffee shop?" Mary asks.

"I actually work at a hot yoga studio now," I tell her.

"Some things change so quickly. It's hard to keep up!" she says.

"Conflict of interest at the coffee shop," Kirk adds.

"Indeed," his grandmother agrees.

We continue to eat, and the room is silent; but it's not awkward.

"How do you like your new job then?" Mary asks again.

"I like it," I smile.

She smiles back and nods at me. She had her hair trimmed earlier, although I can't really tell the difference.

Dinner finishes up, and I am relieved everyone cleaned their plate.

"You cooked, I will clean," Mary smiles at me.

"That's not necessary," I reply.

She ignores me as she clears the table.

"Come here, Vero," Kirk calls from the couch.

We all sit around the couch, and Kirk turns on a movie; I didn't catch the name.

"Grandpa and I are going to spend the day with you at the shop tomorrow, Kurtis. You and your grandfather will have to get all the things you need tomorrow because we must leave early Wednesday morning," Mary says to Kirk.

"Sure," Kirk agrees, with his eyes glued to the TV.

"I'm going to turn in, I am exhausted. Vero, before I forget, I put your diamond studs in Kirk's top drawer in his bathroom. They are sure beautiful," Mary expresses.

"Good night, Grandma," Kirk says to Mary as he gets up and hugs her tight.

"Good night, sweet girl. Thank you again for dinner," she says to me as she kisses my head.

I figure I should shower and leave Kirk with his grandfather. It just becomes awkward when it's the three of us. I feel like they can't say the things they want to say because I am sitting there.

"Good night," I announce to Tory.

"Good night, dear," he responds.

"Going to bed?" Kirk asks.

"Getting ready," I nod.

I disappear into Kirk's room, and I don't see him until the morning. I was so spent; I hit the pillow and slept right away.

Mary drives me to work because Kirk left much earlier with Tory to do inventory at the shop.

"What is this 'hot yoga' trend?" she asks me as we drive.

"I've gone to a couple of classes, I am finding it hard to find the urge to go," I say.

"No kidding. In my day, there were no such thing as this 'hot yoga' or that 'snowboarding.' You kids are much braver nowadays," she laughs.

"Yeah, this is definitely new," I agree.

I admire her Chanel sunglasses. They are black with thick rims and the famous logo on each side.

We are shortly at the studio. I thank her graciously. She turns their black 7-series BMW around and drives away.

Today at the studio, we are doing an open house to try and attract new yogis. I see outside that Zelda is already setting up for the barbeque.

"Veronica, sweetie, please just watch the phones all day. Be familiar with the directions so when people ask, you are able to easily give them," she orders.

"No problem," I answer.

The studio is basically empty, just the janitor washing the floors from the morning class.

This day drags on forever. There are no classes today, and everyone is outside. I am stuck inside in case someone calls. I don't know how many times I have caught myself in a yawn.

At long last, two o'clock hits the clock and I'm free!

I walk home and find a letter stuck to my front door.

V,

Thank you for the letter. I don't know what to say. My life has changed a lot in the last month. I think we are growing onto separate paths and I didn't mean to leave you hanging with all the responsibilities. I have done things to you that I won't be able to forgive myself for. The things that I have done, you did not deserve.

Please be happy and know that I will never have a friend like you again.

Fio

# Chapter Nineteen

I read this note three times before I begin to understand what this says. This is Fiona's official statement saying we are no longer friends. As if a friendship like the one we used to have would have ever come to this.

After everything she has put me through in this last month, I feel she is right. We will never be friends again. I would not ever be able to forgive her for what she has done.

Fiona taught me lessons all the time in high school. This time, I have to be the one to teach her. From now on, Fiona is no longer a part of my life. She is not my concern and certainly not my problem.

Her parents messed up badly with their decisions. They ruined Fiona's life with their selfishness. She will never be the same girl after this.

I rip the letter into small pieces and throw them away. I don't need to keep that piece of paper as a souvenir.

I become emotional as I think about all the wonderful times I spent with Fiona. I used to envy her free spirit, now I couldn't respect someone less. We used to talk about our future lives together, marrying brothers and sharing the same last name. Becoming real sisters and not just make-believe ones. She promised she would always have my back, but really she didn't. She saw Kirk as an opportunity to distract me while she was busy seeking adventure.

Fiona wants to numb her pain with drugs and alcohol, take her clothes off for money and attention. This lifestyle will never require her to settle down and have a family. That is something she is petrified of. She is scared she will make the same mistakes as her sick father.

Fiona is so far into this life, she was even considering coming onto Kirk so she could sabotage my relationship with him. I now remember what Fiona is talking about when she says she won't be able to forgive herself. She followed Kirk and me, helped vandalize his truck, and had the audacity to call him nauseating.

I don't feel so emotional anymore. I feel betrayed and used. She won't sabotage my relationship with Kirk. In fact, no one will. I love him, and even if he has not been honest, well, neither have I. I forgive Kirk for everything that has happened, but will he forgive me after he finds out what I have done? There is only one way to find out.

I walk to Kirk's shop and find him there with his grandparents. Mary asks me if I will drive the truck back to Kirk's and let in the repairman for her. Apparently, the washing machine is acting up and he is already on his way there. She offers me her set of keys; I agree and head to Kirk's apartment.

As I am approaching his front door, I notice a man who resembles Kirk walking out of a door a few condos down. Since his condo building has all outdoor entrances with no closed-off hallways, I have no choice but to hide behind a pillar. Then, I see Penny walk out of the same door. The man takes Penny's hand, and they walk together toward the elevator.

Could that be Kirk's dad? Is Penny his new catch of the week?

This man had the same hair as Kirk but was dressed in a business suit, and his face was slightly different. That would have to explain it! Of course, Penny would do this. She wants to continue managing the club, and she is going to make sure Kirk's dad helps her. What a sneaky bitch!

I hustle inside just in time for the repairman. My heart is beating so fast. I am sure I will probably die of a heart attack sometime soon after the week I have had.

Forget about drawing; I am destined for a life of undercover police work!

I give the guy the money he charged as he tells me the washer is all fixed and is as good as new. It's probably been broken since the last time Mary was here. Kirk definitely wouldn't know the difference. He left all his dirty clothes for his poor grandma to wash.

It looks like she has done all his laundry, cleaned all his dishes, and rearranged all the deck furniture. She is certainly the closest thing he has to a loving mom.

It makes me miss my parents again.

In walk Kirk, Mary, and Tory. I greet them each, but give Kirk an extra hug and kiss, as I am now solely committed to making our relationship better.

I think he notices the extra attention because he gives me a genuine smile and winks at me. There is just something about that boy. It's hard to stay mad at him.

For dinner, Mary makes us ribs. Evidently, it's Tory's favorite meal. She adds mashed potatoes and a Caesar salad. She makes the salad dressing herself, and it's delicious. Of course, the entire meal is scrumptious.

Tory goes to bed right after dinner. He tells us he is not feeling well, so Mary follows him to bed, and they turn in early. I notice that the last time we were over there, he went to bed because he was ill; but at that time, I just figured he was mad at Kirk. I hope there is nothing wrong with him.

Kirk and I decide to watch a movie in bed, as we are both tired and I need to talk to him about what I saw earlier. Kirk puts on *Fight Club* as I let him choose. Typical.

"Kirk, I swear I saw an older man that looked just like you today," I tell him.

"Oh yeah? Where?" he asks casually.

"Coming out of an apartment down the hall," I admit.

"What?" he says uncomfortably.

"Yeah, I had to look twice, I thought it was you," I lie.

I watch Kirk's reaction as he takes in this information. He becomes stiff and looks worried. His mood switches quickly.

"Wasn't me." He smiles and gives me a kiss.

He is not going to tell me it was his dad, but I know it was. It's getting harder and harder to play dumb about all of this. He doesn't tell me anything!

I speak rationally to myself, remembering this is all for a reason. He doesn't want this life.

*   *   *

Saturday comes at long last. The only social event I have been looking forward to all week—really, the only social event all week. Tonight we are having a very small get-together down on the beach for Bridgette's birthday. Konner and I have arranged everything. He bought her red velvet cake—her favorite—and I picked up some fixings to make s'mores. She is a simple girl; she will love her birthday party.

I am off work at two, after a horrendously boring day. Bridgette and I head to the spa for our greatly anticipated pedicures.

"This is so nice of you, thank you!" she gushes.

I even gave us the added bonus of a paraffin wax. I'm not high-maintenance; you won't catch me at the nail salon on a weekly basis.

"What's going on with Kirk?" she inquires.

My foot massage was so marvelous, the only thing I wanted to do was keep my eyes closed and enjoy, but I am not the birthday girl.

"Everything is great." I smile.
"So what have you decided about the club?" she insists again.
"I'm just letting it go," I reply.

I think she gets my hint as her foot massage begins and she goes silent. My feet were in bad shape, this could not be better timing.

I decide on a hot pink color for my toes, and Bridgette chose to have a French manicure—or is it pedicure?

Our feet look and feel incredible. I give myself an invisible pat on the back for the idea; seems to have been a hit.

Next, we will meet our boys and head to her bonfire birthday party. She invited a few girls from the studio, and Konner invited some of his buddies from work. They are hoping on doing some matchmaking tonight, but my goal is to have a smooth evening with my main squeeze.

The first bonfire party we ever went to together wasn't exactly enchanted.

The boys really raided Konner and Bridgette's alcohol stash. At their apartment, there is everything under the sun. I realize this is the first time I have ever been inside. I look around to get a feel for her taste.

Their apartment is very simple, a small one-bedroom apartment with a den, kitchen, and bathroom. Konner has turned their den into a TV room, Bridgette explains as she notices me peeking around. She offers to give a short tour.

Their bedroom has a queen-size bed with a dresser and the same type hole-in-the-wall closest as mine. It appears Bridgette has completely taken that over. They don't have a lot of furniture, but it works for them.

Bridgette explained to me once that they have moved into this apartment to save money. They eventually want to do a lot more traveling, like a safari in Africa and skiing in the Alps. They would also like to have an unforgettable wedding and neither have a lot of their parents' support financially, so they are making due on their own.

The bathroom and kitchen are basically identical to mine. I compliment her and tell her their place suits them perfectly. You can tell they have put love in here. It's a warm apartment.

After a few drinks, we all walk to the beach. Kirk carries the cooler, I carry a bag with the fixings, and Konner carries the cake. The beloved birthday girl walks hands-free.

The boys get the fire going, and they move logs around so there is adequate seating. A few of their friends begin to show up, and the atmosphere is fun and casual. It's a warm-enough evening out, and the ocean's breeze has opted to leave us alone. Must be Bridgette's good karma!

She and I take a seat around the fire. She is drinking rum and juice in her red Solo cup. She looks content.

"This is perfect." She smiles.

"I knew you would like something like this," I answer and hug her.

"I am still so confused what is going on with you and Kirk," she states.

"Just a clean slate, we're fine," I say.

"So you have no hard feelings with him about the club or anything?" she asks.

"No," I smile.

"Good, because if you held a grudge for him making mistakes, what kind of person would that make you when you make them? No one is perfect." She smiles back.

I am introduced to some of Kon's work buddies. Those corporate guys don't hold a candle compared to my man. I like him rough around the edges, just the way he is.

My phone begins to buzz like crazy in my purse resting by my legs. It could be my mom, so I pull it out. Five text messages all sent from Fiona. My heart begins to beat fast as I can guess what they say.

-Fio: I saw Kirk cheating on you with one of the stripper girls last weekend. I walked in on them and I know we are not friends anymore but I felt guilty and had to tell you. You need to be careful with him. He owns a strip club and I admit I danced a few times. More for the thrill and the experience, and the money wasn't bad. I couldn't face you, I know you would totally not approve. I also admit I was jealous of you once I saw Kirk and how much he liked you. All the girls I know here think he is the guy to have around. I am so sorry. Ivory and I are moving away to chase the Hollywood dream. I wish you the best, V, and I know you will do the right thing about Kirk, whatever you decide.

That was the kind of honesty I would have appreciated two weeks ago, but now I just find her a coward for running away and finally coming clean. She still hasn't mentioned the fact she has stiffed me on the rent money. Why did she even bother sending that? She left out other important things such as vandalizing his truck and having a party in my apartment. I decide not to reply to her.

The bright side to this is that I can finally confront Kirk about the strip club. I can show him these texts without being an emotional wreck. She might have lit a fire to a lot more truths than just her pathetic ones.

"Kirk, come here," I say as I signal him over.

He walks toward me and sits down. I hand him my phone and tell him to read it. He does and hands it back to me. I look at him for answers, and he doesn't open his mouth at all. The blood drains from his face, and he becomes pale.

"You look kind of guilty, Kirk," I say to him casually.

"I am guilty, Vero," he says and hangs his head.

"Okay. We can talk about this tomorrow. Tonight is Bridgette's birthday, and we will not ruin it for her," I tell him.

"If you insist," he answers.

I kiss Kirk on his cheek, and he looks at me with a puzzled frown.

"Leave it alone tonight, Kirk," I whisper and take his hand in mine.

I feel so relieved now that he didn't get defensive and argue with me. I am so happy he didn't jump up and dramatically leave.

I decide not to tell Bridgette about the texts. She worries for me, and there is nothing to worry about. I glance at her, and she is beaming as Konner is embracing her. They are such an inspiring couple.

For the rest of the night, everyone enjoys themselves making s'mores and having drinks. At around ten, Konner brought out her birthday cake. It melted in the mouth; I understand why it's her favorite. All in all, I think her birthday was great, and I don't think she would have wanted it any other way.

Kirk drank way too much to be able to drive home, so we ended up crashing on my single bed. That goes down as one of the most uncomfortable sleeps of my entire life. We agree that today we will sit down and have a big talk about the texts I received last night.

Of course, I know I cannot get angry and hostile. I will admit to Kirk one day what I did at Erotica, but not today.

I plan to be mellow, and I hope he has it in him to admit all the things that have been secrets these last two months. I am growing up.

Kirk and I take a seat on my couch in the living room once we are awake and comprehensive. I read out loud the texts from Fiona again as a refresher. Kirk better tell the truth, because it will have been a mistake for him to take this last twelve hours as time to make up a story.

"I do own a strip club, but not because I want to. It was passed down to me from my dad. I did have an indiscretion with one of the girls recently, but she was not yet a stripper. I am not sure why Fiona said I am a guy every girl wants as I have treated most girls like shit my whole life and have had nothing but problems with them. I think it's fucking stupid she is moving to Hollywood, she will go nowhere," Kirk explains.

"This is not about Fiona, so don't start to turn anything around," I say sternly.

"Okay, fine," he agrees aggravated.

"Tell me why you own a club, and why you never told me," I instruct.

"My dad bought the rundown joint from a guy who was basically giving it away. He had a bigger vision for it, but he never had the time or the attention span it needed. He has commitment issues, like I've said before. When I turned twenty-one, he gave me the club. Most kids get a laptop, or a trip somewhere. I got a filthy strip club. At the time, I was stoked. I thought it was the coolest thing ever. I was at a time in my life where I needed something like this. I opened the shop with the money I made at the club because my grandpa made me go to school and start a career for myself," Kirk starts.

"Does he know about the club?" I ask.

"He has no idea and would be devastated if he did know," Kirk admits.

"Okay, go on," I command.

"I never let you meet my friends because they all go to the club all the time and I didn't want them to say anything. I don't want you to ever go to the club. It's for sale. I want out. It fixed a need, but now I am past it and I don't want it anymore. I never told you because I knew you would run away. You're a different breed from those girls, they mean nothing to me," he confesses with sad eyes.

"What happened with the girl?" I ask calmly.

"I drank too much, and she came on to me a couple of times. Finally, I wasn't able to fight the urge. She had so many similarities to you, and you were being so distant toward me. I don't have an excuse, Vero, I'm just really sorry. I could deny all of this, and you probably wouldn't know any difference, but I'm trying to be a better guy. I love you, I don't want to lose you," he panics.

# Chapter Twenty

I sit in silence and look into space mainly because I'm trying to think if I have any more questions, partly because I want to keep him on his toes.

"That was your dad coming out of Penny's, wasn't it?" I confront.

"I think so," he answers.

"Kirk, I would rather you be completely honest with me about every single thing good or bad. From the beginning, I was impressed with your blunt honesty and to find this out breaks me down a bit. It makes me feel naïve and it's making it hard to trust you," I explain.

"I understand. I just didn't want to bring you into the dark side of my life. Especially when I am trying so hard to get out. My grandparents would be so disappointed with me. I have been keeping this from them, and that's a huge reason I can't stand my dad," Kirk explains.

"I forgive you," I say with a small smile.

"Thank you, I have been living with such guilt." He takes my hand and kisses it.

"We all make mistakes. Do you really want to change?" I ask.

"Yes," he answers.

Hopefully, he can be the same way with me when I come clean about all the damage I am responsible for. I am thrilled with how that conversation went. I don't feel as if Kirk is holding anything back. All the information matches mine perfectly, and now we can be honest and open about all the things in our lives.

"Did you hire Fiona?" I inquire.

"No. I never saw her there or even knew she had been approved. Everything usually has to go through me; I would never have hired her, I hope you believe me," he pleas.

"I do," I say, composed.

"There is a difference between wants and needs. I *need* a girl like you. You *want* a guy like me. There is history between our two types of people, but I am real when I tell you I won't make these same mistakes again. I know I am the lucky one," he promises.

I have the day off, and enough is enough on the dramatic end of things. I want to do something fun today.

"Let's go rollerblading," I suggest with a big smile.

"You're on!" Kirk laughs.

We get dressed and decide to head down to the cement path. It's usually very busy with pedestrians of all ages. People bike, rollerblade, walk, and run along the path. This is the perfect thing for us to do on this Sunday afternoon. Get some exercise and do something fun together.

We arrive at a small concession stand-type place. They rent rollerblades to the public, so we get geared up and off we go. We both opt not to wear any padding, not even a helmet. My mom would be freaking out at me, she's adamant about that stuff.

It's a beautiful October day; there are tons of people out around us. Kirk is so terrible at rollerblading; I feel like I have provided entertainment for the whole strip. I grab his hand so he can hold his balance; but before we know it, he loses his footing, and we both tumble down to the ground landing hard on our asses.

"Ow!" I scold sarcastically.
"Fuck, I'm brutal at this!" He laughs.

He's right.

After about an hour of trying hard to teach Kirk to hold himself up and glide, I give up. He will not stop complaining that his ankles hurt and how badly he sucks, so we throw in the towel. It was so much fun laughing at Kirk, even if I possibly broke a bone in my ass. I'm going to have a mean bruise tomorrow!

After rollerblading, we decided to take in the last bit of the warm sun before the evening breeze comes in. There are people surfing the waves and young kids playing in the sand. Kirk and I have had a fabulous day joking around and teasing each other.

My mom calls me.
"Hi, Mom,"
"Vero, I am coming to visit you on Wednesday! I can't wait to meet Kirk!"
"Wednesday? That's exciting! I can't wait to see you!"
"Love you, honey. I will talk to you soon."
"Love you."

I tell Kirk my mom has finally planned a trip to come and visit me. He will get to meet her after all he has heard.
"That's awesome!" he grins.

"Hopefully you win her over," I tease.

I went back to work Monday and Tuesday. It's beginning to get busier at the studio, so my job is more exciting than it has been lately. I've been anticipating my mom's visit. I can't wait to see her; it has been so long.

She said she will arrive by eleven in the morning, and the three of us can go for lunch. Kirk isn't anxious at all to meet her; I don't understand that.

My mom arrives at my apartment building right at eleven. When I see her, I jump on her with excitement. It is so great to see her.

"Hi, honey!" she embraces me again with all her might.
"I'm so happy to see you, Mom," I express.
"You've lost weight! Have you been eating properly?" she asks, concerned.
"Yes, Mom." I smile.

With all this stress, I have lost weight and my skin has totally broken out. I have a pimple on my forehead that could compete with Mount Everest in size. Fine, I'm over-exaggerating again.

"This place isn't so bad, Vero," she says as she looks around.
"I have put a lot of work in," I defend.

I show her all around the apartment, and we spend extra time in my room.

"Those are beautiful lilies!" she gushes.
"Kirk gave them to me," I beam.

She smiles at me and puts her nose to them to smell.

My mom agrees that my bed is awful, and she promises she will get me a new one next time she comes.

"You really have made the most of this situation, sweetie," she approves.

"I need to decide what to do with Fiona's room now that she's definitely not coming back," I express.

"You can make that room whatever you would like. Why don't you turn it into a drawing room?" she smiles as she squeezes my arm.

"Maybe. I hadn't thought of that," I reply.

"Honey, how are you honestly holding up about Ty? Have you thought of him at all? Are you still hurting?" she inquires with worried eyes.

"No. He has a new girlfriend already. I'm fine, I haven't thought of him at all," I answer.

My mom gives me another hug and tells me how good it is to see me.

"Here, all your presents. Dad and I got you a few things from our trip, and of course, here is the care package I've been promising," she explains as she picks a medium-sized cardboard box off the ground and a pink gift bag.

I open the gift bag and find a beautiful necklace, some candies, and a new white linen sundress. My mom knows how much I love sundresses; she's the one who got me hooked on them after all.

Inside the box are the basics—a new toothbrush, hairbrush, shampoo, conditioner, magazines, new running shoes, a few movies, a new drawing portfolio, ballet shoes, more candy, and new sunglasses.

"Wow! Thank you so much, Mom!" I shriek as I give her another huge hug.

"You're welcome." She smiles.

"Ballet shoes?" I say with a raised eyebrow.

"Just in case." She winks.

We leave my apartment and walk to Kirk's shop. I really want to show my mom Kirk's apartment because that is where we spend a majority of our time together.

"Kirk!" I call when we arrive.

He comes out in a button-down white shirt—first three buttons loose—famous khaki shorts, and black flip-flops. He gelled his sun-kissed brown hair up so it's tidy, and he sprayed himself with an extra dose of his cologne. I gush as I see him. He looks so good.

"So nice to finally meet you, Mrs. White," Kirk says as he hugs her.

"Please, Kirk, call me Jackie." She smiles.

I can tell she is charmed right from first sight.

"I'm leaving it up to you where I take the two of you for lunch," she says to him.

"I think I know the right place." He smirks.

He guides us to a neat little restaurant overlooking the ocean on the boardwalk. He tells the hostess to sit us outside in the best table they have. She ushers us to a patio table with four chairs. The view is perfect.

"So tell me about yourself, Kirk," my mom starts.

"There's not a whole lot to me. I own an auto body shop I opened when I finished school. My only brother is two years older and lives up in Canada with his wife and baby girl. My dad and I are not on speaking terms, and my grandparents have been my parental influence basically my entire life. My mom left when I was young, I don't really remember her," he declares.

"Wow, and how old are you?" my mom asks.

"I'm twenty-two," he answers.

"I'm sorry to hear about your biological parents, that must have been hard for you," she says sympathetically.

"I'm fine." He smiles.

"You know, maybe you could help me. Veronica is a breathtaking ballet performer. It breaks my heart that she has quit. Maybe you could encourage her." She smiles.

"Mom!" I scold.

"I would love it if she started dancing again. I think it's very cool." He smiles back.

Lunch went extremely well. Everyone got along great, and I feel like my mom now has a real good sense of what Kirk is like. He paid for the meal and even ordered my mom a very classy glass of champagne to enjoy.

He invites us to his place to sit by the pool, and my mom accepts. I am ecstatic because I really want her to see how beautiful Kirk's condo is.

"Here we are, home sweet home," Kirk invites as we all get in his condo.

"This is quite a nice place you have here, Kirk," my mom compliments.

"Thank you," he accepts.

He gives my mom a tour of his place and explains how his grandparents bought it as an investment property. He prepares us a pitcher of lemon ice water for the pool, and we all head down together after I put on my bathing suit.

"Do you think she likes me?" Kirk asks as my mom steps back to answer a phone call.

"Of course she likes you," I reassure and squeeze his hand.

I have never been comfortable with PDA, especially in front of my parents. My dad is very vocal about the proper etiquette a young girl should have. I never swore in front of my parents. That would really get my dad red in the face.

My parents are very old-fashioned. I know she is playing polite around Kirk, but she is always thinking something else is her head. She will give an earful when we are alone. She notices every little thing.

My mom plants herself on one of the loungers. She has her sunglasses on and appears to be relaxed. Kirk and I dip into the pool. I forgot to warn him that my mom hates PDA, so I am just praying he doesn't try anything in front of her. She will not appreciate that.

Kirk climbs out of the pool and pours all three of us a glass of lemon water. He and my mom make small talk together about the weather as I lie in the pool and float. My mom tells us all about her and my dad's trip in complete detail. They had such an amazing time.

My mom decides after an hour of lounging with us that it's time for her to get back to her car and start her trek home. We pack all our things up and drop them back off at Kirk's.

I need some alone time with my mom to hear her out. I know she will have a lot to say, especially right after she just met Kirk.

"So you can drop us off at my place and I can spend a few minutes with my mom before she goes back," I instruct.

"Sure, babe." He smiles.

Kirk drops us off at my apartment, and we make our way back to my place.

"How was the day?" I ask my mom.

"It was wonderful, honey. I just have a couple of concerns," she starts.

I *knew* she would.

"First of all, I like Kirk. I think he is a very nice young man with a lot of charm. However, he is a few years older, and I don't want that to influence you in any way. This is not why you moved here. I am just not convinced getting into a new relationship right away is going to help you heal from your last one," she says.

"Okay." I shrug.

"Listen to your mother, Veronica. When your father and I first found out about Kirk, we were upset. We were not impressed that he took you to his grandparents on a small vacation before he had even met us. He seems like a nice boy, but it seems his family values are out of order. You love your parents, you don't understand that part of his life," she judges.

"Mother, he is extremely respectful. He loves his grandparents like crazy. Don't forget a wonderful day because you are remembering how angry you were days ago. He is only helping me to move on, he is not holding me back," I demand.

I shift awkwardly. I wasn't expecting it to go this badly. My mom continues to watch me intensely as she rests against my kitchen countertop.

"I love him," I admit.

"That's great, Vero. You are a hopeless romantic, and you may think that you love him, but you are just being ambitious," she doubts.

"Please don't be negative, Mom," I beg.

"I told you, I like Kirk. Just take this one step at a time. You are not walking down the aisle any time soon. You are only eighteen years old. You have your entire life ahead of you. Don't forget that in your search for love," she says.

Now, I just want her to leave. What an awful way to end a great day. I wanted this to go so much more smoothly.

"I have to get going," she blurts out and grabs her purse off the floor.

"I'll walk you out," I say.

I hug my mom a few times, realizing I probably won't see her again until Christmas. I can't get so down on her. I have to remember she is just being protective of her only child. I tell her I love her and will miss her so much.

I watch her drive away and tears fall from my face gently. I hate saying bye, especially to my mom in these circumstances.

# Chapter Twenty-One

I wipe my tears and pull myself together with a few deep breaths. Another big breakthrough that Kirk and I have made. Now he has met my mom. She will come along the more time that passes.

I call Kirk and tell him to come back and get me. He says he will be here in fifteen minutes and to wait for me on the road. I decide to just stay put and wait.

"You don't have to put my laundry away for me, hun," Kirk offers.

"I don't mind." I smile.

I open his closet and begin to put his clean clothes away. He watches me entertained. I know I don't have to put his laundry away, but someone has to or there are just clothes in piles everywhere.

"I'll let you continue if you take off all your clothes." He winks.

"Are you challenging me?" I tease.

"Yep," he answers.

I decide to play along and take off all my clothes leaving me completely naked as I carry on. I spot the shirt that Penny dropped off on a different shelf.

"What's this shirt?" I ask him.

"I don't know where that shirt came from. It's my dad's," he answers.

"It's your dad's shirt? Well, where do you think it came from?" I probe.

I know where the damn shirt came from, but why did Penny drop off Kirk's dad's shirt?

"Yeah, it showed up on my dining-room table a couple of weeks ago. I've been trying to figure out where it came from. I really don't think he was actually here, but where the hell else would it have come from?" he asks.

I can't bring myself to say anything. I don't know why, but I get nervous and decide to clam up. This new information really bothers me. I need to find a way to solve this for Kirk. Why is Penny involved with his dad? How can I find out?

"Forget the clothes, I am way too horny to continue watching you. Get into my bed!" he yells in a teasing tone.

"Ah!" I tease and try to run away from him.

Kirk corners me and throws me over his shoulder. He tosses me onto his bed and begins stripping off his clothes. Soon enough, we are both naked in bed and Kirk has an idea to introduce whipped cream into our sex life.

He runs to the kitchen and takes the fresh whipped cream bottle from the fridge. He returns and rips off the lid of the bottle. I lie nervously on my back, staring at him. Soon, there is a trail of whipped cream from my navel to my femininity.

He begins to lick the whipped cream off my stomach until the trail has evaporated in his mouth.

"Mmm," he releases.

Kirk hands me the whipped cream and lies beside me.

"Your turn," he smirks.

I copy him as I make a line from his navel to his package. I lick all the whipped cream off.

This game carries on for quite some time. I am so happy I have been persistent with my birth control.

Kirk goes back into the kitchen, takes the blender out and decides to make us blended lime margaritas. He doses them with a lot of tequila. He says he will put them in plastic cups and we can drink them in the hot tub.

We put our bathing suits on and go back down to the pool area. We slip into the hot tub with our margaritas in hand.

"What did your mom say about me?" Kirk asks.

"She said she likes you a lot." I smile and move to sit on his lap.

"You know, hun, I think you should take ballet up again. Before your mom even mentioned it, I felt that way," he says.

"Nah," I answer bluntly.

The margarita is strong. With the heat from the hot tub, I am already feeling a little lightheaded.

We are alone in the pool area; it's six o'clock at night, and the sun is still up. For dinner, we are going for Greek food.

After cuddling in the hot tub for thirty minutes, we go back up to the apartment and shower off to get ready for dinner. Bridgette and Konner are coming with us tonight, and we are meeting at the restaurant at seven.

"Is this okay?" I ask him as I twirl my new white sundress around.

"You look beautiful, baby," he compliments.

My style is very feminine and simple. I don't try so hard to keep up with the latest fashion trends. I like solid colors that are form flattering and easy to match. I have always been this way.

Kirk comes out of the closet in a navy blue V-neck and white khaki shorts. Kirk doesn't wear any jewelry ever. No bracelets, no necklaces, nothing. His style is very masculine, clean cut. He wears khaki shorts basically every day.

"My brother called me earlier, he's doing really well. He wants us to make a trip up to Canada sometime soon," Kirk tells me as he puts on his deodorant.

"I would love to go," I smile.

Kirk will definitely have to win over my parents before they are happy to let me leave the country with him.

I see Kirk's dad's shirt again. It brings me back to Penny and how I am going to find a way to stop to her. She is disgusting. Sleeping with both the father *and* the son. That's Jerry Springer material. No normal woman would do that.

My simple makeup application is done. I am fresh and clean and ready to have a wonderful dinner with great friends.

We slip our flip-flops on, and Kirk locks the door behind us. I peer down at my toes—the polish still looks awesome.

"I have hired a guy to come and change my locks tomorrow," Kirk tells me.

"Why?" I ask.

"If my dad has been hanging around here while I'm not home, that's not okay with me," he admits.

His dad hasn't been hanging around. Why can't I just tell him the truth?

"I have to work tomorrow. I have a lot of progress to catch up on after slacking the last few days. When you get off work, can you head over here and let him in for me?" Kirk asks.

"Sure, I get off at two," I tell him.

I suddenly have an idea I think could work. I could bring Bianca back to pay Penny a little house call. I need to go home tomorrow before I come back to Kirk's so I can take Bianca's traits and stealthily get away with this one last time.

We meet Bridgette and Konner outside the restaurant. Bridgette looks very pretty with a long turquoise blue maxi dress and gorgeous gold bangles hanging from her slim arm. She is wearing her straight hair a bit wavier today. Konner is casual in jeans and a black and white striped sweater. Both sport flip-flops like Kirk and I.

"You look like a Greek goddess," I compliment with a laugh.

"You're looking flawless, as usual," she compliments back and hugs me.

Throughout dinner, we have smooth conversation. Bridgette and Konner are going to Florida to visit her grandparents as a birthday gift from her parents. They are leaving first week in November. Kirk invites them to a Halloween party at his condo on Saturday night.

My boyfriend treats me with pure affection all evening. He rubs my back, orders my food, and compliments me. I am beaming with warmth.

Kirk treats us all to dinner as an extra birthday present to Bridgette. They are both very grateful and beg Kirk to let them treat us all to ice-cream so we can walk on the beach together and eat it.

The boys fall behind us as something silly amuses them.

"That is probably the best I have seen you and Kirk yet," Bridgette admits.

"Things are going so well right now, I am so happy." I grin.

"That's so wonderful. He seems like he really appreciates you, you should embrace that." She smiles.

Bridgette is like the big sister I never had. She never says anything that's out of line. She is so genuinely sweet and comforting; she's really an amazing person.

The boys catch up to us and are hyper as can be.

"Let's go in the water," Konner suggests.

"Seriously?" Bridgette confirms.

"Yeah, why not?" he answers.

"Okay," she agrees and smiles.

I look at her with my eyes popping out of my head. She laughs again and shrugs at me.

"You only live once." She winks.

I can't believe we are about to go in the ocean at nine at night with no bathing suits, towels, or spare clothing!

Bridgette and I get to the edge of the water. Kirk and Konner strip down to their underwear and we do the same. My white dress becomes covered in wet sand. I look at Bridgette again, and she reassures me by taking my hand.

Luckily, the tide is out, so we have privacy and no one can see us. We stand there in our bras and panties, shivering as our toes touch the water.

"Are you kidding?" I shriek.

"One . . . two . . . three!" she counts as she runs for the boys.

Without putting much thought into it, I follow her running and crashing into the approaching waves. The ocean is absolutely freezing; I am numb.

"Come here, baby!" Kirk yells to me.

I can barely see him from the reflection of the moon on the ocean.

Konner holds Bridgette as she reaches him. You can see the silhouette of their two bodies embracing each other; it's a picturesque sight. I wish I had a camera.

Kirk grabs me and pulls me toward him. I jump up so I am stuck to him like glue with my legs wrapped around his hips and my arms resting around his neck. I am shivering like crazy.

He gives me a long passionate kiss as he holds me up. He doesn’t seem nearly as cold as I am. Goose bumps fill my entire body as a breeze picks up.

We arrive back at our clothes. We laugh as we watch Konner struggle back into his jeans. That was an experience I won’t soon forget.

We drop them off at their apartment after an eventful evening of half skinny-dipping on the public beach.

# Chapter Twenty-Two

My eyes are heavy and I begin to yawn several times on the way home. I hold Kirk's hand as he drives, and I sit right up close to him so I can rest my head on his right shoulder.

"Tired, babe?" he asks.
"Evidently," I say and yawn again.

We get home and crawl right into bed, bypassing the TV and everything else that could be distracting.

Kirk lit candles all over the room while I was brushing my teeth and washing my face. I have decided to wear an outfit a little braver to bed tonight. It's a pink see-through lace corset with matching thong panties. I had bought it to wear for my ex but never got around to it.

I take a deep breath and strut confidently out to the bed to meet him. His eyes focus in on my outfit, and I stand at the end of the bed returning the glance. He says nothing, and he doesn't move. He just continues to stare at my body in its lavish new look. The room is so romantic with the ambience from the candlelight.

I get onto the bed and crawl toward him, giving him a good glimpse of my cleavage in the corset. Kirk just continues to watch. He doesn't say a word. He wasn't expecting me to approach him like this. He had already tucked himself into bed.

I slowly pull the duvet off of him and notice he is excited through his underwear. My hair is down, so it bounces around me as I move.

I straddle Kirk gently, and I begin to kiss his neck and trail my nails softly over his broad shoulders. He still doesn't move a muscle. As I reach his lips and kiss him, he begins to cooperate, moving his tongue around in my mouth. He runs his hands delicately over the fabric I have chosen.

"This is sexy," he pants.

He moves his hands down to my butt as he grabs a firm grip. He slaps one cheek, but not hard so it doesn't hurt.

"You make me crazy," he whispers in my ear.

His whisper sends a sharp shiver down my spine and I am extremely turned on now. He undoes each clip on my back, holding the corset together. Soon, he slips it off and places it on the floor, leaving me in my panties.

I continue to straddle him as he cups each of my breasts. He brings his mouth overtop one and licks it swiftly.

Kirk drops me so I fall onto my back. He removes his underwear and then tenderly pulls off mine. He is now on top of me and inserts himself into my sex gradually. I let out a whimper of pleasure as he slowly thrusts back and forth.

Kirk and I make love for what seems like hours. Neither of us is in any rush to reach our climax. We explored each other's bodies and created a captivating connection. We are completely in love with each other, and it's a beautiful thing.

The morning arrives far too soon. We both grunt and moan as the alarm clock sounds and it's time to face reality again. The candles are all still out from our night, and I find my corset and panties pair resting neatly on the floor beside me.

"Time to get up, sleepyhead." I smile.
"Come lie with me for a few more minutes," he muffles.

Finally, I am able to drag Kirk out of bed. I do not feel like working today. I just want to stay in bed all day. I am so sleepy.

"Stop keeping me up all night," Kirk jokes.
"You love it!" I reply.

After work today, I will have to find a way to get information out of Penny.

I arrive at the studio, and Zelda is outside the door, placing a note over the door.

"I forgot to call you. We have to close this morning. I have a sanitary inspection in three hours, so I have called a janitorial crew over and we are going to blitz the place. Take the day off, sweetie, I'll see you tomorrow," she dismisses.

I nod my head and head on home. Kirk gave me an extra set of keys to his apartment and said he won't be home until six tonight. This gives me time to execute my plan with Penny. I reach for the "Bianca Box" under my bed and place all the appropriate things I need in my overnight bag. I have time to get to Kirk's, talk to Penny, come home, stash this stuff, and go back. He will never know.

I rush home, change, and I go out in public as Bianca. I hop on the bus and sit there impatiently as I wait for it to drop me at Kirk's. I feel so guilty. I feel like everyone around me knows what I am up to and the devil is waiting for me to rot in sin.

I am wearing tight dark denim jeans, push-up bra, a black tank top with spaghetti straps, and flip-flops. I hide behind the same large sunglasses. I arrive outside Kirk's condo and hustle in. I am unseen, as far as I can tell. I throw my bag into his front-door area and take a few deep breaths before I find the courage to knock on Penny's door.

"Bianca?" Penny answers the door.

"Hi, I know this is so random. Could you tell me which apartment is Kirk Floyd's? I need to talk to him," I explain.

"How do you know I live here?" she asks confused.

"One of the girls told me. There was some drama that happened, I need to apologize," I continue.

"Come in," she says as she ushers me inside.

I take off my sunglasses so I can glance around. Her apartment resembles Kirk's except it has a much more feminine vibe. She has white couches in the living room with light furniture throughout. It's spotlessly clean and smells very nice.

Penny is wearing pajama shorts and a revealing white tank top. She must have just woken up; probably had a late night.

"Do you want some coffee?" she asks.

"No," I answer.

"Why are you looking for Kirk?" she inquires, cutting to the chase.

"I really want to dance, but he won't approve me," I lie.

Penny invites me to take a seat at her dining table. She sits across from me with a giant coffee mug. I can see the steam coming out of the top. She blows on the coffee as she stares at me.

"Is that it?" she tests.

"Well, I came on to him after one too many drinks. He didn't like that," I explain.

She looks at me with intense eyes as they really focus in on me. She is quite intimidating now that I am in her condo alone. I probably made a mistake coming here—surprise, surprise.

"Kirk is going through something right now," she starts.

I listen.

"I've been dating his dad for a while now. They are quite similar, yet nothing alike. His dad is strong and charismatic. Kirk is lost and persuaded easily. This is interesting now, an attractive young girl coming to beg for his forgiveness. You know, he wants to get rid of the club altogether," she confesses.

"Why?" I ask.

"He's too weak. He can't handle the pressure anymore. He wants the wife-and-kids story, just like his brother. All because his grandparents have loved and nurtured him. He wasn't always like this. He used to be a little prick," she says.

"I see," I answer.

"Kirk fired me, Bianca. I can't help you, not yet anyway. I'm working on getting back in. His dad is hours away from pulling Kirk off his title anyways. It's over for little Kirky. If you want to meet me next week, we can talk about you dancing. I am giving that place a whole entire overhaul once I get my roll back. If you ever find out who trashed Kirk's truck recently, you'll let me know, won't you?" she asks.

"Of course," I answer.

"Here, this is my number. Call me one week today and you and I can figure something out. I admire your bravery. He'll probably explode on you like he did to me last week. Ever since his new little wife came along, he has had an attitude," she says as she lights a cigarette.

Now I know why she uses strong scents in here—to mask the nicotine.

"Do you want one?" she asks.

"No," I reply.

These contacts are really starting to itch, especially after she lit that cigarette and smoke filled the air.

"So I probably shouldn't even bother tracking down Kirk if he has nothing to do with the club now?" I confirm.

"I guess not. He and all his cheap buddies will be strictly banned from ever stepping foot in there again," she answers as she takes a deep drag.

"Okay," I answer.

"So don't worry about that." She smiles deviously.

"I better get going," I announce.

"Sure," she agrees as she rests her cigarette in an ashtray beside her.

She rises from the chair.

"How did you get into this building anyway?" she asks.

"I followed someone in at the front door," I answer.

"Clever," she grins.

I show myself to the door and open it.

"Thanks," I say to her.

"Anytime." She smirks as I shut the door.

I exit the building down the elevator like I would do if I were really leaving. I come back up through the emergency exit stairwell and duck into Kirk's place as quickly as humanly possible.

I remove the wig, sunglasses, clothes, and even quickly wash my face so I don't resemble the same girl at all.

I leave again with my overnight bag so I can get home and stash this evidence.

I make it back to Kirk's just in time to let in the locksmith.

My phone buzzes with an e-mail.

**From: Jacqueline White**
**Subject: This Week's Visit**
**Date: October 27, 2011**
**To: Veronica White**

Vero,

Dad and I have drafted this note together. We realize you are growing older and much more independent than we are used to. It is hard for us to think of you as such a liberated young woman.

I am sorry you felt I was harsh about my comments regarding Kirk. This is your life, sweetie. If you are happy, we are happy for you. Please don't be angry with me.

Dad is looking forward to meeting Kirk as well. We figure if you two are still together in December, he should come for the holidays.

Love you forever and for always,

Mom

That's a step in a better direction.

**From: Veronica White**
**Subject: Re: This Week's Visit**
**Date: October 27, 2011**
**To: Jacqueline White**

Mom & Dad,

It's fine. It's been an adjustment for me, too. I didn't mean to move here and wind myself up in a relationship right away either. Kirk is great for me. I am sure he would love to come at Christmas and meet Dad.

He really enjoyed the afternoon we all shared together. I am more independent now, but I know you guys will always worry.

I love you,

Vero

After the summer I just put them through, I am not surprised they are not happy about the idea of Kirk. The fact that he doesn't have two loving parents to go home to every night does not make him a bad person. My parents are close-minded because neither of them grew up in a "broken home."

I call Kirk.

"Hey, baby."

"Hi, the locksmith just left your place. What's our plan for dinner?"

"I can pick something up on my way home. What do you feel like?"

"I feel like bringing something down at the beach."

"Are you sure you're ready to go back there?"

"I am positive."

"Okay, I'll see you later, babe."

The door has a loud startling knock. I walk to it and look through the door hole. It's a deliveryman.

"Yes?" I answer curiously.

"Could you please sign here," he orders as he pushes a machine in my face.

I sign the machine, and he hands me a thin sealed package. There is an orange sticker on it that reads "CONFIDENTIAL" in black bold capital letters. It's addressed to Kirk, so I shut the door and place the package on the dining-room table.

My curiosity is burning, but I know I definitely can't open it.

Kirk returns home with a bag of groceries. He drops them off in the kitchen. He meets me on the couch as I am curled up in a ball relaxing. He comes over to me and gives me a big kiss.

"How was your day?" I ask.

"It was great, really productive," he answers and stretches out on the couch.

"What did you get for dinner?" I probe.

"I picked up some sushi for my favorite girl and me." He winks.

I remember the delivery.

"Some deliveryman dropped off a thin parcel for you," I inform.

"Really? Where?" he asks.

"Dining-room table." I point.

# Chapter Twenty-Three

Kirk gets up and retrieves the package. He brings it over to the couch area and opens it. He scans it over and puts them down on the coffee table.

"What is it?" I ask curiously.

Kirk passes me the papers, I read.

*Attention: Kirk Floyd*

*Please find enclosed the documents pertaining the dissolving of our partnership effective immediately.*

*I have willingly accepted your resignation. Due to a nonmonetary investment in this company, there will be no equity shares owing.*

*As of today's date, October 27, 2011, you have been released as management at Erotica.*

*Please sign your name where it is stated and return them to the address provided.*

*Timothy Floyd*

"So that's it? You're free from the club?" I ask.

"I will swing by my lawyer's office in the morning. I'm not worried about it. My dad is just such a fucking asshole," Kirk says as he shakes his head.

"Are you upset?" I probe.

"Nah, I'm good." He smiles.

We get going so we can eat dinner at the beach. Kirk seems fine after what just happened.

"I need a new truck," Kirk expresses.

"I need a car, period." I laugh.

"You never need to drive anywhere!" he defends.

"Yeah, I don't have a desire to get one," I agree.

We arrive at the beach. It's seven at night, but the sun has already set, and it's dark out. Summer is undeniably gone now. I shake out the blanket and drop it to the sand. We both sit on the blanket, and Kirk brings out the sushi and sets it down in their individual plastic containers. He also brought us two cans of Coca-Cola.

"Dig in." He smiles.

I can't wait to eat this. He has a variety of rolls and sashimi. Soon enough, we have managed to scarf down all the sushi.

The weather is mild this evening, and as usual, our spot is totally secluded.

"Did you eat enough?" Kirk asks.

"Yes, I am happily full." I laugh.

"I got you a present today. For Halloween and for being an amazing girlfriend to me." He smiles.

"You got me a present? What kind of present?" I ask, intrigued.

Kirk pulls out a long Tiffany & Co. jewelry box with a white ribbon around it. My eyes widen as he hands it to me.

"You didn't have to do this!" I gush.

I unwrap the box to find an absolutely gorgeous diamond and pearl tennis bracelet. It has three round diamonds and three pearls all spaced out on a platinum chain. My mouth drops open. It's stunning.

"Oh my god!" I gush again.

"I didn't actually have to work late, I've been spending some time at the sparkly store." He laughs.

This bracelet cost Kirk a fortune. This is likely the most expensive thing I own.

"Really?" I pinch myself.

"I thought it would go nicely with your diamond studs. It's an Elsa Peretti design apparently." He shrugs.

"I absolutely love it! Thank you so much!" I shriek as I throw my arms around him and kiss him.

"My pleasure." He grins.

I put the bracelet on straight away. It sparkles and shines; I never want to take it off!

I cuddle right up to Kirk and hug his arm. I look up and smile sweetly at him.

"I'm so glad you like it," he whispers as he runs his fingers over the bracelet.

"I'm still shocked." I smile.

"I'm crazy about you. I hope you understand what that means to me. You are the best thing that's ever happened in my life." He looks at me with sincere eyes.

I look at him with adoring eyes. I'm speechless, so I just smile at him.

We climb over the rocks back to the truck. Luckily, there is no damage done this time. Kirk throws the aftermath of our dinner into the closest garbage bin. I sit and admire my bracelet as I wait for him to get in.

Kirk opens the driver's side door and climbs in. He goes to put the keys in the ignition, but I stop him.

"What's wrong?" he asks.

I don't know what has come over me, but I am full of craving.

I look around the parking lot again to make sure we are totally alone. I lift off my shirt and sit in my bra. I take Kirk's left hand and place it on my breast. He understands what's going on now. He moves toward me, and we begin to kiss vigorously. He lays me down so I am on my back now, taking over both the passenger seats. He pulls off my jean short-shorts. Kirk peels off his shirt and awkwardly removes his shorts. There is not a whole lot of room for this.

He meets my kiss again as he starts to stroke in between my legs. I moan with desire as that familiar feeling fills my veins. He rips off my panties and tosses off his underwear. He lubricates his hand with his saliva and doses his erection before he powers through me. My back arches as Kirk thrusts. My legs are bent, one resting on the dashboard the other resting against the back rests. Things become really heated between us, and there is a loud knock on the driver's side window.

I frantically look for something to cover my naked body as we both become aware someone is looking in on us.

A parking-lot security man waves his pointer finger at us. My face burns with humiliation. This is *so* not like me.

Kirk waves him away, and he bursts into laughter.

"That's a first." He smirks.
"Oh my god! How embarrassing!" I cringe and laugh too.

We both dress ourselves quickly wanting to get the fuck out of there.

"You are full of surprises lately." He grins.

He can say that again.

"Don't sweat it! I'm sure that's not the first time he saw something like that taking place in a parking lot. We didn't exactly just invent that," he reassures.

"Just drive!" I tease.

We get back to Kirk's apartment. He is so different tonight. So carefree; you can tell he's been stressed out about the final decision of the club. I think he made the right choice. I know I couldn't stay with him if he continued to be involved in that repulsive operation.

"I have another fun thing for us to do," he suggests.

My dirty mind automatically directs its guess toward something sexual.

"I have a fondue set that is great with chocolate. I bought all kinds of fruit for us to dip into it," he enlightens.
"That's such a great idea." I smile.

Kirk goes off into his kitchen to prepare the fondue. I decide to contribute by making a giant bed on the floor. I move his coffee table out of the way, allowing much more room for the blankets and pillows I am about to throw down. I go into the bedroom and take the duvet off the bed. I also grab all of Kirk's pillows and drag them along.

Kirk puts the radio on. Country music fills his sound system—totally not what I was expecting. We are still learning so much about each other.

I remove the pillows and blankets from the couch area as well and add them to my newly formed floor bed.

I lie down to test it out. It's comfortable enough.

"I'm just waiting for the chocolate to melt, hun," he yells from the kitchen.
"Okay," I reply.

Kirk brings out a giant plate of cut fruit, everything from strawberries to pineapple. He places the plate on the floor bed and goes back into the kitchen to get the chocolate.

He returns with the pot and its stand. It's milk chocolate, I can tell by the color.

"Let it sit for a second," he orders as he goes and gets the fondue sticks.

We sit down together on the floor bed and he hands me a stick.

"This little floor bed is a nice touch." He smiles.
"It makes it very cozy." I smile back.

Kirk digs into the chocolate as he sticks a strawberry on the end of fondue stick and places it in the pot. He pops it in his mouth a moment later.

"It's hot," he mumbles.
"I can see that," I tease.

I choose to stick a piece of banana in the chocolate. I stick it in my mouth, and it melts right away. So yummy.

He picks up another strawberry and dips it. This time, he offers it to me as I open my mouth. How romantic and cheesy is this Thursday evening? The only thing we are missing is a mass amount of lit candles and rose petals.

I would have never thought when I first met Kirk that he had this side to him. Underneath his steel armor is a soft, adoring man.

I peer down at my new bracelet and admire it again.

Kirk moves all the food onto the coffee table.

"Now, where were we earlier?" He winks as he begins to take off my shirt.

It's Friday morning now. Only one more day until the Halloween party Kirk won't stop talking about.

Bridgette comes into the studio and tells me Konner surprised her with a puppy as a late birthday gift. She is so spoiled this girl; her birthday seems to be dragging on even a week later!

"A puppy?" I gasp.
"A little baby girl," she beams.

"What kind?" I ask excited.

"She's a Morkie—a cross between Yorkshire Terrier and Maltese," she explains.

"I *have* to see her!" I gush.

After work, Bridgette has agreed to let me meet their new addition to their little family. She named her Rosie.

"Isn't a puppy going to be a lot of work?" I ask.

"She'll be a lot of work," she confirms.

Now, as usual, I can't wait to get off work. This job has turned out to be *a lot* more boring than I was anticipating.

I requested tomorrow off so I can get ready for the party. Zelda didn't seem to mind letting me have to day off at all, she's so strange.

Two hits the clock and I jump out of my seat like my ass was on fire.

"Let's go!" I shriek to Bridgette.

She laughs and agrees as she goes into her locker to gather her things.

"How old is she?" I inquire.

"She's eight weeks old," Bridgette smiles.

How did she even come into work today? I remember when my dad bought my mom our last dog; she wouldn't leave its side for weeks. She was completely and utterly obsessed with poor Buddy.

We get to Bridgette's apartment, and she runs to a little doggy house and lets Rosie out. The puppy gets so excited when she sees Bridgette she begins running laps around the TV room.

"She is beyond adorable!" I gush as I bend down to pick her up.

"She is so nicely tempered," Bridgette gushes.

The puppy is black and tan in color; she is no bigger than a bunny rabbit. Her hair is soft and curly.

"What made you call her Rosie?" I inquire.

"Right when I saw her, the name just popped up in my head and it felt right. She suits it in my opinion." She smiles.

"I think so too," I agree.

# Chapter Twenty-Four

I hope this doesn't mean they are not coming to the party tomorrow night. I know that's selfish, but I was really looking forward to them coming.

"Does this mean you guys aren't coming to the party tomorrow night?" I ask.

"Of course we are still coming! It's good to leave her for a few hours. She needs to be independent so she doesn't develop a separation anxiety," Bridgette explains.

Phew! I am so glad to hear that.

"Hey, I was thinking tonight you and Kirk could come over here and the four of us could do game night? I haven't done a night like that in forever!" she proposes.

"That actually sounds like the perfect plan!" I agree.

"Excellent. I will make dinner too. I hope you guys are in the mood for pasta. Konner wants fettuccini, I agreed I'd make it," she offers.

"That sounds great," I smile.

"Things are good with you two?" she asks.

"If something tragic happens between us, you will be the first to know. He gave me this gorgeous bracelet last night," I brag and show her.

"That's stunning! Don't show Konner, he's competitive and that is not a bracelet he'll be buying me anytime soon!" she teases.

I leave Bridgette and her puppy to return to my lonely apartment. I haven't gone for a run in days; I decide it's time to change that. I change into my running clothes and off I go. The sun is out, and it's perfect weather to jog. I run along the boardwalk past all the other people stretching their legs today. It's an amazing privilege to be able to exercise with such a beautiful view.

When I come home, I run my shower and send Kirk a text message.

-Vero: Game night at B & K's tonight!

I shower off and go through all the motions of my routine. I'm going to surprise Kirk at the shop once I'm done. He never texted me back, so I hope he's not super busy.

"Surprise!" I yell as I walk into the shop.

"Baby!" he answers with a smile.

"Is this a bad time?" I ask.

"Never a bad time." He winks.

I look around to see if it's still organized. It looks pretty good.

"Hey, babe, do you want to answer the phones and shit for me? I really have to focus on this," he asks.

"Sure." I smile.

I sit in the front of the shop and act as his receptionist for the rest of the day. This could be an interesting role to play. I only have to answer the phone call about pricing and one person walked in and asked if Kirk sells car air fresheners.

At five-thirty, he shuts down shop and we go through the car wash. He is right; he probably could use a new truck. I think it's an attachment thing since he says he bought it with money he saved up in high school and has taken care of it since.

We sit in the car wash and it goes through all the cycles—washing, drying, soap, washing, drying, etc. It's so complex.

"Let's do something while we wait for this to finish," Kirk winks.

"I've had enough public display of affection to last me a while." I laugh.

I still can't believe a security guy walked us in on last night. With my luck, I would give in to Kirk and the car wash has a camera sitting there taping the whole thing and we'd be on the eleven o'clock news later.

"That's all part of the fun! I've had way worse happen!" he defends.

I don't want to know, so I pass on the interrogation this time.

"What should we bring to Bridgette's tonight?" I change the subject.

"We'll get her flowers, girls love flowers." He laughs.

That's not such a bad idea.

"Good idea, honey." I laugh back.

I realize I didn't even tell Kirk that Konner bought Bridgette a puppy. I don't want to sound too excited because guys get competitive and I really *don't* want a new puppy.

"Konner bought Bridgette a new puppy yesterday so there is going to be five of us tonight," I mention casually.

"Unreal! What kind of puppy?" he asks.

"A little girl puppy named Rosie. She is a Morkie," I inform.

"What is a Morkie? He didn't get her a little rodent, did he?" he says dramatically.

"She is adorable! She's not a rodent at all!" I defend.

Why is it that almost all guys hate small tiny dogs? I think they are adorable!

"Don't ever expect me to buy you one of those," he adds.

Phew! Too much responsibility!

"So I was thinking next week we could take the day to drive over to Anaheim and spend some time at Disneyland. Go on some rollercoasters, a little Splash Mountain action?" Kirk suggests.

"What a great idea!" I gush.

This just keeps getting better!

I send Kirk into the flower place as I call my mom and check in.

"Hi, honey!"

"Hey, Mom. How are you?"

"I'm great, how are you?"

"Good. I'm just with Kirk. We are going to Bridgette's for a game night."

"That sounds like so much fun. I hope you two win."

"Thanks. Is anything new?"

"No, sweetie. Just plugging along. It was so great to see you this week. I miss you so much, honey."

"I miss you too. I'm glad you came. I'll call you this weekend and we can talk more, okay?"

"Sure, honey. Say hi to Kirk. We love you!"

"Love you guys too."

Kirk returns to the truck with a premade bouquet of fresh-cut beautiful flowers. It's an assortment of colors and kinds. She will love them. They smell amazing too.

"Anything else we need?" he asks.

"No, just our competiveness!" I laugh.

We get to my building and park on the side of the road. Kirk carries in the flowers for us, and I stop by my apartment quickly to put on a sweater. We knock on their door, and Bridgette opens the door to greet us.

"Hi! Come in!" she gushes.

"These are for you," Kirk says as he hugs her and hands her the flowers.

"Wow, this wasn't necessary. Thank you!" she gushes again.

She's in a really good mood tonight.

"This was a cool idea," Kirk says.

"I love game night. That's why I'm so excited, it's been way too long," she explains.

Konner approaches us.

"Hey," he greets.

"Good to see you, man," Kirk says as he pats him on the shoulder.

I give Konner a hug, and we all settle into the living room.

"I hope you guys are hungry, dinner will be done in thirty minutes," she informs.

"Can I toss you a beer or anything?" Konner offers.

"I'd love one," Kirk accepts.

"I would love any kind of juice or even just a water," I smile.

I am not in any kind of drinking mood tonight. We have that huge party tomorrow night, that will be more than enough.

"We are going to start with Life!" Bridgette jumps in an excited manner.

"Excellent choice, hun," Konner approves.

You can tell he is being so patient and supportive of how excited Bridgette is for this game night. None of us would dare bring her down, even if board games really were not our favorite thing.

The little fluffy puppy running around quickly finds us after being distracted by one of her many toys. They have only had her a couple of days and she is already the most spoiled animal I have ever met. Bridgette bought her a bling—a tiny collar to go around her neck—and her cage is a bright pink.

"Rosie!" I call as I pick her up.

She is so playful and hyper. Rosie licks my face and continues to jump around my arms. I hand her to Kirk and she calms right down.

"She is pretty cute," he admits as he hands her to Bridgette.

"She's the fluffy love of my life," she beams.

Bridgette settles Rosie down with one of her dog toys so we can start our game.

We all pick the color of own cars. Bridgette, Konner, and I choose to go down the education path and Kirk decides to jump right into the career path. He draws the "entertainer" career card following a fifty thousand dollar salary card.

"You're a pretty shitty entertainer," Konner teases.

The game goes on. I end up being the doctor card, Bridgette the athlete, and Konner the salesperson card—the three of us pulling much higher salaries than Kirk. This board game is a lot more fun than I remember. Konner wins with the most money at the end.

Bridgette serves us a plate of chicken fettuccini Alfredo and a mixed green salad in a side bowl. We held off on dinner so we could finish our game.

"Amazing," I compliment.

This isn't the healthiest meal I've ever had, but it's so satisfying I don't care.

After dinner, I help Bridgette hand wash all the dishes. I instantly wish we were at Kirk's so we could just throw them in the dishwasher and let it do its job. I can't stand washing dishes; I just hate it.

We stick around to play a game of Cranium and decide once that finishes, it's time to head out.

"Thank you guys for dinner and for the fun game night," I smile graciously.

"Yeah, we had a blast. Next time, no one's beating me!" Kirk jokes.

"It was a pleasure. We can't wait for the party tomorrow night," Bridgette says as she holds open their front door.

We wave good-bye and off to Kirk's we go.

Every year, Kirk's building has a giant Halloween party. Each floor invites each other to an open-house-type-style party, and the pool and hot tub area is a free for all. If a condo doesn't want to participate, they put a red paper on their door, indicating no one can come in. Everyone else who is taking part puts a green paper on their door, and their door remains open the whole party. Each condo has to supply his or her fair share of alcohol, as it's sort of like a potluck and everyone shares.

Kirk tells me people also put out food if they are generous. I think it's clear that Kirk's apartment is the one with most booze and the most food being offered. He is bighearted and overly offering.

This year, I am so excited to take part. It's a costume party, and everyone dresses up. I've been hearing for the last week how much fun it is and how every year it's over, people can't wait for it to come again.

Kirk is being a pilot, and I have lied and told him I am being a butterfly. He will see what I am really dressing as later tonight.

Kirk has been out all day grocery and liquor shopping. He is so excited; it's so cute to watch. I have been at home making Jell-O shooters and cleaning. It's October 29, and the party starts at seven.

My parents got home from their cruise last Sunday. They had the trip of a lifetime, taking in all of the breathtaking sites Europe offers, like the Leaning Tower of Pisa and the Coliseum. My mom even thinks she knows how to speak Italian. I fear after all the wine she probably drank, she did really attempt to speak it.

We invited Bridgette and Konner to the party so they will come over at eight to join us. Bridgette knows my plan with my costume. She says she is only coming in case she has to guard and keep me safe.

Kirk finally gets home at five. We ate a steak dinner, and we begin to put our costumes on. I wear a tight white dress, butterfly wings, antennas, and put glitter on my face, arms, and legs. I sport my dazzling new piece of jewelry on my wrist. Kirk is so convincing in his pilot's costume. He looks sexy! I am immediately relieved he works in a grease field all day and that there are no hot, tempting, flight attendants there.

Once I see him, I have to have him to myself. I pull him onto the bed and begin harassing him. I am sure it's not as arousing for him as I am dressed as a butterfly and I'm positive he feels like a pervert. However, he does accept, as I demand he join the mile-high club with me.

Soon, we are not in costumes anymore. My butterfly outfit and Kirk's pilot uniform lie somewhere on the floor as we get playful on his bed. Expecting our friends any moment, we finish up and quickly change back into our getups. I have to pick a few sparkles off his face to hide the evidence.

There is a knock on the door, and Bridgette and Konner come in with a large bottle of vodka and granting us each a big Halloween group hug.

"Let the party begin!" Kirk yells.

Bridgette is dressed as a uniformed schoolgirl with high pigtails, fake glasses, a buttoned-down white shirt, loose tie, short kilt, and white knee-high socks with flat black shoes.

Konner is dressed as an army solider. He has some camouflage pants, white wife-beater, a camouflage headband around the crown of his head, and army boots.

They both put effort into their costumes, and they look fantastic. This is going to be a seriously fun night!

Kirk mixes a few drinks and gathers the four of us in the kitchen so he can make a toast.

"To my beautiful butterfly and good friends! Happy Halloween!" he cheers.
"Cheers!" the three of us yell in unison.

Bridgette and I snap a few pictures of the two of us and then a few of the four of us. She has the first picture Kirk and I have ever taken now on her camera. I have to remember to ask her for copies.

Kirk blasts the music in his apartment; so soon, the party vibe is really going strong. There is a disco ball hanging from the living room, and he moved and covered all the couches so there's a dance floor. The lights are dim, and he is being overly affectionate with me, constantly kissing and caressing me.

"Are you wearing underwear?" he asks.
"Of course!" I laugh.

I can tell he is becoming tipsy already.

The open-house portion of the evening has now officially started, so people are coming and going. I meet a lot of Kirk's neighbors; there are way more than I would have ever expected.

Bridgette sticks by my side as Konner and Kirk go off to mingle. She doesn't want to miss me when I do a transformation into my next costume.

"I'm so nervous for you," she squeals.

"Don't worry," I reassure.

Time goes by and Kirk's alcohol contribution is getting quite the beat down. I think the word has spread that he has a generous display sitting here in the condo. The dining-room table is covered in a black plastic tablecloth with all kinds of finger food being offered. I haven't seen him for probably close to an hour now. It's nice that he and Konner are developing their own kind of friendship.

A guy comes up to me and begins to chat me up. He is probably about twenty-five. He says he lives in the building and is a civil engineer. He is decent-looking; too bad I don't have a single friend to stick him on.

He continues to hang around like a bee on honey. Bridgette and I don't have the heart to send him away.

"Can I help you?" I hear an angry Kirk confront.

"No," the guy replies.

"Well, you seem to be spending a lot of time bothering my girlfriend. Would you mind laying off?" he growls.

"Sorry, man," the guy apologizes as he staggers off.

Kirk puts his arm around me and keeps a steady grip on the drink occupying his other hand. I wish he would sober up before I change into my other costume.

Something distracts him, and he wanders off to observe something.

I pull Bridgette into Kirk's room so she can help me. I make absolutely sure the door is locked behind us.

"Are you really sure about this, Vero? You don't have to do this. You've really thought it through?" she worries.
"Yes," I answer.

I change into my costume, and she helps me with finishing makeup touches.

I clean up my mess and open his bedroom door to reveal my costume. Bridgette and I sit and wait for Kirk to return.

"I am so nervous I can barely stand it!" she shrieks.
"Stop worrying!" I order.

I have become quite good at this sneakiness over the last little while. I have managed to learn to control my own nerves so they don't get the best of me.

I see Bridgette's eyes enlarge as she takes a step away from me. Soon after, I feel a firm grip on my arm from behind me.

"*What the fuck are you doing here?*" Kirk spits in a downright malicious tone.
"I need to talk to you desperately. Can we go somewhere private?" I say to him.

I am about to reveal the truth about Bianca as I stand there in front of Kirk in his apartment dressed in my shameful disguise.

He pulls me into his bedroom and locks the door behind him.

"You need to leave and never come back. I don't even know how you know where I live! What are you? A psycho or something?" he panics.

"Kirk, listen," I begin.

I quickly remove the wig before Kirk throws me out.

His eyes widen as I shake down my hair. Next, I remove the contacts and toss them on the bedside table.

"Kirk, I haven't been honest with you entirely, but after this, all my cards are on the table. First of all, I have to start off by telling you, I am madly in love with you. I can't imagine myself with anyone else. I decided to dress up and go to the strip club dressed as a girl no one knew. I was trying to find a way to communicate with Fiona. When I got in, I immediately saw your business card on the ledge of the coat check. My entire heart dropped, and I was mortified. I decided to investigate more by calling you from a blocked number and seeing how you interact with the girls there," I start.

He looks at me with a wide-open mouth.

"It all just became too easy. I was right there in the thick of things, and then before I knew it, I was in too deep. I learned a lot of shocking things about you that I would have never thought possible. I knew everything about you before you came clean to me the other day. This seems awful, and I am sure you are fuming mad, but this hasn't been all bad," I explain.

"I can't believe this," Kirk adds.

"Fiona and Ivory were the ones who messed with your truck. Penny is dating your dad so she can weasel her way into a more permanent job there, and your dad hasn't been in here.

Penny dropped that shirt off to me the night Bridgette and I had our girls' night here," I say.

"Fiona and Ivory . . . that's interesting," he contemplates.

"I touched you and came onto you because I couldn't help myself. You looked so miserable, I just wanted to put a smile on your face. I am so sorry, I hope you understand," I plea.

He walks over to his bedroom door and turns the knob to make sure it's locked. I begin to fidget, as I can't read what's coming next. I look at him with sad eyes.

"Let's worry about this tomorrow. Right now, get on my bed. Put that wig back on and take off those clothes."

Yes, Captain.

CPSIA information can be obtained at www.ICGtesting.com
Printed in the USA
LVOW080218270912

300532LV00001B/2/P

9 781466 959002